where two rivers meet

Peter Damen

BUNYA
PUBLISHING.com

Where Two Rivers Meet

Gary Taaffe
BunyaPublishing.com
Gary@BunyaPublishing.com

B BUNYA PUBLISHING.com

Thank you

To the people who knowingly and unknowingly gave me the idea to write:

Where Two Rivers Meet!

A story about our early ancestors who began to shape this country into what it is now.

A special thanks to my wife Maureen and my friend Jeanette Pidgeon who made sure all the "I's" were dotted and "T's" were crossed plus their great assistance in the editorial work.

Endorsements

You won't put this book down before the last word. A great new author and a fascinating introduction to Australian Literature.

Valerie Munroe, Australia

A totally readable book which becomes a practical aid in facing the battles of ordinary life.

Maureen Turner, Australia

Set in the 1890s Peter Damen gives us a glimpse of the hardship and complexities of life in outback Australia. An intriguing story of life, love and family, which makes great reading for all.

Major Eva Phillips, Chaplain

— CHAPTER ONE —

Anno Domini 1898

Slowly the horse wended its way up the side of the steep hill. The rider let the horse make his own way. At times branches from the eucalyptus trees tried to sweep the rider from his saddle as if they didn't want him to reach the crest. The smell of eucalyptus lay heavily on the air. Clouds, almost low enough to reach by hand, looked ready to drop their load of life saving water, drifted overhead. Apart from the noise his horse made they were surrounded by an overwhelming but ominous stillness. Hoping to reach the top before the weather changed for the worse, the rider spurred his mount on.

Finally they were there. Dismounting near some large boulders from which eons ago the surrounding soil had washed away, the man tethered his horse to a tree, removed the saddle and gave his steed a quick well deserved rub down, then efficiently began to erect his own shelter. You could tell by the deft movements of his actions that he was no new comer to this task. Under the overhanging part of the large rock he lit a fire over which he hung a stained billy that he filled with water from his flask. Raising his face to the sky he tried to estimate how much time there was left before the elements would show their power. A flash of forked lightning robbed him of his eyesight; however it didn't take long for his vision to be restored. Judging he had about five minutes he walked towards the precipice before him. Looking down into the valley he could see where two rivers joined to continue their journey down the valley as one. Much as he appreciated the streams, it was the land lying in between them he was studying.

He had first come across the valley by searching for a young steer which had separated from the mob he was droving to Albury. Somehow the land had spoken to him, never leaving his thoughts. Ever since he'd seen the lush grass between the streams, the land had been calling him. Since then he had been saving literally every penny he earned to be able to purchase his dream. While in Albury he had contacted the proper Government Authorities who informed him that whoever laid claim to any land in that particular district could have title to it.

Throwing some dry wood which he had collected, when returning to the camp, on the fire, soon helped make the billy boil. A sudden clap of thunder nearly made him spill the water he was pouring into his well-used tin mug. As he sat down heavy drops of rain poured around him. The horse whinnied trying to evade most of the rain by leaning closely against the boulder.

Sipping from his mug while sitting relatively safe from the storm that was exploding around him, his thoughts ran to what he would have to do in the next few days. The area of land that wouldn't leave his mind and that he so desperately wanted would have to be marked out so that there was no possible way anyone else could lay title to it while he was back in Albury legalising his claim.

Slowly he thoroughly chewed some dried biltong, as it looked like it would be the only nourishment he'd have tonight. Pouring another strong mug of tea with some heaped spoonfuls of sugar, throwing another log on the fire he hoped that the wind wouldn't change direction because so far the boulder had been a Godsend. Making himself as comfortable as his saddle that was used, as a pillow, would allow him, he closed his eyes to soon fall asleep while thinking that it wouldn't be long now before his dream would begin to take shape.

Giving the area where he had camped one more glance, he threw some more soil on the dead ashes to ensure there would be no fire risk. All seemed safe. Nothing left behind? Mounting his horse, he gave another last look to ensure nothing had been overlooked; he then prodded his horse that seemed eager to be on its way.

Riding along the ridge he caught glimpses of the Valley below him. He'd have to discover another way to reach his land; in no way could he expect his herd to struggle through the route he had just come. Seeing a mob of wallabies he smiled to himself; it wouldn't be long before they would notice that soon there would be competition for the succulent grass. Aiming for a spot where he could safely cross the stream with reasonable ease he finally found himself standing on the land, which he hoped he would soon own. A sense of being at home enveloped him. Walking the land, his horse trailing behind him, he felt there was no better way to obtain a feel for the land than to walk on it. Walking proudly, he felt almost eight feet tall, but looking at the high hills that surrounded him he knew it was an illusion. It was nice to know that the power of Mother Nature in this valley brought to him a sense of presence and reality.

Eventually he mounted his steed again, mainly for the better view it gave him. Yes! That looked the right place to build the homestead, further over to the left would be where the corrals and the barns should be located. With a smile in his heart he continued on.

***

Thud! With a solid clunk the heavy wooden entrance door of the Department of Lands and Agriculture Office closed behind him. Once on the footpath he stood still. Taking a deep breath, he looked at the activity of the township of Albury bustling around him. The world appeared different now that he was officially a property owner. Sunlight was brighter, people passing him were more cheerful and the ladies looked ever so much more attractive and colourful in their attire than he had ever observed before.

Marvellous what becoming a landowner did for you! No more bowing and scraping to other people from now on. When people discovered he owned over a thousand acres they would treat him with reverence and respect.

Anyway there was no need to worry about that at the moment. Right now he should be attending the sales at the stockyard to purchase the cattle he required to form the nucleus of his herd. With light but swift determined steps he strode towards the sale yards. Soon he heard the sound of brisk bidding while inhaling the typical aroma that attended every sales yard he'd been at. Confidently he meandered past the holding yards, casting his eyes casually over whatever beast was held in there. Suddenly his left hand shot out to grab hold of a thin arm. The owner squealed in a loud protesting whining voice.

"What did you do that for, I can't help it if I walked into you when you stopped suddenly, can I now?" Not letting go of the arm the man replied,

"Maybe you can't? But I hadn't stopped! You were aiming to part me from my wallet weren't you? I only stopped walking after I grabbed your arm."

With a morose look the skinny urchin half-heartedly tried without success to jerk his arm away from the strong grip holding him. Looking down at him the man noticed that the kid needed a good bath and some decent victuals inside him wouldn't do him any harm either. When their eyes locked he recognised a kindred soul. His memory went back to when he had been a struggling undernourished lad fighting to survive. In a kinder voice he asked, "Did you need the money to obtain something to eat?"

Sensing a change in the man's attitude the urchin's eyes wavered shiftily for a moment, then returning to look at the man's face he murmured in a soft voice,

"I haven't had anything decent to eat for nigh on a week. Me stomach thinks me throat's bin cut." Silently with the crowd surging around them they studied each other. Letting go of the kid's arm the man suggested,

"I'm feeling a mite peckish myself. Why don't you and I walk over to the pie shop I noticed near the entrance of the sales yard to partake of some of their pies?"

The urchin's eyes lit up brightly. Gaining confidence fast, he replied, "Yeah, I won't argue against that suggestion," licking his lips in anticipation.

Like old friends they aimed towards the pie shop. Both wondered how quickly a situation can change for the better. The urchin soon found some stools near a table while the man went to order beef and curry pies with peas in mint sauce and mugs of ginger beer.

With his finger scraping the plate, then licking the finger clean, making sure his mug was drained of all its ginger beer the urchin placed it back on the table.

"Wow! That was nice. I haven't had a treat like this for a long time I can tell you that for nothing. Thank you ever so much, Sir."

The man had been sitting back watching the urchin enjoying his feast.

"So you think you had enough then do you?"

Emitting a light burp the kid nodded in agreement.

"I couldn't possibly swallow another mouthful even if I poked it down with a stick."

The man withdrew a ten shilling note from his wallet, and gave it to the kid saying,

"I have to pop down behind the shop to see a man about his dog; while I'm away could you pay for the meal we had with this. I won't be long."

The kid looked at the money in his hand.

He was sure the whole meal wouldn't cost any more than half a crown. That meant he would still have seven shillings and sixpence in change. He could live for at least two weeks with that amount of money. Of course if he scarpered now he would have the whole ten shillings to survive on. Looking around he couldn't see the man anywhere. Slowly he walked towards the shop. Hesitatingly he gave the note to the serving girl behind the counter. Without looking at him or asking him anything she gave him the required change. Holding the money in his hand he stood waiting. His mind was in turmoil. You are a fool if you don't take the money? Yes, but the man treated me so nice why should I do the dirty to him now? What to do?

"Ah, there you are?"

Relieved the urchin turned toward the man handing him the money.

"No, you keep the change. I think you earned it, don't you?" The man looked at him, "You see, I could see how you were fighting with yourself to remain here or to run away. Now that you made the right decision why don't we walk around and get to know each other. You might even be able to help me select the cattle I need?"

"I do recognise good beef when I see it," the kid replied modestly. "By the way my friends call me

Tommy; Thomas Matheson is my full name, Sir."

"A right good name it is Tommy!" The man said seriously. Together they meandered through the yard.

"Begging your pardon, Sir, but did you notice that Hereford bull we passed just now? I reckon, I could recommend for you to purchase that animal, Sir."

Tracing their steps back they stopped to study the animal. The boy was right the Hereford had all the lines a thoroughbred required. The young bull was standing in the far corner with its distinctive woolly face towards them returning their looks as only cattle can do. Tommy had great delight in sharing his knowledge to his new friend.

"See Sir, the Hereford breed originated in England. It is vigorous yet docile, matures early but is productive for many years. The Americans and Canadians love it as it is the only breed which survives on grass alone in sub-zero temperatures."

The boy stopped as he realised he might've overstepped his mark. The man smiled indulgently saying, "You seem to know what you are talking about Tommy, have you dealt with the breed before?"

Tommy nodded his head eagerly; explaining that before his Father died and their property had been taken off them they'd owned a herd of Herefords. The man noticed the sad expression on the young face and wisely refrained from asking for any more details. Pointing back to the bull he continued, "At a guess I'd estimate this one to weigh in at over 2500 lb and he's not all that old yet."

While they had been watching the animal a man had come up behind them.

"Like what you see, do you?" Both the boy and the man jumped in surprise.

"Sorry, didn't mean to frighten you but I am the owner of this animal and as you looked interested I thought I'd come over."

"Is there a special reason why you are selling the beast?" Not expecting to receive an honest answer, but there was no harm in asking, as people had been known to blurt out the truth in surprise.

"The only reason I can give as to why I have to reluctantly sell the bull is because of my dear departed wife."

"I am ever so sorry to hear that your wife passed away." The man replied with a concerned note in his voice.

"No, I am the one that should apologise in giving you the wrong impression, Sir, my wife didn't die!" The farmer retorted with an angry frown on his face. "She just departed! Gathered her kit and caboodle to leave me run the farm with two small children. Eventually I'll have to sell the remainder of the herd but as I needed some ready cash I thought to get rid of the bull first."

The man looked thoughtfully at the farmer.

"I have an idea. I have only recently obtained a

property in the hills and am looking for some cattle to stock it with. Seeing this bull, I assume that the rest of your herd would be in a similar condition." The man nodded. "So I suggest that if I could ride over to your place to see what you have to offer, we could make a deal that would benefit us both."

The farmer accepted a card with the man's name on it, and smiled when he was informed that he would be paid in cash. Also the offer of paying a monthly agistment fee until the cattle would be ready to depart helped to make his eyes light up. A time to meet was organised. Farmer McGregor wrote his address down on a note, which he handed to the man, shaking hands they departed.

The man walked away from the sales yards. Not having been told otherwise Tommy stuck with him. Muttering to himself the man appeared to be in deep thought.

"Sorry Sir, I didn't understand what you were saying?" The man looked down at him acting surprised to see him.

"You must excuse me Tommy, I am trying to work out my next step, and it could be a bit tricky. You'll have to put up with me being rather quiet while I plan."

Tommy's heart lifted; at least the man hadn't told him to go. Silently he walked next to his newfound friend. Turning into a treed avenue the sound of children voices could be heard. Soon they came upon a school. The children were out at play, a teacher who was suppose to supervise them was busy helping a youngster up who had tripped and hurt his knee. To Tommy's amazement the man entered the schoolyard walking directly to the teacher whose long blond hair nearly reached the ground as she leaned over the hurt child.

"Wish me luck, Tom," whispered the man. Astonished Tom dropped back, what was going on here? The man walked until he stood behind the teacher.

"Hello, Elizabeth!" He said in a hoarse voice.

At hearing the voice the teacher stiffened, slowly standing erect, to then whirl round. Her long hair sprayed out in a circle to settle down on her shoulders and back as she faced the man. Stepping back, nearly falling over the hurt little boy, white faced with shock she gasped.

"Is it really you?"

"Yes, it is I Elizabeth," the man said hesitantly.

"I did tell you I was coming back!"

"You told me you were coming back? Yes, I remember you telling me that! I also remember it was over three years since you promised that you would come back to see me, Ross Smith!" Walking towards him she began hammering him on his chest.

One of the children yelled out, "Look everyone, Miss is attacking a man!"

It didn't take long for the children to stop

playing and form a large ring around the couple who were so wrapped up in each other they'd forgotten they were in a schoolyard full with children. Tom stood stock-still; to stare at the most beautiful women he had ever cast his eyes on.

"Never once did you write to me. Eventually I came to the conclusion that something must've happened and gave up thinking about you. Well, I tried not to think about you, but you just wouldn't leave my mind. It didn't matter what I did, you were always in my thoughts."

"Hang on a minute, Elizabeth. What do you mean by, no matter what you did? You are not spoken for are you? Please don't tell me you are spoken for!"

"What if I had been? Where were you? Breaking some other girl's heart for all I knew." Frantically she began to thump him in the chest again. Fragile looking as she was she certainly knew how to pack a punch. Tom heard the dull sound from where he was standing.

"Did I hear you say I broke your heart?"

"O, you brute; don't talk to me about my heart! I hate you with a vengeance Ross Smith, for all the agony you put me through. All the pain I suf…"

She couldn't speak any more as Ross had covered her mouth with his. She resisted for a little while, it was only a little while, before she responded to his kiss. The same kid that had informed the others now told them that someone should get the headmaster, as it seemed Miss had stopped hitting the man but was now busy trying to eat him.

"If someone doesn't call the headmaster soon there won't be anything left of him," he commented worriedly.

"Don't panic," another boy said, "They are only kissing!"

Some of the young girls sighed.

Everyone was so busy watching they never saw the short man stepping angrily towards the circle. Pushing some of the children aside he strode on to stop near the busy couple. Red in the face with anger he lifted his shoulders importantly to state.

"Miss Mainwaring, don't you dare behave like this on my school premises!"

Miss Mainwaring was too busy to take much notice of her boss, which upset him even more. To make matters worse the stocky headmaster could see the dream disappearing, the dream which he had created in his mind, of what he had in store for his assistant teacher. Not once in his dream had there been a strong, tall lean man kissing his girl. That part he had always done himself. Now his dream was shattered. Anger and disappointment drove him to push the kissing couple apart.

The sudden shock at being brought back to reality, made Elizabeth's head spin. Focussing her eyes she recognised the head master ferociously snarling bitter words in her direction. A dark shadow flew past her head to connect against the headmaster's nose. Blood spurted as the man collapsed. Every eye in the schoolyard was riveted on the headmaster as silently he stayed on the ground.

"Holy moly," someone whispered. "He's done the old headmaster in!"

In shock Elizabeth turned round to face Ross. "You didn't kill him did you?"

"I don't think so dear, I only gave him a wee little punch, and normally it wouldn't hurt a fly. However he did upset me by the way he talked to my future wife, so I might've hit him a wee bit harder than I meant to. They tell me I don't know my own strength, at times."

"What do you mean by 'your future…'"?

The headmaster who was attempting to raise himself from the ground interrupted her. With his bleeding lips starting to swell he mumbled, "Miss Mainwaring you are fired! You will leave now!"

Angrily he spat out a loose tooth.

"Elizabeth! Stay here with the children!" Ross ordered decisively.

Grabbing the headmaster by his collar he began to drag him in the direction of the school. Elizabeth was too stunned to argue. When she finally found her voice it was to ask Tom what he thought Ross was going to do to the headmaster.

Tom shook his head, totally baffled by what had

happened so far.

"I can't tell you Miss, you've known him longer than I have. I only made his acquaintance today." The woman looked surprised, "How and where did you meet him, what's your name?" With flashing eyes she fired the questions at him.

"Tom, I am called Tom. I met him at the saleyards only today."

Suddenly Tom looked embarrassed. "I tried to part him from his wallet, but he caught me at it. I'm glad I didn't give him any lip when he caught me, seeing what he just did to your boss."

Elizabeth looked even more mystified.

Not obtaining any enlightenment from Tom she decided to take the children back into their classroom. Once they had settled into their seats she gave them some work to do, nodding her head at Tom she indicated that she wanted him to follow her. As they stepped out of the class they saw Ross exit the headmaster's office. When he noticed them a large smile appeared on his face, he waved an envelope at her stating,

"Look what I have here Elizabeth. I have your reference! He didn't want to write one out but when I convinced him that taking you away from his school would be beneficial for him, he saw the error of his ways and relented. Actually he wrote a lovely reference about you, when you read it you will see he held you in high esteem."

"Ross Smith! What did you do to the man to make him write me a reference?"

Ross looked a little bit guilty but soon his brash manner returned.

"Nothing love, I will admit he was very 'anti' you in the beginning but when I pointed out that I knew some people who could help or hinder him in his career he soon saw where I was leading him. After that he couldn't be more cooperative."

She studied his face as if she didn't believe a word of what he had said.

"You don't know anyone with connections to the school, do you?"

"No one at all, but he doesn't have to know that does he?"

"Well, no good standing here looking at each other. Why don't you return to your class to say goodbye to the students, after which we'll walk you home."

Elizabeth was rather stunned as if events had occurred a little too fast for her. Moving slowly to the classroom she muttered softly, "This day is definitely not developing as I had planned it!"

— CHAPTER TWO —

In a subdued mood the trio walked very quietly towards Elizabeth's home. Elizabeth was still overcome by the emotions some of her students had displayed when they were informed that she was leaving the school. Small girls began to whimper and one boy cried out aloud (who will tie my shoe laces when you are not here Miss?) on and on it went until the teacher walked from the room close to crying herself.

Elizabeth's Mother was in her front garden cutting some roses for display inside when she saw her daughter come down the street accompanied by two males. Walking to the gate to meet them she enquired in a worried voice,

"What are you doing home at this hour, love? Aren't you well?" Then she must have recognised the man who was standing close to her daughter.

"Goodness gracious me as God made little apples. Is that you Ross? I thought you'd died!"

"You have to be good to die young, Mrs.

Mainwaring!" Ross replied, trying to sound jocular. Somehow he felt that he had lost a few points in Elizabeth's esteem since they met again this afternoon.

"Good he definitely isn't!" Elizabeth muttered under her breath to her Mother. Her Mother studied her daughter's face enquiringly?

"He's only seen me for about two hours. So far he's punched the headmaster in the face and made me lose my job. I'd hate to see what he could do if he really tried?"

"He did what; surely you are having me on?"

"No Mater, that's what he did. I don't know what possessed the man but when he saw me greeting Ross he came out of his office and rebuked me horridly. Ross stopped him by punching him in the nose."

Elizabeth began to giggle hysterically as she recalled the moment. Tom and Ross looked at each other. Maybe her nerves were falling apart? Then to her Mother's dismay she started to laugh out aloud. In relief Tom and Ross shared her laughter.

"Will you stop your unseemly behaviour Elizabeth? I thought I'd brought you up better than this. That poor man was interested in selecting you as his wife."

"You are right, Mater," Elizabeth answered while trying to stifle her laughter. "But you never saw the horrible things he tried to do to me when he manoeuvred me into a corner. Thinking back on it now; I feel quite grateful to Ross for flattening the mean little weasel. He probably saved me from a fate worse than death."

Turning away from her Mother to affectionately lean against Ross, she burst out in laughter again. Ross took quick advantage of the situation by holding her tightly, purely to prevent her from falling over of course!

"I think we should go inside before the whole street is watching this spectacle you are putting on." Trying not to smile until she was out of sight from the neighbours, Mrs. Mainwaring led the way in to her home.

After finishing the strong but sweetened tea and the buttered scones Mrs. Mainwaring nudged Tom, saying in a loud voice, "I'll show you through the garden Tom, seeing as you'll be here for another month or so I'd better make you familiar with the place."

When they were outside she told him that the other two wouldn't mind being on their own, as surely they must have lots to say to each other.

"While you are here Tom I hope you won't mind if I borrow your muscles at times because I am getting too old to keep the garden in tip top condition and your arrival has been very timely. I am sure the weeds have been anticipating your coming, as I have never seen them as large or as plentiful as they are presently."

Tom looked around; there was going to be plenty to do around here alright. He was also sure that the pleasant old lady had plenty of other jobs stored up for him. It looked like she was going to make sure he earned his keep.

With a wry smile he said that he looked forward to helping her during the times that Ross didn't need him of course. They'd come to a shed, and she opened the door. Tom noticed it was set up as a bedroom cum sitting room.

"This is where you'll be living while you are staying with us Tom. You'll have your meals with us at the house but this is solely for you to use. Ross will have to remain at the hotel, neighbours will talk you know, at this stage with Ross returning so unexpectedly I believe we've giving them enough to gossip about."

As no reply seemed to be expected Tom remained silent. Until he knew a bit more about this family (nice as they seemed to be) he wasn't going to say too much.

Now that they had the room to themselves Ross and Elizabeth fell silent. The pleasure of being able to look at each other was enough. Finally Elizabeth let out a heavy sigh, muttering, "You really have done it this time Ross! I expected a change in my life if we ever were to meet again, but what occurred today never entered into my deepest fantasy."

Looking directly at him she raised her voice.

"Do you realise that you have ruined my reputation as a school teacher in this town? Most likely I will never be able to apply for a job again regardless of how nice a reference that weasel wrote. You don't expect him to hold his mouth forever do you?" Ross was sitting looking very sorry. Once Mrs. Mainwaring had taken Tom outside he'd expected Elizabeth to come over, sit on his knee and make up for lost time, so to speak.

"I think you are making a mountain out of a molehill dear. You won't need a job with the school department anyway. I haven't had a chance to tell you, but you are looking at a landowner now. Over a thousand acres, you know!" Seeing the look of surprise on her face made him feel a lot better, he continued, "That's why I came to visit you. Now I have something to offer you we can finish that discussion we began over two years ago."

"Oh," she replied innocently, "What discussion would that be?"

This flustered him; surely she was making him pay for what had happened to her today? Hesitantly he replied, "You know what I am talking about Elizabeth?"

Her eyebrows lifted, as if to say, please enlighten me?

"Remember that night when we walked home from the dance? We stopped to sit on that old log in the park and were talking about what we would do if we had money. You know, set up a farm, raise beef, and have our own milk cow and some chickens to supply us with fresh eggs." He looked at her again. "You even mentioned how many children you'd like to have."

"Oh, that was you, was it? You must forgive me; so many gentlemen have spoken to me since that night. It is hard to keep them all apart."

Ross cursed himself again, for not writing to her during his absence. She was definitely making him suffer for his neglect. There was only one way to stop her. Standing up so suddenly that the chair scraped over the paved floor he moved towards her.

"Well if your problem is that you can't remember who was who, I can soon remedy that," he said sternly. "There is only one way I can think of to right this matter." Her eyes opened wide in apprehension as he strode towards her. He ignored whatever signs he could read on her features. Moving behind her he placed his hands firmly under her armpits, raised her from the seat, and then turned her face towards his to give her an old fashioned kiss, which was so hard and long that there was no reason to misunderstand the signal he was giving her. Elizabeth's knees began to wobble; Ross kissed her with more determination still. Finally they both came up for air. Shaking her shoulders firmly he said hoarsely,

"Can you remember who I am now?" Ross looked at her fiercely.

Trying to keep her face straight, the nearly hidden sparkle in her eyes however gave the game away. Soberly she replied while returning his look mischievously,

"Yes Ross, I believe it is coming back to me. I'm sure my memory will be more complete if you kiss me like that again. Do you think you could?"

Ross shrugged his shoulders; life was going to be ever so exciting trying to understand this woman. Lowering his head he murmured,

"I'll do whatever my lady desires if she thinks it'll help bring her memory back." They moulded together once again.

Leaning against the back of his chair, Ross contentedly watched Elizabeth prepare the necessaries for the evening meal. What a lucky chap he was. Due to Elizabeth's Father passing away while she was in her early teens she'd missed out on a lot of the male domineering that the unchallenged head of the house insisted the females under his domain adhered to.

Hanging against the wallpaper was a picture of the family that had been taken just before her Father passed away. It depicted all the trappings of his class. An almost grimfaced Father standing rigidly upright holding a Bible in his right hand, a golden watch-chain known as an Albert hanging from his waistcoat. No decent person would ever shed his waistcoat; it didn't matter how high the temperature reached that day. Also in the photograph were his wife and daughter who knew their place in the household only too well and so sat demurely on chairs respectfully facing him. Elizabeth would have had to address him as 'Pater', no doubt also being familiar with the instruction that she should be seen but not heard.

Most of her female friends and their 'Maters' wouldn't avail themselves to use lipstick or face powder, perhaps in the direst of circumstances a discreet application to a shiny nose was permissible. Smoking for girls was frowned upon and words like 'sex', 'contraception' or 'pregnancy' were never uttered. The poor girls were completely ignorant on how their bodies worked but could give you precise details on how a sewing machine performed.

Although Mrs. Mainwaring professed to her friends how much she missed her husband, she also realised that she had more freedom than ever before in her life, especially with the reasonable amount of money he had left behind. Thus she could advise her daughter to expand her thinking but at the same time be smart enough not to overstep the boundaries that society set.

"A clever woman is always obedient to her husband's wishes but subtly will win him over to her way of thinking. The same technique should be used with the 'society people' one meets. Always give praise, it doesn't matter how silly the suggestion was, before tactfully proposing another idea. Of course if you are in agreement with their thinking, make sure they know so."

Yes, Mater Mainwaring had learned from her marriage. She'd also made sure that her daughter benefited from her experience.

Each generation should improve on the previous one, was her thinking. After all, hadn't God ordained it that way by creating mankind in such a manner that there was always a younger generation available. Surely this was so that the elders could pass their knowledge on, before departing from earth?

***

"How much do you want for the old wagon?"

Ross had picked Elizabeth and Tom up in a hired Rosa buggy. It looked rather festive with its fringe around the top. When Elizabeth saw Ross proudly sitting in it holding the reins she wondered once again where or how he had obtained the money.

She shrugged the thought from her mind as Ross jumped down to gallantly give her a hand to climb onto the seat. Tom noticed that no one gave him a hand to climb in the cart. Soon they were trotting smartly down the street, with Elizabeth waving at some of her neighbours as they stopped their chores to see who was passing by. They made a smart looking couple, catching many an eye. Out of town she moved a bit closer to Ross who didn't hesitate to place his arm snugly around her waist. Totally content to be with each other Elizabeth was saddened when Ross steered the buggy into a farm driveway. After some jolting and bouncing he finally stopped near the house. Three dogs had been barking loud enough to raise the dead, jumping around the horse's legs in excitement. Luckily the mare took it all in her stride ignoring the lot of them.

The din brought out the inhabitants who screamed at the dogs to quieten them - making more noise than the dogs had in the first place. Eventually peace was restored. Before farmer McGregor could assist Elizabeth, Ross jumped from the buggy, ran round to the other side, arriving just in time to push the farmer away so he could lift her gently down to slowly release her when she stood next to him. The act had been so obvious that the farmer's daughter a girl of around thirteen or fourteen summers said with a delighted grin on her face.

"Did you get the feeling Dad, that he wanted to do that job himself?"

Tom was halfway out of the buggy when he'd noticed the girl coming gracefully down the steps to stop behind her younger brother laying her hands protectively on his shoulders. He couldn't keep his eyes off her. She to his dismay ignored him completely.

Farmer McGregor introduced his offspring casually as,

"This is my daughter Tracy and that young scamp is James."

Ross introduced Elizabeth and Tom. To show how grown up he was Tom shook hands with the farmer and James but when he aimed his hand towards the girl she'd turned to start walking towards the stables.

He went red in the face, what was wrong with the girl? Maybe she was just plain ignorant!

After making sure his horse could get to the water trough plus nibble on some of the green shoots of grass surrounding it, Ross grabbed Elizabeth's arm to guide her towards the old wagon he had seen out of the corner of his eye.

Ross made no comment when the farmer told him the price he was hoping to obtain, but walked away to the enclosure that held the bull. Murmuring in his beard, "I only wanted to know the price of the wagon, not the whole farm!"

Speaking to Elizabeth he pointed to the animal, "What do you think? Is he good enough to be the originator of our herd?" Her eyes opened wide for a second.

Did he say our herd? A shiver of excitement went through her body. Composing herself she answered him seriously,

"If he's going to be the father of the herd you better name him Abba or Abraham."

They burst out in laughter. "Abba it is then!"

Ross replied with a twinkle in his eye.

Then looking at McGregor he said, "Are you sure he has the stamina, we are asking him to do a big job. We won't be able to purchase a new bull of his calibre every year?"

"Don't worry, Mr. Smith, he won't let you down!"

"Right then, we better see if we can find some wives for him!"

Off he stamped to the paddock dragging Elizabeth behind him. Tom noticed that Ross's mind was now focussed more on the herd than on the long haired blond woman. Suddenly Ross stopped. As Elizabeth wasn't prepared for the sudden stop she collided against him.

"Sorry love, you're not hurt are you?" As the wind had been knocked out of her all she could do was shake her head. Colliding against his muscular frame had made her body go weak. Why did this man have such an effect on her?

"Good," he said in a preoccupied manner. "I've just had a thought."

Turning to face McGregor he said in an abrupt way, "What are you going to do with yourself after you've sold the farm?"

McGregor's face showed that he didn't really approve of the question, but as he didn't want to lose a potential customer he answered nonchalantly,

"I'd thought to pick up a small grain outlet in

town so that the kids didn't have to walk too far to attend their school. At the same time I still would be in contact with the farming community and their animals."

Ross nodded his head in understanding while studying McGregor's face he countered with, "You wouldn't be totally happy though, would you now?" McGregor looked as if he'd been caught out.

"Tell me if I'm wrong?" Ross continued remorselessly. "I have the feeling that you would rather remain on the land?"

McGregor replied in a miserable voice.

"What you feel you should have and what you can actually do is not always the same is it? If you think that I'm happy having to abandon this farm, you have another thing coming. But my circumstances dictate that I have to sell. If James had been another ten years older we could've worked the farm together. However if I have to pay wages for a labourer to help me there wouldn't be enough money left to fulfil our needs."

"Exactly, that's why I like the idea that entered my head."

Everyone had stopped to study Ross.

"Well Ross, don't keep us in the dark, explain what this brilliant idea is all about." Elizabeth nudged him as if that would help Ross to speak.

Once again Ross faced McGregor.

"Why don't you come with me when Tom and I

take the equipment I've ordered in town to my property? Not only will I pay you for your time but at the same time it will give you an opportunity to survey the land. When you sell your farm you'll have plenty of cash to start out again. You only have to sell the land with the outbuildings and your home. Take your herd and anything else you feel you need, with you. As you won't have to pay for your new property I can't see how you can lose. At the same time we can help each other to build our estates up."

Ross had run out of puff, he stood with his hands hanging loosely against his thighs studying McGregor's reactions.

"Mr. Smith, you are placing me in an invidious position," McGregor weakly protested, "But what about my James' education? Tracey is old enough to start a job. I have to take their future into consideration too, you know. There won't be much work available where we'll all be going, will there?" Ross answered coolly. "Oh there'll be plenty of work but maybe not the kind that Tracy would be interested in. However, that is a decision Tracy will have to make. If she wants to remain behind I'm sure she could find board with Elizabeth's Mother. She'll be only too glad to have some company once Elizabeth and I are married."

"What do you mean, once we are married?" Elizabeth interrupted, "Aren't you jumping the gun a bit Mr. Smith? You haven't even proposed to me yet."

Ross turned to face her with a disarming expression on his face, "Yes darling, that's true. But after all, how could you say no to me when I eventually come round to your place to propose."

That was true. Elizabeth knew, even if she didn't want to admit it, she wouldn't be able to refuse him. All the same a girl had her pride; she would make him suffer just that bit extra when he finally came round to ask her to become his wife.

Turning back to McGregor, Ross said, "You don't realise that my Elizabeth is a teacher, James could become her pupil. Just think it would be like having a private tutor, exactly the same as the toffs' children have."

Elizabeth was fuming!

It had felt ever so nice to be called 'my Elizabeth', but who did this Ross Smith think he was? Without ever having asked her permission he was organising her time as if she was his lackey. He had made himself scarce for nigh on three years and now he behaved as if he was the only one who knew everything. At the same time she couldn't prevent herself from admiring at the cocksure way he could control other people, leading them to his way of thinking.

With a shock she returned to the present, to discover everyone staring at her. Flustered she said, "What are you looking at me for? I was thinking of something else so I didn't hear your question. What did you want to know?"

Ross explained that they'd asked her if she would be agreeable to teach James and any others between her other duties. She studied his face intently before replying,

"How can I give an answer to this when you haven't had the decency to discuss any of your plans with me anyway? For all you know I might want to teach at a school in Sydney. Now that I am free I can apply for any position I like."

Ross looked shocked, sensing he had moved too fast. Seeing the looks on the faces around him he realised he'd better come up with something that would put him in charge again. Cursing for not thinking about Elizabeth again, for letting his eagerness to become a successful property owner overlook the feelings of his beloved Elizabeth.

"I am ever so sorry Elizabeth; this plan of mine has been in my mind for so long I feel that anyone I am close to knows just as much about it as I do. Please forgive me, you also Mr. McGregor, I've been far too hasty, forget what I've said. I'll come back to you when Elizabeth and I have had our discussion on what we should do to make our future."

McGregor replied. "That's fine with me, it will give me some time to think about the direction my family and I will go."

Ross went on with selecting the beasts he thought were best, but somehow the atmosphere had changed, the lighter mood had disappeared. Everyone was quieter in their dealings with each other almost to the sense of being subdued.

After Ross finished choosing thirty animals he went inside the house to finish the financial business with McGregor. Elizabeth and Tom went to sit in the buggy to wait for him. After saying goodbye, James disappeared with his sister into one of the many sheds to finish their chores.

Elizabeth sighed, but sat up straight when Ross followed by McGregor who was all smiles, stepped out from the house.

Even the dogs were silent when Ross made a clicking noise to indicate to the horse it could begin to move.

On the road Ross sensing that all was not right, placed his arm around Elizabeth's back murmuring softly, "Do you still care for me then?"

"I'll have to think about it," she replied in a soft hurt voice.

He pulled her a bit closer, Tom noticed with relief that Elizabeth didn't move away.

Eager as Ross was, the next few days he set aside to spend time with Elizabeth. Among one of the outings they did was a day trip spent on a ferry ride up and down the Murray. Elizabeth loved to sit next to him while Ross was excitedly telling her what he had in mind for the house they were going to live in on their property. When Elizabeth asked him what sort of a residence he had in mind he hastily explained that he couldn't afford to build a palace just yet. Seeing the question of what he could deliver in her eyes he said, "At this stage I can offer you a tent or at the most a small galvanized iron shack complete with windows of course," he added hurriedly seeing her frown. But when we have settled and sold some stock we'll be able to build a proper size house where we can display our Rembrandt and Constable paintings."

Elizabeth interrupted him, "How large will these paintings be?

"What? Oh I see. They'll be big enough to impress your friends and relations don't you worry yourself about that!" Ross smiled.

Elizabeth smiled sweetly back at him.

"Maybe you should purchase the paintings first, then you'll know what size walls will be required?"

"Where could we keep them?"

"You purchase the paintings then build the walls and to stop them from getting wet you might as well add a roof and since the house will be nearly finished by then you might as well add all the other rooms. Remember to add plenty of bedrooms as I feel we might need them for all our children."

Ross looked at her askance. "What do you mean plenty of bedrooms for all our children? You are having me on aren't you?"

He grabbed a giggling Elizabeth close to his chest.

"Well, you were dreaming out loud and I thought I'd add my dream to yours!" Elizabeth leaned with her eyes closed against Ross's strong shoulder. My, she loved this man!

The two remained in this close position as the ferry sailed slowly on.

From two seats further down the aisle an elderly spinster had been watching the young couple, jealously thinking, "How absolutely disgusting those young people are behaving! They have no sense of any decorum whatsoever."

With a great show of disgust she turned her face away from them but making sure however that she could still observe them by watching their reflection in a window.

— CHAPTER THREE —

With eyes open wide McGregor whistled in surprise, "As sure as God made little green apples, never have I seen a sight like this!" Tom was also impressed, while Ross had a contented smile on his face.

"Ross, please point out which part of the valley belongs to you."

Ross moved next to McGregor. He pointed his arm towards the meeting place of the two rivers.

"See the land in between the two rivers? That's mine! As you can see there is plenty left over for you or anyone else interested in good farmland."

Tom piped up and said, "Anyone that's not blind can see that you've selected the better section though. Having water on both sides of your property can only be seen as an asset surely?" Ross glanced at Tom; once again he was impressed with the boy. In one glance Tom had seen what Ross had noticed when he had first come across the valley.

"I suppose that's why they have the saying Tom,

'The things that come to those who wait will be the unwanted items left behind by those who got there before them'. Anyway you've seen what's on offer here.

We'd better return to see if we still have any cattle; the longer we hang about here the more they can disperse."

Ross noted that McGregor moved regretfully away from the view. He was pretty certain that the farmer inside McGregor was bursting to own a part of the valley.

The setting sun indicated the day was drawing near its end. Being in the valley meant the days were shorter than when you lived on the plains. The cattle were settling down now, they realised they had arrived at their destination. Ross was discussing with McGregor where he thought the best location for the shed they were going to build would be. McGregor thought nearer the trees would be a better spot than where Ross suggested building them.

"You are right, I agree that would be the better place if the shed would be our house," commented Ross, "but the shed will return to being a shed once the main house is built." He looked at McGregor. "That is the spot I've selected to place our home. The trees will give us some protection from the wind, also, not only can we see along the whole of the valley but we'll also be able to view our own property."

While the two of them were discussing the finer

details of the land, Tom decided to see if he could supplement anything different to their evening meal which wasn't that far off. Picking up some fishing tackle, which was stored in the wagon he went towards the creek. In the evening light the water had a silvery sheen, similar to a wide silver ribbon he had seen on a carriage that was taking its occupants to their wedding service.

Trees growing on the bank trailed their overhanging branches lazily through the smooth current while water bugs and insects were darting in whichever direction. The shallower part of the creek had pebbles that the setting sun made to look like large gold nuggets resting on the clean white sand. All was silent. The wallaby on the bank of the creek raised its head; saw all was safe so returned to nibbling the fresh green shoots that grew plentiful on the bank.

Making himself comfortable on the bank Tom got his gear ready, using some old bread for bait he dropped his line into the nearest billabong; it didn't take him long before he had a bite. His equipment might be makeshift but that didn't stop the fish from biting.

The sun had well set when Tom dropped his nice string of perch close to the fire that Ross had started, a cleaned shovel had a Damper on it waiting to be covered by hot ashes. Ross winked at Tom when he saw the harvest he held in his hand.

"This meal will definitely be worth waiting for tonight, and it'll really improve the Damper, that's for sure."

McGregor said impatiently, "How about doing less talking and some more cooking. I don't know about you lot but I'm starving."

Tom and Ross simultaneously turned to McGregor, "Pour the tea from the billy and give us something to drink instead of sitting there moaning."

"Pardon me for breathing," muttered McGregor. "I've had to work for my living today; I'm only trying to survive."

"Sorry we spoke sir, here have another spoon of sugar that should keep you going until the food is cooked." Tom threw a generous amount of sugar into McGregor's stained tin mug.

"Thanks mate; at least you know how to sweeten someone up."

When the last piece of burned crust was scraped off the shovel and there was no more fish meat left on the bones McGregor leaned back against the cart wheel making a contented sigh. "Ah, what a feast, never have I tasted better."

"It only tasted this good because this is the first day you've had to work hard for a living." Ross commented.

"That's not true!" McGregor replied quickly. "Ever since my dear wife departed I've had to work quite hard. I never realised how much that woman did around the house until she left!"

Without thinking Tom said, "Maybe that's why she..." He stopped suddenly realising what he was going to say.

"You could well be right Thomas; the same thought entered my head at the time. All the same, looking back, there must be more to it than that, because since she has left we've had more peace in the house than ever before."

Casting his mind back to the only time Tom had seen the family he'd noticed at the time that there seemed to be no stress among them. No mention of the missing woman had been made; they were very comfortable with each other's company. At the same time it came to him that he had been the only one who hadn't bowed his head before eating his meal. He had noticed this a few times but had always been too hungry to worry about it. Remarkable though, McGregor had admitted he was starving but still took time to say Grace before taking a bite.

The fire had turned into a collection of glowing embers when the two men and the boy decided to go to sleep.

The three lay on half a tarpaulin with the other half thrown over the top. The night was mild enough that no more covering was required. Tom lay on his back studying the stars. There seemed to be millions of them, at one time someone had told him that the Northern hemisphere was even more studded with stars which made him wonder how big the universe really was.

He gave up thinking about the possible size of it, as he had no idea on how he could measure it anyway. It wasn't as if you could take a yardstick and measure how far apart the stars were. If men could only fly! Just think how handy that would be. You wouldn't need to use winding tracks anymore, just flex your knees, push off, and up you would soar, way up into the wild blue yonder. It had to be a marvellous feeling, much better than swimming under water; at least you wouldn't have to come up for air. If his memory were correct he'd read in a newspaper that someone had reported that a Frenchman had invented something called a balloon which when filled with hot air would rise and float in the air. He'd had a dream once, where he found himself flying, it sure felt great. Perhaps, if you could dream about it, it could mean that man was able to fly if he spent some serious time in thinking how to go about it? If you thought about it; leaves floated gently down to the ground when they departed from the branch that held them. Large sails maybe?

Not tonight anyway, he was too tired. Slowly the stars went out of focus as his eyes closed. The wallaby near the creek sat up hesitantly to investigate the rumbling noises coming from the three strangers, saw that all was safe so continued nibbling at the fresh green shoots the last rain shower had helped bring up.

The shed started to take shape. Straight saplings from the forest were cut to length to be placed in the holes that had been dug at set intervals. The wood was still green of course, which meant that it would shrink when dried, but at least it would make it easier to hammer the nails in to hold the frame together. Ross commented, "This shed will only have to last for a certain amount of years. Once the main residence is erected we can rebuild at our leisure, the proper size shed we'll need. Fortunately the corrugated iron will still be as new."

As soon as the sheets were fastened to the roof, McGregor harnessed his horses to the coach to return and see if his farm had been sold in his absence. It was now up to Ross and Tom to complete the shed. Extra care was taken in making sure that vermin would find it difficult to enter, which meant that each sheet had to be painstakingly positioned. Ross pointed out to Tom, "A wife and mice don't get along, so let us try to keep one of them contented!"

Once they had finished the floor, which consisted of mixing cow dung and then working it into the earthen floor until they ended up with a reasonable polish, the inside looked quite homely with the sun streaming in through the only window that was there.

Stepping out Ross looked at Tom - with a smile on his face he said, "I think we've been in the middle of cow dung long enough! How about a swim in the river and tomorrow we give our horses a run. Let's spend a day or so to see what else the property has to offer. With a bit of luck the smell will have disappeared by the time we return."

Tom didn't disagree, like most youngsters he always wanted to see what was around the next corner. Undoing his shirt as he began to run towards the water he yelled, "Last one in is a slowcoach!"

The splash they made entering the water sounded as one.

"How did you get on with your Father?" The question came from Ross as they were waiting for sleep to overtake them. Tom took a while to answer. Just as Ross thought Tom had fallen asleep he was answered,

"I miss him; I miss him now more than ever. The times are too numerous to mention when the thought enters my head, wish I could speak to my Dad about this, or wouldn't Dad enjoy being here with me now? Dad and I were mates; there was nothing that he and I couldn't talk about. At times I had the feeling that my Mother was jealous of me as she wanted more of Dad also, but despite all that we were a close family. I suppose I was lucky to get to know him that well for the short time he resided with us on earth."

Once Tom started to speak there was no holding him. Ross realised that his question had opened a floodgate. Eventually Tom ceased speaking, after a quiet moment he asked Ross if he had got on with his

Father. After some silence the soft reply came.

"Not as well as you got on with yours, Tom. My Father was a very hard man and even now I find it hard to speak about him."

There was another long silence; Ross began to speak again.

"You are the first person to whom I've spoken about my Father. We owned a large property near Hahndorf in South Australia. Being not only the eldest son but also the only one I was groomed by my Father to run the property according to his wishes. No expense was too large to help educate me in the direction he wanted me to go. Once I began to mature however I started to push for the directions I thought that modern farm management techniques should be applied at our property. Mentioning that cattle should be circulated from one paddock to another to facilitate better fodder growth and prevention of disease was one thing. However when I brought to his attention that if you let land lay fallow for a while it would perform better after the rest, I found out I should've kept my opinions to myself because all it brought forth was sarcastic comments from my Father. It was the day I questioned him why he had spent so much money on my education when he would never heed or listen to any of it I discovered what he really thought of me.

"That's a good question," he had replied sardonically,

"because I've started to think that your education has been a waste of time. And I tell you now; you will never apply any of your silly know-how on this property".

"Well," I replied, "it seems that I am wasting my time here; I might as well go." All he said was,

"Yes, you might as well leave now and I'll inform your Mother."

So with nothing else but the clothes I had on he walked me to the front gate, opened it and closed it after me. That was the last time I saw any of my family. To this day I don't know if my Mother or my sister are alive or not."

A long silence hung over them both - time seemed to stretch out. Finally Tom said, "That's one of the saddest stories I've heard, I'm ever so sorry for you and your family."

"It's been a bitter lesson Tom, and I have to make sure that I will never become like my Father, although the older I am getting the more I see some of my Father's traits reflected in me."

Quietness descended upon them as both lay on their backs staring into the dark sky above them. Each one was absorbed by his own thoughts.

It took an awful long time before the silence was broken by the regular sound of Tom's light snore.

— *CHAPTER FOUR* —

They'd been on the way for a couple of hours. Tom had saddled their mounts albeit with a heavy head due to his lack of sleep, while Ross was making sure that the equipment needed was on their packhorse. The grass they were travelling through was so tall it scraped against their legs, annoyingly leaving prickly seeds probing in their socks.

Regardless of all these small discomforts Tom was enjoying himself as he discovered more of what the land had to offer.

The view obtained from the horses back was spectacular. On each side of the valley there rose magnificent granite cliffs with the occasional waterfall looking like a long white ribbon cascading from the escarpment. Beautiful green and red coloured king parrots flew screeching noisily from tree to tree.

Twisting his body around he smiled at Ross who prodded his mount to walk along side Tom.

"Stop for a moment Tom and cast your eyes back to where we've come from. What does the sight remind you of?"

Tom looked back; all he could see was the tall grass weaving back and forwards with the wind. Then it came to him what Ross was referring to.

"Seeing it from here gives me the feeling that we are standing in the middle of a large lake! The wind is pushing the top of the grass just like the effect it has on water."

"It certainly is a sight to behold. I can't wait to show Elizabeth and see her reaction to all this. I just hope she feels she'll be in Paradise; that is the only place I can compare it to. Can't you see God's hand in this?"

Tom didn't reply. At times he wished that Ross didn't speak so openly about God, as if he had a personal relationship with him, it made him feel embarrassed.

"Well can't you?" Ross prodded.

"I don't know him that well!" Tom replied angrily. "Our minister kept telling us that God will never do anything bad, he can only do well. All the same, my Father believed in Him wholeheartedly, and he was taken away from us when we really needed him. Mum became melancholic when we needed her, our farm was taken from us and my brother and sisters are all disbanded." Angrily he faced Ross and continued, "At this stage I'm not very impressed with God's handiwork or his goodness!"

Ross saw the bitterness reflected on his young companion's face. He could relate to Tom, as he had felt very similar when his Father had made him leave home and family. Somehow he had to diffuse this anger. He knew that if Tom stayed this way he would become an embittered man and never enjoy the goodness that was to be grasped by those that were willing to look for it on earth. He was hoping that God would place the right words in his mouth so he would be of some help to Tom.

"Look at it from another point Tom. He has given you the opportunity to bring your family together. You have enough intelligence to survive on your own. You have a job, which means you can save your money so that you can find out where the members of your family are. I promise that if you can locate them, I will do everything possible to make them comfortable. If that is what your family members would want to do. You must remember that their conditions have also changed and they might not want the same things you want!"

With a surprised expression on his face Tom looked at him. Pulling up his horse he said in a husky voice, "You would do that for me? We've hardly been together long enough to really know each other!"

"How long do you have to be with each other before you know when you can trust a person? I've only known Elizabeth for a short while, but it took me only a few hours after meeting her that I knew she was the girl for me. She must've felt the same, as she was still waiting for me even if I had been away for over two years!"

Ross shook his head as if he didn't believe the wonder of it all.

Suddenly Tom felt rather ashamed. Within his heart he knew that Ross trusted him, right from the time when they sat together sharing the pies after they'd met; he had felt the bond between them. Why did he make these silly statements that in the end only hurt Ross and upset his own feelings? Was it because he didn't want to be close to anyone because they might disappear and he would have to suffer being alone all over again? Ah, life was confusing! At times his body felt as if it was filled with so many complex emotions that he'd thought he would explode. Wouldn't it be nice though to have his family around him again? Tears came to his eyes. Hoping he wouldn't be noticed wiping his eyes with his sleeve he turned towards Ross, who was watching him with a bemused but understanding expression.

"Well Ross, you've certainly made me think. I'd be ever so grateful if I could have my family with me, however, it would take some saving so I realise that it might take some time." Ross stared at Tom a while before saying, "Think about it deeply and do some praying, it might happen a lot faster if you have the Lord on your side."

Looking straight into Ross' eyes Tom stretched his arm towards Ross who grabbed hold of his hand. Tom stated clearly, "I will take your advice and promise to do what you suggested!"

Resting at a place where the cliffs only reached the height of a man sitting on his horse, the grass was at a convenient height so you could walk through it and a small stream came burbling down the cliff nearby supplying them with the sweetest tasting water they had ever drank.

Both were sitting quietly around the small crackling fire enjoying their mugs of coffee, when Tom suddenly reared up. "What's that?" he exclaimed.

A drumming sound quickly drew nearer. Before they could stand up a large black ball exploded from the trees on the cliffs above them. Floating through the air over them was a large stallion followed by the rest of the herd of brumbies. Time seemed to freeze; the large animals hit the ground effortlessly. The neighing of our horses brought the stallion to a sudden stop, as he turned around to protect his herd, which were thundering past him. The air cleared of the dust created by the wild horses giving a clear view of the spectacular beast.

"Grab hold of our horses," yelled Ross. Not knowing the reason why, Tom blindly followed the instructions. Grabbing hold of their bridles Tom tied the restless animals to the nearest tree. Leaderless, the brumbies had stopped galloping to begin grazing not far away from their leader who standing on his hind legs, was neighing shrilly in our direction. His coat was so black and shiny it looked a dark blue where the muscles rippled under his skin.

Ross came over to stand next to Tom to assist him in holding back the three animals who were straining to break loose from their leases.

"He's calling them to join him," whispered Ross. "Can't say I can blame them for wanting to join him, life must be so much better when you are free!"

"Isn't he a magnificent animal?" Tom exhaled deeply.

"He sure is." Ross replied. "We've been very privileged to come across him, in more ways than one. Once we have established ourselves we know where there is a supply of good quality horses available. We keep the best for our use and sell the rest making sure there are enough mares left remaining to start a new herd."

"Wouldn't you want to own and ride him?" Tom asked eyeing Ross who nodded his head stating.

"I sure would love to own him but at the moment he is better off here where he can improve and build up the herd. There has to be a foal among that lot over there that takes after his sire?"

Ross pointed to the grazing brumbies. Eventually the stallion realized he was wasting his time and joined the herd to lead them away.

"We'd better sleep lightly tonight," Ross remarked. "I have a feeling that we haven't seen the last of him yet. He's bound to return and have another try at taking our animals from us."

Once the stallion was out of sight, the horses calmed down. As it was still a few hours till sunset Ross decided to continue on and find a nice spot to camp.

It was nearly dark when a suitable location to bivouac for the night was found, after making sure that their horses were well tethered and watered, Tom lit a small fire to boil the billy. Not many words were spoken as their senses were honed in on listening to see if the stallion would return.

After a restless night Tom woke up with the birds; or as one of his schoolmates used to say, 'at sparrow fart'. The birds were trying to outdo each other with their songs. Exploring the area around the camp Tom heard a rustling in the bushes across the fast flowing but narrow creek. Nimbly jumping unto a long dead tree that looked as if many years ago it had fallen across the creek, he carefully moved along it towards the source of the sound. Glancing downwards Tom observed that he was crossing over another stream that seemed to come straight out from the side of the cliff. With all the ground cover and scrub surrounding the creek you would never realise that it was there when standing on the bank from which he had stepped onto the tree. Suddenly a large emu flew out from a bush; Tom's presence must've frightened it. Desperate to escape it only barely missed Tom, who had such a fright at the suddenness of it, lost his balance. Wheeling his arms to remain on the fallen tree he realised he was fighting a losing battle as he tumbled backwards to fall in the creek below him.

Tom thought, "What a great start for the day. It'll take most of the day to get myself dry."

Turning around Tom attempted to stand up when he noticed something yellowish in the water that made his heart beat faster. Falling back on his knees his hand groped towards the yellow stone. When extracting his hand from the stream, Tom stared in amazement at the object that covered most of the palm of his hand. Turning it between his fingers he felt how heavy it was. This had to be a gold nugget, surely?

If there was one, was his next thought, there had to be more nuggets! Sure, there was another. It didn't take long before he had both his pockets and his hands full. Walking back towards the camp he could hear Ross muttering in a disgruntled voice.

"Useless, he is absolutely useless. Why do I hire staff who are never around to do a day's work. All I need is a pot of coffee and I have to make that myself!"

Tom softly crept up behind Ross, who was busily attempting to organise his breakfast. "Did you say I am useless, Ross? How much money have you made today then? At least I earn my keep. See if you can beat this!"

Tom dropped the nuggets from his hands onto the hessian chaff bag that served as a tablecloth, while all the time watching Ross' face.

Ross said very little, in fact he was too flabbergasted to say anything at all. Tom was now emptying his pockets while all Ross did was sit and watch the amount of nuggets grow. Eventually Tom's pockets were empty. Sitting down next to Ross he stated, "Well Ross, what do you think of this effort?"

Then with a smile on his face Tom continued, "And I haven't even had breakfast yet!"

Ross dragged his eyes away from the gold to look at Tom.

"You were mistaken in what you heard me say Tom. I was just contemplating on how 'useful' you've been since we've known each other. Whatever gave you the idea that I could ever call you useless?"

Ross placed his hand tenderly on Tom's shoulders.

"I believe you Ross, thousands wouldn't, but I am naïve enough to believe you."

Tom gestured towards the pile of nuggets stating, "Not a bad little find though, is it? If you organise breakfast I might even show you where I found it."

Ross salaamed, "Sure my lord and master, I'll serve you your breakfast. As long as you realise that once you've consumed it, I am still your boss!"

They both fell on the ground in hysterical laughter. Suddenly Ross stopped, looked at Tom and queried, "How come you are wet all over?"

Tom sat up, grabbed hold of the bread pulling a hunk away from it.

"I think the coffee is ready to pour Ross, let's sit down and I'll tell you all about it."

When Tom finished his narrative Ross kept looking at him. Tom began to feel embarrassed and was opening his mouth to say something when Ross spoke.

"Tom, do you recall yesterday's remarks about looking for your family?"

Tom nodded his head.

"Well, I have a feeling this gift you found is a direct sign from God for you to start looking for them!"

"You think so Ross?" Tom's voice shook with the enormity of it. If Ross was right God was taking a personal interest in him. His heart was hammering in his throat; this was an enormous responsibility. Tom felt so weak and small, he was certain that he would let God down. Suddenly a calmness descended over him, he was sure he heard someone say.

Be still; I'll be with you always!

Tom raised his eyes at Ross. "Did you hear someone speak then?" Ross shook his head negatively. "I just heard a voice telling me to be still and that he would be always with me."

Ross' mouth dropped open. "If I were you Tom, I'd heed that advice."

"Golly, this spot is certainly hidden? You must've been meant to find it that's for sure." Walking through knee high water Ross was eagerly searching for more nuggets. It didn't take long before he had a similar amount as Tom had found. Wading towards the cliff they discovered that the stream came out of a hole similar to what a wombat might make. Once again there were nuggets for the picking.

"Let's not be greedy Tom, we know now where the gold is and we can come back anytime if we ever are desperate for cash in the future. I feel that we should keep this knowledge just between the two of us. Also, it's a pity that you are too young to take this gold to the bank to open an account. If you believe you can trust me I'll open a trust type account in your name and we'll trickle small amounts of nuggets into it, as we don't want them to become suspicious as to how it is we are in possession of such a quantity of gold. One of the last things we need is an army of gold diggers on our farm. 'Our farm', Tom liked the sound of that.

The horses must've realised they were returning home as they needed no pushing. Time seemed to fly for the riders, as they were busy planning on how to make their dreams come true.

— CHAPTER FIVE —

'What am I going to do? Who'll help me run this place?'

These thoughts were running around in her head as Jessica was sitting with her knees under her chin in one of the large chairs in the drawing room. This was her favourite place and position when she was trying to sort out a problem that required some extra effort. It was only two days since Mother's burial and her Father was expecting her to take over Mother's duties as if she was away on holidays. Nothing had been discussed; just that statements were made and orders given. If Jessica queried anything her father stood there, just looking at her, not making any helpful comments, his eyes cold and disdainful.

Jessica had never understood how her Mother could've loved her Father. In all her seventeen years she had never seen her Father display any warmth or love towards her Mother or anyone else in the family.

Times hadn't been too bad when Ross had been

at home; plenty of stolen moments of fun and laughter then, although even Ross went quiet when Father was near. Somehow a cold aura surrounded her Father at all times.

Mother had been sick for a long while and Jessica had fulfilled many of the duties that her Father expected to be done by the lady of the house. During the last month of her Mother's illness she had asked Jessica at least three times a week if any news of her darling son Ross had arrived. Always the answer was to be in the negative. Ross had departed a good four years ago. To this day Jessica wondered what had really occurred on that day. All she knew was that her Father had come to the table for his meal and informed her Mother that Ross' place setting could be put away as he would not require it any more. Mother had gone white and her hands had started to shake when she asked softly, "why?"

"He's decided to move on!" Was the only comment her father made! No mention of Ross was ever made by her Father again. Mother from that day on had never acted the same. To be more accurate; nothing had been the same for anyone working on the estate. Until that time Jessica hadn't been aware that Ross had had such a large influence in the running of the farm.

Staff began to disappear, with replacements never being as good as the previous workers. Two of the girls who used to assist her Mother with the housework never came back after attending the funeral which hadn't helped her Father's mood. If everyone was leaving, Jessica thought, maybe it was time for her to depart also? There definitely was no fun in being at home. It was a frightening thought, but remaining at home with her Father felt scary also. There would be no chance that any of the local boys would arrive on a white horse to take her away from her predicament. Her Father let the few who had had the courage to call on her know in no uncertain terms that they weren't wanted here. Anyway where could she go? If she moved to Adelaide her father would come and drag her back home as soon as he discovered where she was residing.

"No," Jessica said to herself, "I'd have to go further away? Go to Melbourne maybe?" It was a long way away. There'd be plenty of places to hide though especially if she changed her name.

A door slammed, heavy footsteps were coming up the passage.

Jessica panicked. What had she forgotten now? The door opened and not much later her father stood in front of her.

"What do you think you are up to," he hissed through his tight thin lips. "I went to the kitchen to have my afternoon tea, not only was there no one there but there was no tea laid out on the table. You'd better get your act together my girl or things will change around here!"

Sliding from the chair Jessica carefully slunk around her Father saying, "I am so sorry Father it won't happen again I'll go and make your afternoon tea right now."

Placing the cup and saucer on the table next to the biscuit jar in front of her Father's chair, she walked to the door and called out that his tea was ready and waiting for him.

In silence he entered the kitchen, remaining that way until he finished drinking. His chair scraped on the tiled floor as he rose to push himself away from the table to leave the room. Jessica sighed despondently, wouldn't it have been nice to hear him say,

"Thank you, dear daughter, that was an excellent afternoon tea, I really appreciated the effort you made to have it ready so quickly!" These were words you would never hear in this household said Jessica to herself. "Dear Father," she sarcastically thought, "you mentioned that there would be changes around here. You've just made up my mind, tomorrow after you have left to ride into town, I'll be riding out on my way to Melbourne. Thank heavens that Mother left instructions to have my share of her inheritance placed into my personal bank account. At the first National Bank I come to tomorrow I'll withdraw half of my money and I'll be off to Melbourne."

Jessica shivered slightly. She'd better start organising herself, as there was a lot to do.

The bank clerk looked strangely at her when he read the figure written on the withdrawal slip. Then shrugging his shoulders he opened his drawer and counted out the money. Before any of the other customers in the bank could see the size of the wad of notes, Jessica whipped them into her bag. Returning to the pony trap she'd used to come to town in she grabbed a Gladstone bag and her portmanteau; she left the trap behind as she began walking towards the railway station. She'd felt concerned about leaving the poor animal waiting there but she knew that someone would contact her Father when they realised that one of his horses and trap was still reigned to a post in front of the bank. After purchasing her ticket it fortunately only took ten minutes before she was sitting facing the direction she was travelling in a reasonable empty carriage. The deed was done! She was on her way.

It wasn't all that many years ago that Cob & Co. coaches had been replaced, Jessica looked around and thought that this style of travelling was far superior to that of the past. Now if only they could control the amount of soot that seeped into the carriages, as no matter how hard you closed the doors and widows the soot entered. However it was a small price to pay for not having to put up with her father.

Jessica felt as if she had been catapulted out of Spencer street station. Never in her life had she been surrounded by so many people. Surely all these people hadn't been on her train? Her bag became tangled with another bag. As her eyes followed the arm that was holding the culprit bag, she eventually looked into two merry eyes of a girl about her own age.

"I think our bags like each other," the girl said. "How about we move together until we are away from this rat race and can do something about separating our bags?"

This was easier said than done. There seemed to be no end to the crowd that surrounded them. Suddenly the crowd seemed to be sweeping past them, never had that little unoccupied space been so appreciated.

"Phew," said Jessica. "I sincerely hope I don't have to do this every day? I don't think I could cope with it!"

"It's not all that bad!" The other girl replied, trying to remove a strand of hair that insisted on hanging over her right eye. "It looks and sounds as if you are an out of Towner that's why it seems so frightening?"

"You are right I am from the country, I didn't think it looked so obvious?" Jessica answered anxiously; she studied the girl thoroughly wondering how it was that you could feel so at ease with a person whom you had never met before?

"Have you seen enough?" The girl said smiling. Jessica blushed as it came to her that she had been very rude in staring at the girl before her so blatantly.

"Oh, I am ever so sorry, I didn't realise I was using you as a staring post. Why don't we separate our bags and as I have no idea where I am going we could perhaps have a coffee together so that you can enlighten me on where a young girl can stay safely in this large town. Please say yes?"

For some unexplainable reason Jessica didn't want the girl to move out of her life just yet.

"Gloria is what my parents named me!"

Jessica had introduced herself formally as soon as they had found an empty table at the coffee place around the corner from the station. While waiting for the drinks to arrive Jessica looked around at the hustle and bustle that was going on around her. Everyone seemed to be in such a rush. Adelaide was never like this, everything happened at a slower pace over there. Here young boys were yelling out the latest headlines and the name of the paper they were selling, horse drawn cabs were picking up and discharging customers while other horses were impatiently pawing the ground with their well shod feet waiting for their masters to return from dropping off goods they had to deliver to various shops in the street. The smell of horse dung was overpowering much stronger than it had been in the country, Gloria explained that this was because it hadn't rained for a while.

"If you think this is bad, I'm afraid, things don't

become much better when it rains, at least now you can cross the street, if you keep a watchful eye, without slipping on something nasty, or have your skirt trailing through the wet muck. Why do we women wear the outfits' men design for us? It makes no sense to me whatsoever. Although, I suppose if we are silly enough to try to please their little minds, it doesn't say a lot for us women, does it?"

Gloria looked enquiringly at Jessica to see what sort of a response she'd come out with. However all Jessica said was, "How would you like me to answer that?"

"That's fair enough!" Gloria stated after a pause. "We've only known each other less than an hour there's no need to spoil the moment by airing my views on politics. Changing the subject, where are you planning to work and live in this large City?"

Jessica shrugged her shoulders, looking very young and unsure.

"To tell you the truth, I haven't the foggiest? The decision to come here was so sudden that I haven't had time to really think about it yet. Work-wise I expect to find a position as an office girl. That was one of the reasons I learned to type, but now that I am here and see so many people milling on the streets I wonder if there are any positions available anywhere at all?"

Gloria laughed.

"Don't worry about the people on the streets;

most of them don't seem to need a job. I think your first need is to find somewhere to be able to lay your head down. The reason I asked where you were going to work is that by pure coincidence there are two rooms available at the house where I am staying as one of the tenants left to go home last week to get married. If you are interested and trust me I could put in a good word to the owner and at least you'll have a bed to sleep in and a roof over your head while you're looking for work."

Jessica couldn't believe her luck, once again she studied Gloria intently, then her face cleared as she made up her mind, all her instincts cried out that this girl was to be trusted.

"You must be an angel; I am starting to believe that our bags tangled due to heavenly intervention. Someone definitely wanted the two of us to meet!"

Gloria stood up brushing some imaginary crumbs from the front of her dress, saying,

"We'd better get a move on then or it'll be late by the time we arrive home. I'll give you a hand with your unpacking and tell you about the type of work-places that are located in the area."

With a heavy bag but a light heart Jessica followed Gloria to the tram stop that was going to take her to her new abode. Within a half hour Jessica was standing on the footpath in front of a house that had known better days.

Gloria had to lift the gate to open it and was

accompanied by so many different squeaks - it sounded as if an orchestra were tuning their instruments.

Turning to face Jessica she muttered, "We boarders believe the owner leaves it in this state so that he can hear us coming in at night."

"Oops, there is Mr. Lorrimer now."

Confidently she walked up to the man and began talking to him. Jessica could tell that they were discussing her as his rheumy eyes peered over Gloria's shoulder at her from under a shock of greying red hair.

Acting as if she was totally unconcerned Jessica studied the area around her. The garden could be made into something quite respectable if one took the effort to do something about it. Dreaming of how she would improve it she was interrupted in her thoughts by a voice saying, "Room six is yours but I want two months' rent first thing tomorrow morning, after that we'll see. We aren't running a charity here you know?" He turned round to carry on with whatever he was doing completely ignoring her.

With a bewildered look Jessica looked at Gloria who winked at her and led her to the front door whispering, "Ignore him, you can tell he is kindness itself. You are in and that's all that counts. If he was really ruthless he would've taken your rent money from you now before you even entered the place."

The kitchenette cum dining room was just as

neglected as the outside of the house but at least had a window that was large enough to let a decent amount of light in. The bedroom was dark and dingy but then Jessica thought, fortunately the lights are out and your eyes are closed when you are asleep so it doesn't really matter what the room looks like. At least I have arrived in Melbourne, found lodgings and a friend all in the first day. I'll just have to take it day by day.

Just before falling asleep in her new bed Jessica fleetingly wondered what her Father's reaction on discovering that his daughter had disappeared would've been?

***

For the first time in his life Jessica's Father was confused. Sitting in the same chair that his daughter used when she had to do some heavy thinking he was doing some heavy thinking himself. Sipping from his third glass of brandy he observed that the liquid remaining in the decanter had gone down considerably since he had entered the room. However even the large Cuban cigar he was smoking hadn't been able to assist the brandy to dull his mind. Something was nagging at him that it could be his fault why he was in this predicament. This was disturbing, for a man who never before in his existence had made a mistake. In the past anything that had gone wrong was always blamed on someone else. Even he had to admit to himself, that there weren't too many people left whom he could lay the blame on now. He took another large gulp. A wave of self-pity washed over him. It was going to take a long time for him and the town to forget how his daughter had made a fool of him.   Never had he felt as embarrassed as when the Bank manager had dropped in on his way home to inform him that his horse and trap were parked in front of the bank. To rub it in the fool had left the horse and trap in town - surely it wouldn't have taken too much effort to tie the horse to his own trap and bring it here. All the same it had been clever of the little minx in how she had departed. He had never guessed that she was so cunning. Against his will a grain of pride entered his mind. Fiercely stabbing the butt of the cigar into the ashtray he poured the remaining liquid in the glass down his throat, and then sank back into the chair to stare into space. Slowly his breathing slowed down, his fingers relaxed releasing the glass to fall on the floor. A tear trickled down his cheek and he emitted a light snore as sleep finally overcame him.

— *CHAPTER SIX* —

Tom was standing in the shade of a large eucalyptus watching the shanty across the road. He'd been there for a while and so far hadn't been too impressed with the clientele that wandered in and out from the hastily put together three-roomed shack. Two cattle dogs were lying in the dust near the front entrance waiting for their owners. Each time a person exited the place they raised their heads hopefully but had to lay their heads back disappointedly between their stretched-out paws.

The solicitor, who had been hired by Ross, had informed him that his sister was 'working' at the premises. At this stage Tom had seen no hide or hair of her and was beginning to wonder if the man had his facts right.

"Something had better happen soon," Tom thought. 'I've been here for three days running and people are beginning to look suspiciously at me."

Six months had passed since he had started to

bring his family together. It hadn't been easy trying to follow a trail of paperwork but all he had to do now was locate his sister and they'd all be together again.

"If it hasn't happened in three days why do you think it should happen today?" Deep in thought, it took a while to register that the words had been addressed to him.

"Are you speaking to me?" Tom asked as he turned to see who was speaking to him.

"You are the only person I know that's been acting as if he hasn't been here for the last three days, that I know of," the man replied.

Tom studied the individual who was speaking to him. Never had he seen so many whiskers on a man's face, however there was still room for a nose to poke through the hair although the friendly sparkly eyes were hard to find.

"Have I been so obvious?"

"I don't know if the whole town knew you were standing here but I can advise you now that if you don't move to another place the owner of that residence will become so jittery that he'll set his boys on to you. Mark DeVilliers does not take kindly to people taking an interest in his business activities."

Tom recalled that name being associated with a court case only a few months ago. The locals had laughed, albeit softly, to each other that once again the jury had proved that the law was an ass. DeVilliers had claimed that he had been standing on the corner of the main street trying to remove a splinter from underneath one of his nails with his knife blade when a man had rushed up and accidentally run into him. All of this was believable and no one was denying that it couldn't happen. However the evidence brought forward by the coroner stating where the knife wounds were located, proved that the man must've done it four times and he had to be running backwards at the same time.

Toms' hair stood up on the back of his neck. The solicitor had never advised him what type of company his sister was in.

The whiskered man grabbed Tom gently by the shoulder to push him nearer the tree. A smart single brougham drawn by a magnificent groomed horse pulled up at the front of the pub's entrance. A tall man dressed like a dandy jumped out to run and open the door on Tom's side and assisted a young lady to step down from the vehicle. Tom gasped, when he recognized the girl was his sister. He stepped forward but the man held him back, "Don't do anything silly," the stranger whispered. "The girl is his latest bit of fluff, she sings and entertains his customers, but for some reason he is more smitten with her than he has been with any of his previous talented girls. I do admit this girl has more talent than the others, she sings like an angel, and there is an innocence about her that would intrigue a man like DeVilliers. He believes that there's evil in everyone, in some people it just takes a little while longer to come out, that's all."

In spite of himself Tom shuddered at what he was hearing. DeVilliers and his companion had gone inside. Tom looked at the man who most likely had saved his life.

"Why don't you and I go somewhere where we don't look so conspicuous and at the same time we can discuss DeVilliers in greater detail? You seem to know a lot about him?"

The bearded stranger nodded his head and led the way.

Soon he stopped at a seat that was conveniently placed in a small park behind some shrubs. Making sure that they could not be overheard the man spoke.

"It wasn't hard to notice that you were very interested in the girl that accompanied DeVilliers; you wouldn't be Tom Matheson would you?"

Tom nodded his head in bewilderment. "Yes, how do you know?"

"Plain deduction that's how Tom, you don't mind if I call you Tom, do you?"

Tom shook his head, not sure if he did it in agreement to the question or just in pure bewilderment of the situation he was in.

"You seem to know a lot about my sister and DeVilliers? Why are they of interest to you? Who are you, anyway?"

Tom would've liked answers to all his questions

but all the man said was,

"You may call me Jason. I've had a close interest in DeVilliers for a long while."

Tom studied the man. There was something not quite right in his appearance. Something must've reflected in Tom's face as Jason began to wriggle on his seat as if he felt uncomfortable.

Suddenly it clicked in Tom's brain; Jason was wearing a wig, the skin around his eyes gave away that he was a lot younger than he wanted you to think he was.

"Why are you disguising yourself?" Before Tom could ask anymore Jason placed his hand on Tom's arm. Looking around to see if no one was near he said,

"You are very observant Tom, I'm glad that we met up because I think we could work together; kill two birds with one stone, if you are receiving what I'm talking about."

"Jason, you have to explain yourself a lot clearer than you have done because at this stage I haven't a clue what you are on about."

Jason looked steadily at Tom then shrugged his shoulders.

"Right, am I right in thinking that you are here to take your sister away from that place?"

Hesitantly Tom replied, "Yes, that was my original quest and that is my final aim. I want my family to be together again." Jason nodded his head.

"That's what I thought when I observed you standing under the tree. You see, three years ago I was in the same predicament as you. My younger sister who was the darling of our family got into his clutches, he promised to train her to become an Opera singer while she was singing in one of his dives. The girl had music on her brain; all she ever spoke about was how she was going to be the most appreciated singer after Nellie Stewart. So it wasn't all that difficult for that weasel Mark DeVilliers to gain her attention and believe his smooth oily talk about all the large Opera houses she would visit to sing in if she stuck with him.

Then one day she realised what she was really there for; he had become bored with her; dropping her for another woman and forced her to begin entertaining his guests. Knowing what she'd become she felt so degraded that she believed she could never look her family and friends in their eyes again. In her desperate depressed state she took her own life, possibly thinking it would take away the shame. Of course the result in the end was that it took away my sister! My parents were devastated, their daughter, the idol of their existence had never given them a chance to tell her that they would stick with her and love her regardless of what she had done. To this day they are suffering and I am hoping to ease their feelings by bringing that scoundrel DeVilliers to justice."

Jason went silent and stared at the grass; a deep sigh passed his lips.

"That is why I restrained you from walking over to your sister. Once DeVilliers knew you were interested in taking away Kathleen he would make life a misery for both of you. What we need to do is plan this thoroughly so that no one ends up being hurt apart from DeVilliers. What we need to do with him is to have a sound case against him so that even his clever lawyers can't get him off."

"Well, how can we do that? I only want my sister to come home with me, how will that make him end up in gaol?"

"Don't you worry about that, we, I mean I have plenty on him, what I need is the opportunity to take him in. There is always a guard somewhere close by, so that you can't get near him. We need to distract him while he is in the middle of one of his illegal activities. That's where you and your sister can help. Do you think you can talk to Kathleen without him being too surprised that you have found her?"

Tom kept silent. What had seemed a simple job of finding his sister and explaining to her that they could live together as a family again had become a huge complicated affair, that wouldn't be solved in a couple of days. In the back of his mind he always had a reservation that his sister wouldn't be that keen on coming home. Once she had had a taste of freedom with no added responsibilities of having to look after any siblings. Now that he had seen her dressed in her finery and been made a fuss off by a rich man who she thought was her swain, it would be very difficult or nigh impossible to ask her to come back home. His head was spinning with possible solutions but none came to mind that would solve his predicament.

Be still; I'll be with you always!

There was that calm voice again. Last time it had spoken Tom had been worried and not long after his problem was lightened. If only he had more faith. He still felt guilty about receiving help from above. After all he was or should be old enough to solve his own problems. Maybe though, this was a situation beyond his control, Ross always said that if you could get someone who could do the job better than yourself you should be humble enough to let him or her do it.

Jason nudged him. "Are you awake?" Tom looked at him, he hadn't realised so much time had passed.

"Sorry Jason, I was communicating with my Maker!" Jason studied Tom as if he had gone bonkers. "You mean!" He raised his eyebrows heavenward.

"Yes, I hope you don't mind but He has helped me in the past and just now he spoke to me again.

"No, I don't mind Tom. If anything I feel jealous. I seem to have to solve all my own problems. I wouldn't mind a bit of assistance at times."

"I can't help you there very much Jason, I don't

know why He helps me but ever since He has, I've been very grateful and that is why I am going with his advice again."

"Good heavens, what did He tell you to do?"

"Nothing solid really, the voice tells me that He's with me always. I think that in this case it means that I am going to have to leave this situation in His hands for my Maker to do with it what He wants."

"Come on Tom, don't you think that's the easy or the coward's way out?"

"Maybe, but I feel very comfortable with it all the same. I'll tell you what I will do though; tomorrow I'll visit Kathleen and leave my home address with her so that in case she has to leave suddenly she knows where to go. Then I'll continue on my way to finish my business at Gundagai and on my return I'll contact my sister again. Surely Mark can't do anything to me if all I do is visit my sister when I'm passing through?"

Jason sat back on the bench to have a better look at Tom. He really wasn't sure what he was hearing; it all sounded a bit unadventurous for his liking.

How could you walk away with the sense of having achieved something when you didn't have to raise a hand towards achieving a result? It was all beyond him! However, he had been trying for some years now without achieving any results whatsoever so why not run with what Tom was suggesting. Thinking back on it he did have an easier way of living when he used to attend Sunday school. The rules were so much easier to follow then; all you had to do was please your teacher, God and your parents. If things did go wrong there was always someone nearby that either forgave you or gave you a helping hand.

Somehow he had drifted away from everything he had learned as life had only too quickly pointed out that there were many people living by another set of rules. It was more like man eats dog, than to be kind to your fellow man. Then when his sister did what never should've occurred in the first place he really got uptight with his Maker for letting a wee innocent girl come into a situation like that anyway. Somehow with the anger that was deep inside his heart and trying to get even with Mark DeVilliers hadn't dissipated any of it, so maybe he was on the wrong track and should give Tom's method a go.

Making up his mind he said to Tom, "Okay mate, we'll do it your way. I'll hang around here until you return and then we'll have another talk. I've wasted so much time on that weasel already a little bit more won't hurt.

The shiny brougham was parked near the front entrance again; the horse was pawing the dirt as if it was bored. With a thumping heart Tom entered the building whispering,

"Give me some strength Lord, I feel I need it." As he walked towards the bar he ordered a drink. Before he could raise it to his lips a voice screamed out, "Tommy, Tommy, what are you doing here?" Next minute he was in a bear hug.

Acting surprised he called out, "Katy, how come you are here?"

Lowering her eyes modestly, she said, "I work here, I'm their main singer."

"Here, you sing here?" Letting his eyes go around the room. "Surely you could sing somewhere better, especially with your voice."

"Alright, I know what you mean but a girl has to start somewhere and at least dear Mark gave me a go when no one else was interested." Her voice turned sulky.

"Anyway changing the subject, have you heard from the others?" Tom knew what she meant, "Indeed I have, and we are all together again. I've had a stroke of fortune and as I'm now a partner, at the place where I work, our little family are living in my house. We only found each other a few months ago but we are settling down very nicely."

Stepping back so that he could give her the once over he said, "Looks like you are not struggling too much either. Those clothes look very expensive!"

Once again she lowered her eyes.

"Oh Tom," she whispered, "if I could only tell you what it is really like…"

Before she could say any more a voice interrupted her.

"What have we here then?" The dandy pranced towards them speaking in an effeminate manner. "Introduce me to your handsome friend. Oh dear, looking at both of you I could swear I can see a similarity." There was a small hiatus in the conversation as each person studied the other, then in a simpering babyish voice Kathleen explained,

"Yes Mark, you are right, as ever, you are ever so clever. Please meet my brother Tom who happened to come in for a drink on his way through." Turning to Tom she continued, "You haven't told me where you are off to." She turned to face Mark again.

"We haven't seen each other since we were separated, there's so much to tell."

"Where are you off to Tom?" The question might've been asked nicely but Tom could detect a heap of suspicion in the depths of Mark's mean eyes.

"I am on my way to Gundagai. My partner and I purchased a dray complete with four draught-horses from a farmer who is in desperate straits. I'm travelling up there to finalise the deal and drive the whole lot home." Interest showed in Mark's eyes.

"You'd better be alert then; there have been a few hold ups on that road lately."

"Gee, thank you Mark, that's worth knowing, I'll keep my eyes open." In the shadowy part of the tavern Tom noticed there were two men who were making sure they would not be recognised although both of them were keeping a sharp eye on him.

"Well, you know Tom there are always people who like to make some easy money! Anyway I'll leave you to talk with your sister. Kathleen, tell the bartender that the drinks will be on me."

With this he walked away - as he passed the two men he gave some instructions, which no one would've noticed unless they like Tom; had been observing them out of the corner of their eye. Remarking to his sister, "He seems a nice guy Katy, I can't say the same of the surroundings though, I don't know how you stand it?"

Kathleen looked rather surprised at how Tom had described Mark.

"Eh? Oh I see what you mean. He can be nice when he wants to be, and I must admit it did surprise me how nicely he treated you. Normally he goes berserk when he discovers me speaking to anyone." Concerned Tom looked at her.

"He hasn't hurt you has he? I'll fix him right now if he has!"

Holding her brothers arm she said, "He'd better not hurt me! I'm only using him to get to where I want to go."

Tom told her that he'd better be on his way as he had a long way to go as yet and when he hugged Katy goodbye he dropped his card in her pocket.

"I've left my address in your pocket," he whispered in her ear. If you ever need to contact me, for any reason at all, come to that address, we'll look after you. I'll leave the decision to you.

As he walked out of the place he felt that there was more than one pair of eyes following him.

Before leaving town he had a last word with Jason to bring him up to date. Telling him how friendly Mark DeVilliers had treated him Jason replied with,

"I'd be very careful where I'd rest my head tonight. From what I know of him most of his victims were treated nice just before he had them finished off."

Tom had only been on the road for a short while before he passed two other riders who acted quite surprised as he called out to them in greeting. Their heads quickly swung to face each other before one of them grunted a greeting in return. Tom had the impression they would've been happier if he hadn't seen them, somehow the glance they'd cast his way carried intense annoyance.

A feeling of wariness combined with restlessness overcame him after he had finished his evening meal. Without obviously indicating that he was checking the neighbourhood he had a good look around. There was nothing Tom could put a finger on, maybe it was Jason's parting words that made him feel jumpy or perhaps it was his imagination that was working overtime.

"Dear Lord," he prayed, "I might need your help again."

Suddenly calmness settled like a mantle over him. "Thank you Father!" Tom said gratefully.

It had become dark; the location he had chosen was well away from any traffic that was still travelling on the road. He built his fire up so that the embers would keep him warm till the early hours of the morning. He loved sleeping out under the stars but that time just before dawn was always the coldest. He settled down to rest.

A sharp loud crack followed by a muffled curse woke him. Not moving his body but opening his eyes he saw two dark shapes moving towards the fire.

"There he is," he heard one of them whisper. "Let's get him afore he wakens!"

Slowly they advanced upon the prone body that was in a deep sleep. Both of them aimed their pistols at Tom's body and the night's stillness was shattered as they pulled their triggers. "We've got him!" one of them shouted. "He's stone dead. I never knew this job was going to be so easy! Let's see what he's got on him." Both began moving closer to the dead body.

A low eerie moan brought them to a halt.

"What was that? The tall one whispered nervously. The sound came again, this time it sounded nearer. Branches began to shake and something white fluttered about. The body they'd been shooting at slowly began to rise. The eerie sound was all around them.

Pulling their revolvers from their holsters both

men began to shoot wildly in various directions.

"He's shot me!" the tall one cried! He dropped his gun on the ground so he could get hold of his sore leg better. The man cursed and swore when he felt slippery blood between his fingers.

"Jeepers; I think he hit me too, my arm is hurting like mad," moaned his mate. Both were so frightened and had been so distracted they had actually shot each other. "I'm getting out of here I don't care what DeVilliers says, this is not normal."

The two scampered away as fast as the tall one could limp.

"Wait for me!"

These were the last words Tom heard as he leaned against the tree wiping the laughter tears from his eyes, continuing to fold up a white sheet that had been tied to a branch, which unfolded when Tom pulled the rope to shake the branch giving the sheet a ghostly appearance!   Another rope was attached to the supposed body.

"Lord, you do know how to come up with the right solution. Thank you for making it possible to have some sleep tonight. I certainly would've slept for a long time without you intervening."

Looking at the bullet holes in the old blanket, Tom realised how close to death's door he had been. Settling down Tom slept soundly till morning when the magpies warbling woke him up.

The first thing he noticed on rising was the

revolver positioned in the grass. Picking it up he wondered what he should do with it. Tom had never found any need for carrying a weapon and didn't want one now. Not far away was a waterhole and when he'd finished his ablutions he threw the gun into the middle of it.

— CHAPTER SEVEN —

Tom gazed in amazement at the sight he beheld, a coldness swept over him. His first thought was of his sister as he pulled up his team of four draught horses in front of where the tavern had been. The only remains left to show that something had been there were a few rusty galvanized iron sheets. A smell of burning faintly pervaded the air.

The sight had so upset him he never even noticed the noisy De Dion Voiturette automobile that swerved past to avoid hitting his dray. Ever since Federation occurred on the first day of January in 1901 more of these vehicles were seen on the road to the consternation of horses as they didn't like the noisy rattle traps.

Normally Tom would've stopped and studied the vehicle but presently his mind was otherwise occupied. Seeing a man walking nearby he jumped from the dray and enquired as to what had occurred?

"Place went up in smoke!" The bloke enlightened

him. Even Tom had come to that deduction before asking the man.

"What I meant was, was there anyone hurt?" The man shrugged his shoulders, scratched his behind and stated,

"No, not really, only the owner and another bloke who was paralysed with drink caught it."

Tom looked bewildered. He didn't have a clue what the man meant when he said, 'caught it'.

"What about a girl? Did a girl end up being hurt?" Tom couldn't get the words out fast enough. Enlightenment came upon the fellow's features.

"You mean the nightingale that used to sing here. Many a time I stood here when she was warbling away." He gave Tom a measured look. "We won't be hearing that quality of song here again, I'm afraid." Tom's heart sank to his stomach.

"You mean?" The guy nodded his head sympathetically.

"Yes, I mean how is she going to sing here when there is no building left to sing in? We have to be realistic don't we?" Tom's hopes rose as his heart lifted.

The man continued, "We have to realise when you live in a small town like this you can only have talent like hers for a short while before the people in the larger cities want to enjoy it. Yes, my young fellow, you'll probably have to visit Melbourne or Sydney if you want to hear our nightingale again."

The man became so upset he turned and walked away.

There wasn't much Tom could do so he climbed back on the dray and drove to the rooms where he had stayed earlier, blaming himself for not acting stronger in saving his sister. Walking towards the office to book in for the night he was stopped by someone yelling out his name.

"Tom, Tom?" Turning around he found it was Jason who was yelling his name. It was fortunate that Tom recognised the voice because Jason's appearance had changed dramatically. Gone were the long hairs and the old clothes. Standing smiling in front of him stood a young man who looked only a few years older than Tom.

"Well Jason, it must've taken a few jars of make up to make you look this young?"

"Funny, ha ha!" Jason replied morosely, "this is the real me you are looking at, the other was my disguise you nincompoop! Thank heavens I've caught you Tom, I've been coming here for the last three days hoping to catch you. Have I got some news for you? You know that was the best advice you ever gave me when you told me to leave everything for your Maker to organise it at His convenience."

Wondering what he was going to tell, Tom could do little else but smile modestly while wishing that Jason would get on with what he had to say.

"Well Tom, it was fortunate that we joined up

because as soon as you left town three strangers rode in. From the way they behaved and were dressed you could pick them as heavies belonging to a Melbourne gang.

Leaving their mounts tied up near the tavern entrance the three of them swaggered through the door in a way that only the toughest gangsters do. Kicking away anything that was standing in their path they walked in a straight line towards our friend DeVilliers. Mark was busy playing stud poker with some of his usual cronies when the sudden silence in the room made him take notice that something different was going on. When one of the players suddenly flew backwards and the table raised itself sideways with all the chips flying through the air Mark knew he had trouble on his hands.

"How did you know what was going on in the pub, were you there?" Tom queried.

"No, I've had a spy in there for months. That's why I know so much of what is going on," Jason answered rather peeved as he didn't want to be interrupted in the telling of his tale.

"Sorry do go on. I'll try not to interfere again," Tom said humbly.

Jason didn't hesitate but continued his news.

"When DeVilliers saw who had come to visit him his face turned a sickly white. He attempted a friendly smile saying,

'Nice of you guys to come and visit me; would

you like something to drink?' The leader of the thugs ignored Marks offer stating with a threatening voice,

'The boss wants his money and he wants it now!'

"Mark gave a feeble grimace while protesting.

'The boss knows I'm good for it, why is he using these unfriendly tactics now?' The reply came from the burly faced thug, 'Our boss heard you are in trouble and he wants his money now!' DeVilliers looked around him but saw little support as his crew all had found different jobs to do.

'Isn't it funny,' he thought, 'everyone wants to share your good times but no one knows you when the going gets tough?' Trying his charm again he said, 'Why don't you guys have a drink and I'll go home to pick up the money.' Before anyone realised what was going on DeVilliers had left his chair to run out the front door.

Jumping on the first available horse he disappeared leaving a cloud of dust. The three toughs chased him but collided as the door opening wasn't wide enough to let the three of them through together. The shanty rocked and a sheet of corrugated iron fell from the wall. Once they organised themselves the chase was on. The last words the remaining spectators heard were, 'We know where he lives so he won't escape from us!' A few of the spectators carefully entered the pub; they couldn't believe their eyes,

'We're in heaven,' cried one of them, 'there's

nothing in here but the grog! The lot o' them have scarpered.'

Mark DeVilliers opened the rear door quietly, not that he had any need to bother because the noise made by the freeloaders could be heard a block away. He knew he had only so much time as the thugs wouldn't need a lot of brain power to deduce that they had been had. As he was opening the safe, the door opened and a voice said, 'Thank goodness you are here! What is going on? Everyone is boozing and no one is paying, you are lucky we returned in time from wasting the nark on the highway. He won't cause you any trouble that's for sure! Dead as a doornail he is. Isn't he Mick?'

Mick nodded his head weakly. He was trying to prop himself up against the safe. When Mark rose his eyebrows he was soon informed, 'Eh, yes boss. The geezer is dead but he put up a struggle and winged us both. I got hit in the arm while poor Mick there got it in the leg. Actually we could both do with some cash so that we can visit the old doc whats knows what to do if you gets me meaning.'

DeVilliers was exasperated at the way his underlings spoke to him but he knew only too well to which doctor they were referring. In his early years the man had given in to the temptation to earn some easy money by doing operations on young girls and women who wanted to get rid of what they named 'their indiscretions'. Once started on that road however the criminal element in town soon had a hold on him and the doctor was stuck in the illegal rut forever. The alcoholic mixtures he concocted in his spare time helped to forget how low he had sunk. But there was always that small little gap in time when the truth came to haunt him and he had to quickly down another drink or two.

"To get rid of his two henchmen Mark handed a few notes over. He had better things to do than quibble over who paid for whom. The men disappeared and Mark got on with emptying the safe. Once again he was interrupted by the door slamming against the wall. 'What now?' he thought irritably.

Looking up he froze as he recognised the three thugs. The meanest one had taken in with a glance what DeVilliers was up to. With a nasty grin on his face he said, 'My boss gave me clear instructions on what to do if I caught you doing what I can see you are doing.' Without another word he withdrew his pistol from under his coat and shot Mark.

DeVilliers stepped backwards with the force of the bullet's impact. With an incredulous look on his face Mark tried to say something and move but he stumbled against a small table that was used to stand the hurricane lamp on. As he had no control over his actions the lamp fell off the rocking table and the kerosene inside it ran over the floor. The flame that had remained alight wasted no time in igniting the spilt fuel. Seeing the damage he had done to Mark and assessing the fast spreading fire the leader yelled, 'Let's get out of here boys!' The leader having a last look at DeVilliers saw that he was unconscious and grabbed the bag of money. They disappeared through the back door without the happy drinkers in the other part of the tavern even realising that they'd been there. The flames spread rapidly around the office and over DeVilliers whose fingers spasmodically opened and closed. When the effect of the heat and the bullet finally overtook him the flames had risen to the rafters in their never ending search for more fuel.

"The by now fully sozzled drinkers realised something wasn't normal when the wall from the office exploded into the bar area.

'By George!' one staunch citizen exclaimed while drinking from a half full bottle. 'I believe we have a fire on our hands. Come on chaps let us forthwith depart.' He was sounding very eloquent considering the state and company he was in.

Striding towards the exit but making sure he wasn't going to miss out on more drinks he grabbed another full bottle from the shelf first as he led the motley crew away from the building. At a safe distance they stopped to look at what they had walked away from and observed that the fire had grown into quite a spectacle. Smoke and sparks went shooting up in the air; kids yelling 'Fire, Fire,' came running from every direction as not one of them wanted to miss out. After all there's nothing better to watch than a good fire."

Tom wanted to ask a question but saw that Jason was eager to continue imparting the details to him so he thought he'd better remain silent.

"The children cheered with excitement and wonder as each explosion rent the air while the drinkers groaned and bemoaned their fate as each bang represented a bottle they could've drunk. More smoke blew up from the burning building blotting out the sunrays. A wind change scattered the crowd as ash and pungent smoke fell on them and entered their eyes. It also brought the smell of burning furniture and other articles that had been left in the building. A voice called out above the others 'Someone has been left behind in the pub!' A hush descended over the crowd, it was obvious to all now that a person had remained behind. Some young volunteers edged nearer the burning tavern. They saw the rear of the building had burned out; perhaps they'd have a better chance to see inside from there? Kicking and pulling away some sheets from the wall near the burned rear door they observed the charred remains of what had been a human being lying on the floor in front of the open safe. The local Fire Brigade had arrived on the scene and men were busy pumping water into the tavern dousing the flames, now steam was mingling with the smoke. Seeing a constable attempting to push through the crowd the volunteers urgently gained his attention and showed him what they'd discovered. A daring drunk with the appearance that would give a pub a bad name, ran forward to pick up an unexploded bottle he had seen among the debris but the loud voice of the constable soon brought him to a halt.

'You there!' he shouted, 'Clear orf, from here you'se lot! There is a body on this site! So that means this site is out orf bounds until our investigation is over!' The drunk looked defiant at the policeman for a second or two then gave up and slunk back to his mates."

Tom, sensing that Jason was coming to the end of his tale couldn't hold back any longer, "It is true about what they say isn't it? They who live by the sword die by the sword." He nodded his head wisely.

Jason answered, "Seems that way doesn't it? You reap what you sow, is another way of putting it I suppose. The funny thing is now that my quest is over I feel all empty inside and I am wondering what I've been chasing all this time."

Tom placed his arm around his new found friend's shoulder.

"I believe that is the natural reaction to shock which takes place after something dramatic has occurred. Time helps a lot although it doesn't help you now when you really need it."

Jason looked around as if searching for something. "Ah, there it is." Walking across the road he opened the gate which led into the garden of an elegant double story residence.

Tom wondered what they were doing here. The sun had well and truly set by now but the canopy of the trees nearby made it even darker than it actually was. Jason knocked loudly on the door. After some time a weak yellow light was seen through the window which was alongside the door. The sliding sound of heavy bolts was heard and the door was carefully opened.

"Who is calling?" a gravelly male voice asked as he raised his light to receive a better view. Tom thought that the voice sounded familiar so he took a step forward. Even in the semi-darkness he could see the man's face blanch. He dropped the light he was holding which fortunately was caught by Jason. The man whispered, "You are supposed to be a dead man? We killed you the other night! Have you returned to haunt me?"

Placing his hands on his heart the man moaned and fell in a dead faint on the doorstep. Jason looked at Tom in amazement saying, "What peculiar effects you have on people."

Tom shrugged his shoulders. He knew where he was now. Stepping over the unconscious man he entered the house and heard a female voice speaking.

"Who is it Patrick?" Then in a softer voice said, You'd better go and check Mick, there is something not right at the door, Patrick is taking far too long."

Mick limped through the doorway and there was

enough light in the passage for him to recognise Tom. He stood stock still, eyes popping out of his head; then quick as a flash he turned and ran back into the room he had just vacated.

Kathleen in complete bewilderment; saw Mick ignoring the agonising pain in his sore leg, frothy spittle coming from his mouth, run towards the French doors not stopping to open them but smashing straight through. Splinters of wood and shards of glass flew in all directions while Mick ended his run by collapsing on the patio with a piece of glass sticking from his hip.

"Golly, you certainly do have an effect on people, this is twice now. How come I didn't react like those two when I first met you?" Jason asked.

Tom grinned while replying, "You haven't the deep insight some people have."

"What are you doing here Tom? I didn't know you even knew where I lived, and who is that man with you?"

"Sorry love, but I'd only just returned from my trip when Jason, by the way Jason this is my sister Kathleen, Kathleen this is Jason, informed me of what has occurred while I was away."

Walking over to his sister Tom embraced her as she leaned against him. Speaking softly into her hair he asked how she was coping,

"I'm coping alright," she answered in a tired voice. "It's not as if we were that close, we only had a business relationship after all, but all the same it wasn't nice the way his life ended. Trying to work out the next step is what is the hardest."

A loud groan came from outside, also there was a sound coming from the front door.

"Jason, can you see to the man on the patio and I'll go to the front. Tie him up if you have to."

"What do you mean, tie them up? Patrick and Mick wouldn't hurt a fly."

"You are probably right dear, they wouldn't hurt flies but that didn't stop them from shooting four bullets into me!" Kathleen's face paled, her eyes glancing hurriedly over Tom's body searching for wounds.

"I'll tell you more about it when I finish the business at the front door; I don't want him on the loose." Carrying a light in front of him he noticed Patrick getting up from the floor, the temptation was too great, Tom could not resist it. Raising the light so that it cast shadows on his face he moved in an ogre like manner to the front door.

Patrick saw him coming. He froze with fear! He collapsed on his knees sobbing,

"Oh, holy angels from heaven come and save me." Then he fell once again in a dead faint on the floor.

Tom left Patrick on the floor, he wasn't toting a pistol so was no great threat. Jason entered the room at the same time as Tom.

"He won't be doing us much harm in the state he's in so I think we should plan our next step."

"What will be our next move?" Tom asked looking at the others.

"I suppose you should work out what to do with your sister."

"That's true. But that is simple; she's coming home with me, Tom stated confidently.

"Hang on a minute? I am in this room also you know. Don't I get a say in what I want to do?" Kathleen said vehemently.

"I'm ever so sorry Sis; I just assumed you were..."

"Don't ever assume anything little brother. I am older than you so don't you get it into your head that you can run my life?"

Jason stood still while looking at Tom's sister admiringly. She looked at him. Putting up his hands in a placating manner he said,

"I admire a woman that stands up for herself, it saves us guys so much time."

Kathleen gave him a withering glance but said no more.

"What are you planning to do then Kath?" Tom asked.

"Can any of you men open a safe?"

Tom and Jason looked at each other nonplussed - this was the last question they'd expected to hear.

Hesitantly Jason said, "Show me the safe, I've been taught to open a few."

As Kathleen pushed Tom in front of her to lead them to the safe she whispered, "What does he do for a living? He seems to be well-versed in the shady side of life?"

Tom only shrugged his shoulders. Even he had felt concerned at times. He made sure to find out exactly what Jason was all about when they were on their own.

A smile appeared on Jason's face when he recognised the safe, kneeling in front of it he explained, "We are lucky, this is one of the cheap imitations a Melbourne firm manufactured to give Chubb a run for their money. If I can't open this within five minutes I'll eat my hat," he boasted.

Tom and Kathleen looked at each other. With a straight face Kathleen commented,

"Would you like that with or without butter?" Tom burst out laughing. Jason looked down his nose at him, which is hard to do when you are kneeling on the floor.

In a snooty manner he said, "This is a serious matter and I hope you will refrain from laughing. Could I have some peace and silence please? You ignoramuses don't realise that I have to listen to the tumblers fall so that I know where I am at."

"Pardon us for breathing sir," Kathleen commented digging Tom in his ribs.

She stopped laughing however when with a flourish, Jason opened the door of the safe. All three were astounded at the amount of banknotes that were stashed in there.

"Wow, I am rich!" Kathleen murmured.

"How come you are rich?" Tom queried. "You didn't even know the combination?"

Kathleen's face flushed. Then protesting quickly she replied,

"Well, Mark is not here anymore. So who else should own it? Don't worry I'll pay the others their wages but with the money which is leftover I'm going to keep myself and finance my singing career."

Jason laughed and said, "With all this money you could retire for life, Why bother wasting it on singing?"

"You common peasants wouldn't understand," she spat out haughtily.

"I am a singer and singing is what I shall be doing. We artists live for our art and money is only a vehicle we use to reach our aims!"

After a pause Jason retorted, "With all the money in this safe you'll be able to have a selection of any vehicle you like." Reaching in Jason withdrew a green binder. Casually he flicked through some of the pages inside it when he stopped and whistled softly between his teeth.

"Wow, this explains a lot. The Department should be happy with me for finding this juicy bit of information."

Tom and Kathleen stooped studying the contents

of the safe to turn their eyes to Jason.

"What Department would that be Jason?" Kathleen enquired in a sugary voice.

"Did I say Department?" he replied innocently, realising he had said too much.

"Yes, you sure did!" Kathleen stated; all the sweetness gone from her voice now.

"And if you don't tell us who you really are I'll contact the police!"

Jason shrugged his shoulders walking over to sit on a chair studying them both.

"There is no need to call the police because they are already here!"

Tom and Kathleen looked around the room, but they were the only ones there. Kathleen's face lightened with understanding.

"You mean Patrick and Mick?"

"No I don't mean those two scoundrels, the only association they have had with the police is they have stayed in their lock-ups too often. No, my dear girl, it is I who represents the mighty arm of the law here."

Tom realised that Jason was speaking the truth. So much of what Jason had said in the past made sense now. Kathleen however was still struggling in grasping that Jason represented the law.

"What sort of a policeman are you then if you don't tell anyone? And by the way don't call me your 'dear girl' when you speak to me, as first of all I am not your girl and probably never will be if you keep acting the way you are."

Kathleen realised what she had just said and opened her mouth to say more when Tom laughingly said, "I wouldn't say anymore elder sister because you might put your foot in your mouth again." Kathleen gave him a dirty look while Jason sat smugly in the chair with a smirk on his face.

"Do you mean you could be interested in me if I changed my ways?"

Kathleen made a, "Humph!" sound and quickly directed their attention to the matter at hand.

"The only reason I felt I was entitled to the money is that while I was living here Mark bought my singing outfits and day to day clothing but I never received any payment for the work I did in his club."

Tom was going to say that there was no club, the place was a pub. But he realised that in her mind his sister had elevated the place where she performed. Instead he asked, "Jason, would there be any legal detrimental effect if Kathleen holds on to the money?"

Jason thought for a moment then answered slowly, "The Government always likes to receive any monies found but as the safe at the 'club' was raided by the three thugs from Melbourne we can assume they expect there is nothing left. However if the mob in Melbourne felt that they didn't obtain their fair share and hear that Kathleen is living as a queen they might knock on her door to discover if she is living on what they believe is their money."

Looking directly at Kathleen he emphasised, "They are tough this mob in Melbourne and don't care what they have to do to gain their objectives."

Kathleen went pale and sat down as she felt her legs had trouble holding her. She had just remembered how the mob had treated Mark and although it turned out that Mark had been a crook and a scoundrel he had treated her with some respect. What was she going to do?

Jason could see that Kathleen was in a dilemma, he felt he should help her; maybe it was that she reminded him of his sister but deep inside himself he knew that wasn't so.

"Kathleen, why don't you do what you suggested, pay off all the staff, even these two rogues downstairs and leave these premises. Pat and Mick can remain here in the house and if any of the Melbourne thugs come snooping around these two can honestly say that you had left to go and sing somewhere else as you had a living to make. That would sound plausible to them and if they did get annoyed the only thing they probably would do is set the place alight. What do you think?"

Tom sat quietly thinking, then queried, "That sounds like a good practical legal and moral solution Kathleen. I can live with that, what I do want to know is if you had any intention of visiting your siblings before you go and become famous?"

"Of course I would see them Tom, what do you think of me? It will also give me time to make up my mind if I should go to Sydney or to Melbourne?"

Jason jumped from his chair rubbing his hands.

"Right, let's empty the safe and see what else is in there?"

When they left the house carrying Kathleen's belongings Patrick was still sitting on the floor with a vacant look on his face. He shrunk as Tom walked passed him but Jason stopped to tell him that he had made a deal with Tom not to haunt him anymore as long as he behaved himself. Now you'd better go and see to your mate Mick who needs your help in getting him to a doctor - Kathleen left some money on the table that Mark would've paid you if he had still been here. Also you can remain in the house as long as you like."

Patrick rose to his feet and stumbled in the direction of the main room to find his friend.

— *CHAPTER EIGHT* —

Ross and Elizabeth enjoyed the setting sun while sitting in comfortable chairs on the wide veranda. Playing with the baby on her lap Elizabeth made gurgling noises pushing her face towards the baby's chest to the immense delight of the child.

"He does seem to like what you are doing to him!" Ross stated as he watched with a contented young Father look on his face.

"He's a male, all males like this sort of attention," Elizabeth said with a smile. With concern in her voice she commented, "Young Tom is taking his time, shouldn't he have returned by now?"

Ross smiled fondly at his wife. In his eyes she had become even more beautiful than when they had first met.

"I think you are becoming a mother hen, or do you just miss him?"

"I do miss him. At times I feel we place far too much responsibility on his shoulders. Although he always carries out the tasks we ask him to do," Elizabeth said in a worried voice. "After all he is still only a large child. Ross laughed loudly.

"You're right my love he is large but at times I feel that Tom was never a child. It seems he was born with a mature outlook on life. I am glad I met him that day at the market; my life has never been the same since. Even you must admit we are doing very well financially considering we've only been here a few years."

Elizabeth let her eyes roam around the property. From where she was sitting she could see fenced paddocks full of well fed cattle. There was even a paddock dedicated to the Murray breed which Ross favoured above all. But the Hereford stock they had from the beginning had brought a good return on their investment when they'd taken some of their stock to the Albury market.

They only had to live for a year in the small shack Ross and Tom had built. Both of them had looked so proud when Ross had lifted her from the wagon that had brought them and their goods and carried her through the door. It had taken Elizabeth a lot of self control not to show on her face what she really thought. Her Mother wouldn't have a shack like this on her property and here she had to bring up a family in it.

Now she lived in an up to date home that was painted in the latest Federation colours. It was a joy to behold. Each time they returned from a trip she asked Ross or whoever was driving the team to stop on the side of the hill so that she could take pleasure in looking at it all over again. At times she wondered how Ross had obtained the money. He must have another source of income; of course he had come from a better class. That was evident in how he acted, spoke and behaved with other people.

Maybe he had collected an inheritance? No good thinking about it now!

Others had settled in the valley and their properties could also be seen from the road. The McGregor's were becoming more established and Tom's house which was similar in design to theirs although not as large, gave the place a look of solidity. At first glance you could almost think you had come upon a village. Once you had a good look though you realised that there were only three properties in all. It was the houses with the sheds and the additional two roomed shacks for the labourers that gave the area a look of prosperity. All this growth in only a few years, God has been good to us. Elizabeth sends up a quick silent prayer. Maybe that's why everything went so well. Each time Elizabeth saw the area with new eyes, and she felt as if she had been in the middle of a prayer. Not only was Elizabeth kept busy looking after her own family she also taught the children who belonged to the neighbourhood, their three R's. You might be able to take a school teacher away from the school but you can't take the schooling away from a teacher.

All in all Elizabeth was very content with her married life. Standing up she walked over to Ross and while handing over the baby she planted a firm kiss on his forehead.

"What was that for?" Ross said startled.

"Just for you being you," Elizabeth replied. "You can look after your son and heir while I go to get tea ready. Remember we have Tom's siblings staying with us."

Bouncing the baby on his lap Ross said softly, "You are one lucky little guy. Just remember I picked the best Mum in the world for you."

Junior replied with a loud gurgle, "I'll take that as a yes." Ross laughed, throwing his son up in the air and safely catching him.

Having his own family made Ross think about his parents and younger sister Jessica whom he hadn't seen for a long time. Jessica would be a young lady now, she could even be married. Once his Father had closed the gate in that controlled manner of his it had broken Ross' heart for a long time at not being able to contact his sister or his Mother. If only his Father had slammed the gate shut or had shown some emotion Ross would've been able to cope but no, the man was a control freak and no one was ever permitted to be able to read or see his emotions.

Ross had tried hard to forget his family but how

can you forget anything that close to your heart? The only way you could make thoughts disappear was to take your own life, even now he found it hard to believe that at one stage he had seriously considered in doing just that. Close as he was to his wife at this stage he had never been able to talk about it with her. Tom was the only person with whom he had been able to discuss his family and then it had been only that one time when they'd been busy exploring the area in and around the newly bought property.

The other subject he hadn't raised with her either was how the property was financed. He knew he should mention the gold lode that Tom had found and so willingly shared with him but somehow the right time or opportunity never seemed to occur. Did this make him a bad husband? At times he worried why it had become an issue; not many if any men he knew of ever mentioned their financial business to their wives. They knew that their poor little woman just didn't have the capacity to understand matters of this very complicated nature and was better left to deal with the simple actions of running a household, doing the cooking and raising a family.

However Ross knew that none of these arguments applied to his clever wife. In most situations he found his wife to be way ahead of him. He couldn't use the excuse that his wife didn't understand him, as some men he had met did. His wife understood him only too well. A warm wave of love for Elizabeth seared through his body.

Ross stood up; reality had come to him, as he realised that part of the warm wave of love had been his son wetting his nappy.

This was back to real life, nothing lasts forever he thought sadly. Moving towards the door he called out, "Darling, have I got a surprise for you!"

"The nappies are in the bottom drawer, I'm busy!" Elizabeth called out.

"See what I mean son; your Mother knows me too well!"

***

The dark thunder clouds that had been threatening for days broke that night. Heavy raindrops pelted the corrugated iron roof so hard they almost succeeded in penetrating. Thunder crashed so close above that the whole house shook; brilliant dazzling white lightening flashed so near that at times it looked as bright as day. Wind whipped the top branches of the trees about with such a force that leaves and branches flew through the air, travelling vast distances before falling on the ground to be picked up again and moved further along. One branch was held to the side of the barn for about five minutes before it slid down to be raised up again by another gust of wind.

When morning came it was still raining and

looking through the window Ross found that the peaceful scenery they had seen yesterday had changed into a lake.

"Thank heavens we decided to built on the rise was his first thought, at least there is no water knocking on our front door." The sheds and cattle yards had a foot or more of water swirling through them. Forgetting about having breakfast, being more concerned about his stock he waded through the water to the stables. Water had not entered the stables but the horses were a mite skittish somehow sensing that all was not right in their world. Talking gently to them; running his hand along their withers and giving them their feed Ross managed to calm them down.

Next job after saddling his mount, was to ride alongside the fence to open gates so that his cattle had some chance to survive in case the floodwaters rose higher. So far the water remained at the level he had first noticed it an hour ago. If it stayed there he would have no worries unless it kept on raining. Moving towards the river he noticed that the water was up to the previous floodmarks. With a bit of luck the river had peaked. The problem was no one would be able to get in or out until the river ford became passable again. There wasn't much more that Ross could do so he returned to the homestead where Elizabeth met him at the door with an anxious frown on her face.

"Is there much damage love? It looks horrible

out there when you look through the window!"

Ross took her into his arms. His wife looked tired and he supposed that he did too; as neither had slept much while listening and worrying because of the elements at work during the night.

"As long as the water doesn't get any higher we'll be right. I've checked the stables and the horses are fine, there's water flowing through the other sheds but it is doing very little damage. I think we should have breakfast and then I'll go out and see if there's been any change."

Now that Elizabeth had something positive to do she brightly grabbed the handle of a saucepan saying with a cheerful voice, "Eggs sunny-side up are on their way!"

After his breakfast Ross donned his wet-weather gear and set out on his horse to check if his farmhands and neighbours were in need of any help. The reason he had his breakfast first was that no one had contacted them so he deduced that everything was fine.

That was how it turned out to be. When Ross had first discovered the valley he worked out that if you owned the land nearest the source it would be unlikely that flood waters could be a big problem. The water would be too eager to go down stream and it was only in very low places or if there was an obstruction that any cause for a high flood would occur.

Norm, one of his farmhands was outside digging a trench to ensure water would drain faster from the shack he and his wife resided in.

"G'day, boss, if it doesn't rain any harder than now this drain should keep the water away from our house. We are fortunate that the houses are on stilts otherwise the missus would really be complaining!"

Norm furtively checked the window of the house to see if his wife was watching him or if he could be overheard. No, he was safe so he continued,

"You know it doesn't take much to upset the missus, my missus anyway, she believes any inconvenience that happens is directed only at her."

Ross smiled; Norm was one of his best hands and nearly always made good decisions, however when he proposed to his wife he must've had an off day. Norm's wife was a very attractive woman in appearance but she had a tongue so sharp it could slice meat. Maybe that was why Norm was such a good worker; any excuse for not being at home. At least when they weren't together there was peace in the house.

Ross looked over at the shacks where the other owners were carrying out similar work.

"It seems you have everything under control here. I'd better go and check to see how McGregor is faring?"

"There is no way I could let you travel down there on your own Sir. If you can wait a minute or two, I'll saddle a horse and come with you, Norm said concerned.

"I'll be fine Norm; it is nice of you to offer, but in my time I've crossed faster, deeper and wider flowing rivers than this one."

"That could well be true Sir, but you are older now and you have a wife and child. I would never forgive myself if something happened to you and I could've prevented it."

With a cheeky smile he added,

"It isn't you I am concerned about Sir, it's your lovely wife and that bouncing baby she has. How could I see them grieve?"

"Right Norm, now I know the real reason there is no way I would endeavour to prevent you from accompanying me. While you are getting organised would you like me to inform your wife that you'll be away with me for a while?"

A large smile beamed from Norm's face.

"It is blessed indeed you are Sir, I always tell the others you are ever so clever Sir." Whistling cheerfully he walked towards the stables.

With mud and water splashing from their horse's hooves, Ross and Norm entered the McGregor yard. The dogs barked their heads off from the safety of the veranda which soon brought McGregor's head through the front door opening. Ross wondered why McGregor needed so many dogs around him, ever since he had befriended the man he had been surrounded by dogs.

"Good morning McGregor, we are only passing by to find out how you fared with this beast of a weather we are having," Ross yelled out at the top of his voice hoping he was outdoing the dogs at their noise level.

McGregor stuck two fingers in his mouth letting out a very high pitched whistle; the dogs stopped barking and settled down lying against the dry wall of the house. McGregor peered at the two sodden men.

"Gosh it is hard to recognise you two from the drips that surround you; I meant that in the nicest way of course, I would never suggest that you were drips; that would be rude of me. Why don't you come in for a while so you can dry out in front of the fire?"

Tying their horses to a pole in a place where they wouldn't cop too much of the rain the two trailed a collection of drips on the floor in to the house.

"What do you two think you are doing - I just cleaned that floor!" Tracy yelled out in an indignant voice, and then she recognised who she had been yelling at.

"I'm ever so sorry Mr. Smith, I didn't realise it was you. Everyone looks the same in their wet weather gear." Tracy blushed prettily.

Ross noticed how the girl had grown in the last six months since he had seen her. With Tracy working in town she could only come down to visit her Father every so often. Tom would be pleased to know that she was back on the farm, although lately he hadn't made much mention of her. Ross admitted to himself that Tracy went a bit over the top in how she treated Tom, always treating him with disdain. All the same he was sure that she was interested in Tom because when she thought that no one was looking Ross had noticed that she studied Tom with intense concentration.

Ah, young love, it could be very complicated. Heavens, I am starting to think like an old man. Enjoying sipping his mug of sweetened tea which was so strong a spoon had no trouble standing up in it, Ross answered the questions McGregor threw at him.

"No, apart from the paddocks being covered with water there hadn't been much damage. Norm and I pulled a calf that had strayed from its mother out of the river," Ross drawled.

"The little mite would've drowned that's for sure if Mr. Ross hadn't caught it in time," Norm added with vigour.

"He just plucked it from the water and laid it across the front of his saddle. The old cow was glad to see her calf safe that's for sure." McGregor observed Norm's eyes shone with admiration at Ross, who sat still in his chair with a far away smile on his face sipping his drink with contentment. A quick dart of envy entered McGregor's mind that he shamefully pushed away. Ross had helped him too much for him to harbour such thoughts. But why did no one ever look up to him as they did to Ross?

Tracy came over to offer some more scones. Smiling at her Ross reached for one saying, "Tracy; are you trying to scone me to death? This definitely has to be the last one or my horse won't be able to carry me home."

Ross looked around stating, "We should leave soon and see what else has happened in our district. While we are being spoilt to death here there could be someone out there who really needs our help!"

The menfolk rose from their chairs to walk towards the door.

***

Angrily he kicked the mud from his boots against the scraper that was located near the back door. He was becoming fed up with another ghastly day when nothing had gone right for him. There had been no need for the calf to die and he hadn't liked the way the vet had looked at him as if it had been his fault that the heifer had been too young to give birth. The man should've attended his classes better when studying to become a vet then none of this would've occurred. That was the trouble nowadays. As soon as someone obtained some education he classed himself as an expert. Well, he would show him! The vet could wait for his money that would show him who was in charge! It was about time someone showed these educated experts who mainly came from peasant stock who was in charge.

Venting his anger against the scraper made him feel better, although ever since Jessica had left there hadn't been much happening to raise his spirits.

Spirits! That was what he needed. Giving the scraper another well deserved kick he went inside to open the new bottle of whiskey. In his haste to get to the bottle he ignored the dirt that was still clinging to the boots, spreading it all over the floor which had lost most of its shine since Jessica's departure.

Clarence the only remaining stable-hand; shook his head as he watched his employer's action from the shed. His boss was losing the plot, he thought, while scratching his balding head. To be truthful if things didn't alter soon he might have to take action himself, no decent human being should have to put up with what he had to put up with. At this stage Clarence was confused at why he hadn't disappeared from this miserable farm long ago? But somehow he could never find the energy he needed to walk away. God must've placed him in this spot for a purpose he reasoned because there was no earthly reason why anyone would remain here. With a sigh Clarence went back into the stable. The old man wouldn't be back now until he had slept off the drink and that wouldn't happen until well into the morning. Looking at the dead calf he felt sorrow coursing through his body. What a waste! All the effort of the young heifer had been for nothing. The poor animal was frustratingly mooing and attempting to visit her offspring. It would take a while before time would erase the calf from her memory. Lifting the lifeless remains into a wheelbarrow Clarence wheeled the calf to a spot where the mother would never find it. Picking up a spade he tiredly began to dig the hole wondering how his boss would treat him tomorrow. Alas, gone were the days when the young master had been around, then there had been someone who could lighten up your day.

— *CHAPTER NINE* —

The bell chimed as Jessica entered the milk bar which was only a block away from where she lived. The shop was empty, so with a cheerful voice she called out, "It's only me again Mrs. Jones, take your time." A tired voice coming from behind the counter followed by the rising appearance of Mrs. Jones said, "Don't tell me it's that time already. That's the trouble when you become old, time moves faster, your body moves slower and the floor seems to go further down each time you have to put something down or lift something up from it. Yes, you can laugh you cheeky girl but when I was your age I thought I wasn't ever going to be old, but look at me now?"

"Oh Mrs. Jones you must be joking," Jessica giggled.

"You aren't old, you look hardly a day over sixty five."

"Well, that's encouraging," grumbled the old lady.

"Considering I am only fifty nine you've given

me a real compliment!"

"Oops, I am ever so sorry. That's the second reminder today that I need glasses."

Before she could say anymore the bell rang and a young girl entered the shop. Jessica and Mrs. Jones both stared at her.

"Sorry, if I am interrupting, but I am trying to find a place in this area that has an empty room available and I can't seem to find it," the girl said despondently.

"That would be the place where I am living. One of our girls had to return home as her Mother was ill. When I've finished here I'll show you where it is," Jessica offered.

Turning back to face Mrs. Jones, opening her purse she withdrew some coins and handed them over. "This should see my account settled again, Mrs. Jones. It has been a pleasure as usual and I'll be back tomorrow."

Outside the shop two large portmanteaus stood on the ground.

"You carried these by yourself?"

The girl looked uncomfortable but eventually came out with,

"Not exactly; two young men carried them for me but when we arrived here they wanted me to give something in payment that I wasn't prepared to give so they walked away and left me stranded."

Jessica studied the girl steadily and made up her

mind.

"I'm Jessica Smith and I've lived here for about six months."

"My name is Kathleen Matheson and I've come to town to study music." Before she could say anymore a voice hailed from a cab.

"What in heaven's name are you standing there for Kathleen; I thought you said you'd catch a cab to get to your destination?"

Kathleen went red in the face. The young man in the cab continued,

"Knowing you, I'll wager that you tried to save some money and had some young bloke carry your luggage all the way here."

Stepping from the hansom cab Jessica noticed that the young man was tall and lithe. He turned towards Jessica, smiling disarmingly.

"I hope my sister didn't try to talk you into carrying one of these portmanteaus for her?"

His smile was so open that Jessica felt lost. No one had ever affected her at such a short notice before. Her first thought was, "Thank goodness he is her brother."

Jessica noticed that when Tom, as she discovered he was called, instructed the cab driver to load the luggage into the cab he did so in clear, concise but firm instructions. For his age he acted very confident.

"Tom, stop throwing your weight about, you are after all, only my little brother and you can see that I haven't come to any harm!"

"Yes Sis and I've also noticed that you are still two blocks away from the place that you were supposed to be dropped off at?"

"But you have to admit that she is nearly there!" Jessica butted in.

Tom stopped to study her. He liked what he saw but that didn't mean he was going to give in that fast. Turning to his sister he said with a smile on his face.

"Trust you to find someone to stick up for you at such short notice. Anyway hop in the cab and we'll be on our way I have lots of other things to do you know."

Ignoring her brother Kathleen told Jessica to enter the cab.

"Why walk when you can ride? We girls have to save up our energy so that we'll still look good as we become older!"

Remembering Mrs. Jones, Jessica smartly moved into the cab.

Neat elegant ankles Tom thought as he caught a glimpse of them when Jessica raised her foot onto the step.

When they arrived at their destination Gloria was standing chatting with one of her many admirers who called on her. As soon as Gloria recognised that it was Jessica who was assisted by a very eligible young man she sent her 'gallant' on his way. Jessica noticed the hurt expression on the young man's face but there wasn't much she could do to help him. Not so long ago she had explained to him how Gloria treated her male admirers but he insisted in coming back.

"Who is the handsome hunk?" Enquired Gloria breathlessly

"O that's Tom, he's Kathleen's brother. Kathleen is taking up rooms with us and Tom is making sure that his sister arrived here safely." All this was said as if Jessica had known Tom and Kathleen most of her life.

"Thank heavens he's her brother," Gloria breathed out huskily. "Most of the good-looking men you meet nowadays are married or are interested in each other. This one appears very normal to me."

Jessica was becoming a bit apprehensive at the interest her flatmate was showing in Tom, but what could she do about it? After all, she had no claim on him other than that she had sat next to him in the carriage, and what did that prove?

Tom was too busy handling his sister's luggage to take much notice of anything that went on around him. He had an appointment later that day with a business man and his mind was concentrating on how to best put forward his proposal for an idea he had so that the man would embrace it.

"Right ladies, show me where I have to place these heavy items and then you can chat amongst yourselves for as long as you like, I have to be back in town by four."

As soon as he deposited the load he kissed his sister told Jessica it had been a pleasure to meet her and disappeared from the room.

"I don't believe this," gasped Gloria, "that man completely ignored me!"

"Yes, it is hard to believe but I saw him do it," smiled Jessica to herself, "he was very rude I must admit and he's the only one among your many admirers I have ever seen do that to you." Much as Jessica liked Gloria she felt very content as she could still feel the warm and firm handshake Tom had given her as he departed.

"I suppose he couldn't help it; coming from the country." Gloria consoled herself as she wiped him from her mind and began helping Kathleen to settle in. Soon the three girls were sitting on the bed chatting and discovering that they got on well with each other. Jessica would've loved to hear more about Tom but hesitated to ask as she didn't want to seem too forward. In the end that didn't stop her from finding out as Gloria had no such restraints and asked Kathleen all sort of questions about her handsome brother.

Kathleen was a little bit annoyed as she rather wanted to talk about herself but as Gloria didn't stop asking for details she handed out as little information as she could which only succeeded in wetting Gloria's appetite for more.

"You mean to say that at his age he owns his own farm all paid for and everything! Were your parents well off or something to give him a start like that?"

"No we were poor! Tom was very lucky to meet the man who helped him on his way. When our Father passed away Mum couldn't cope and soon the bank took the farm away from us. As Mum couldn't look after us we were dispersed and it is only in the last year that Tom discovered where we were and now we live together in his home. Mum never recovered and to this day we don't know exactly where her grave is located. Tom wants to find out so that he can bring Mum and Dad together again. Tom is so determined when he sets his sights on something he'll probably succeed in finding her grave."

This last statement from Kathleen kept even Gloria silent, be it only for a moment.

"I might have to alter my thoughts about your brother after all. He sounds like good husband material to me, even if he's a bit rough around the edges still."

"You aren't wrong there. Whoever marries my brother will have him forever, because that is the way he is. Of course, he would have to want you as a wife. Many a girl has tried but so far he is still single."

***

Meanwhile the country boy had finished his

business and was walking down Russell Street when a loud voice hailed him by his name. Stopping to look who had called out his name Tom discovered Jason running towards him from the opposite side of the street. Panting because of the effort of running he spoke, "I couldn't believe my eyes when I saw you walking on the other side of the street. What are you doing in town? I mean, you are a long way from home." Jason was shaking Tom's hand all the while he was speaking.

"If you stop talking for a minute," Tom said laughing aloud, "I'll be able to tell you."

Tom explained that he had dropped his sister off at her rooms so that she could attend the College of Arts to continue improving her career.

Jason nodded his head wisely saying, "This would be the highly talented Kathleen you are referring to then? It surprises me that she stayed with you so long, I would've thought a week or two would've been long enough for her to stay away from the lime light?"

"Come on Jason, she isn't that bad. Once we were together she realised how much she missed us all. At the same time we planned on how she should tackle her career so that she had a high chance of succeeding. I will agree with you though, once she had worked out how to approach everything there was no holding her back."

When Jason discovered that Tom hadn't booked

anywhere to stay the night he invited him home to his parents' place.

"I can't do that," protested Tom, "they don't know me from a bar of soap!"

"You'll be surprised how well they know you. My parents dragged every bit of information from me when I told them

Mark DeVilliers was no more. In the end I had to tell them and that was when you and your sister's activities happened to be mentioned. They'll be ever so pleased to meet the person who can confirm that what I told them was the truth."

Jason was right, his parents who lived in a six roomed Queen Anne brick villa made Tom feel ever so wanted and it was a pleasure to be there. Jason's Mother especially took Tom to heart and couldn't do enough for him. You could tell she loved to have someone to mother. It wasn't long before she was showing him her garden. She was especially proud of their well-clipped pittosporum hedge which bordered their wooden picket fence. A gravel path wound across the buffalo lawn; from the gate to their front door. It was a pleasing picture indeed which reflected Jason's parents' position in the street by the people who judged a person's status by their gardens.

Sitting in a comfortable chair with a crackling fire that reflected the ornate embossment in the metal ceiling Tom realised that Jason's family were enjoying having someone new to air their views to as it seemed that ever since their daughter had died their social life had suffered. Lying in bed that night his mind went over all the discussions they'd had and he realised how much he and his family had missed out on because of the early death of his parents. Funny how you took most everyday things for granted! It was only when you had to go without that you discovered how much you needed them.

Just before Tom fell asleep he hoped that Kathleen wouldn't be too upset that he had asked Jason to keep an eye on her. Jason had promised him that he would arrange to 'accidentally' run into her near her College one day and see how things would develop from there.

Early in the morning before anyone else was up, Tom stropped his hollow ground 'cut-throat' razor and dipped his 'Guaranteed Free From Anthrax' beaver hairbrush into an embossed silver-faced mug while his cast iron bath was filling up with steaming hot water from the chip bath-heater.

Coming from the bathroom Tom could smell the chops and sausages which Jason's Mother was grilling in the kitchen, which was the usual lean to extension to the back of the house.

Jason's Mother smiled at Tom as he entered the room.

"Sit down at the table love, placing a plateful of food in front of him. Make sure you eat it all as you will need it for the distance you'll be travelling."

Stepping from the train at the Albury railway station Tom looked round at the massive structure that surrounded him. The station had seen a lot of trains passing to and fro from Sydney and Melbourne since it was officially opened on 14 June 1883. Having a last look Tom straightened his back and stretched his arms before picking up his luggage from the platform. He moved towards the exit gate where the attendant stood to receive the traveller's tickets.

His horse and buggy were in stables only a block away from the station and it wasn't long before he was riding down the street. Pulling the chain to remove his watch from his waist coat pocket Tom found that it was near lunch time so he decided to drive towards the shop where Tracy worked.

Tracy's eyes lit up when she recognised Tom wrapping his reins around the post which stood in front of her shop. Quickly she glanced into a mirror to see if her hair was in place and with her heart beating fast she began to tidy some of the articles on a shelf. When Tom tapped her on her shoulder she turned around to say calmly, "Hello Tom, what are you doing in town?" Making sure that she showed no indication that she was glad to see him. Even Tracy herself didn't know why she acted this way. Right from the first time they'd met she had acted cool towards Tom. Something inside her seemed to freeze and she could never be open towards him.

Tom was always disturbed by Tracy's behaviour

towards him and he cursed himself each time for putting up with her attitude. The funny thing was when he tried to ignore the girl the pain felt a lot worse. Somehow with her lack of candour he always felt that deep inside her there was that little bit of interest in him that she couldn't hide. As there were no other suitors chasing Tracy and she didn't outright tell him to go home he thought it might pay to persevere.

Looking down at her from his six foot height he saw only a very petite but strong lady. Her hair rested curved on her shoulders attractively framing her face.

"Arriving by train from Melbourne I thought that since I was in town I would drop by to see if you would be interested in having lunch with a lonely tired man before he has to depart to his farm where only more loneliness and hard work awaits him."

Coolly she studied Tom.

"No wonder you are lonely if all you can do is moan."

Hanging the 'be back soon' sign on the door she hooked her arm through Tom's and much to his surprise walked closely with him saying, "There's a new restaurant opened around the corner and since you are paying I wouldn't mind trying it out. What do you think?"

Looking at him enquiringly she clasped his arm tighter.

"Anything to keep you happy dear Tracy, I can

always sell the buggy and eat the horse on my way home."

"Don't play the poor guy with me Tom Matheson, even my Father can't work out how come you've done so well since he met you. He always mentions that on the day he first met you it looked like you didn't have a farthing to your name and now you are better off than he is."

This little comment silenced Tom for a while. Was he acting too fast? Was McGregor the only one that had noticed his quick rise? It looked like he'd better slow down a bit and spend more time on the farm. Come to think of it; in comparison to McGregor he had accomplished so much more in the last four or five years and he could understand why some people would ask questions.

Tom noticed Tracy staring at him.

"Sorry Tracy, I was miles away. I didn't hear your question."

"Never mind Tom, we are here. Will that small table near the window do?"

Tracy pointed towards a small table that stood on its own away from the main traffic. Tom stood for a minute to look around. The decor inside compared favourably to some of the restaurants he had been in during his stays in Melbourne. It was good to know that there was somewhere up-market in town where you could dine in the country.

Sitting opposite Tracy after having placed their

order, he saw something in her face that brought Jessica to his mind.

Why should he be thinking of her when he was with the girl who was always in his dreams? Somehow he knew that if Jessica had been with him she would've shown so much more excitement than Tracy. It's weird where the mind will go Tom thought! I've only seen the girl for no more than half an hour and here I'm comparing her to Tracy whom I've known for years.

Jessica would be craning her neck to see if there was anything she had missed in the establishment while Tracy sits there cool as a cucumber, as if she has been here every day. Tom felt a bit ashamed that these thoughts had actually entered his mind.

"What is wrong with you Tom? You sit there looking at me but when I speak you do not answer. You are making me feel very uncomfortable!" Tracy said in a hurt voice. Never had she seen Tom in this mood. Normally he bent over backwards to please her but today it seemed as if he didn't really care whether she was there or not. Which was rather concerning.

Maybe she had overplayed this 'making it hard to get me' role.

At times Tracy wished she knew what she wanted. All she knew now was that it was hard for her to change the way she behaved when she was with Tom. Tracy looked at him with her eyebrows raised.

"Sorry dear, the trip has taken more out of me than I thought. Also when you mentioned what your Father thought about me it made me think about all the good fortune that's happened since I met Ross."

Looking Tracy piercingly in her eyes Tom continued, "I suppose that it takes a bit of believing how I've done so well. At times I can't believe it myself! You must admit though that your Father hasn't fared too bad since we've all moved to the valley."

Tracy nodded her head in agreement.

"Sometimes I wonder if all this would've happened if we had never teamed up with Ross. Ross has a way of coming up with the ideas; to this day I am not sure if it is his superior education or that he is plain lucky and his luck rubs off on anyone who is near him. At other times I think it is Ross's strong belief in God that makes his ideas become fruitful."

Tom saw when he brought God's name into the conversation how a frown appeared on Tracy's forehead.

"Maybe we should change the subject," Tracy smiled falsely. "Ever since Mother left him Dad has these moods of jealousy come over him. I think what Dad needs is another woman. I don't know why he never remarried? I mean, my Mother has been gone long enough for him to be able to get a divorce. Both James and I are old enough to be able to cope with Father having a new wife."

The idea entered her head - what she was telling Tom sounded quite believable but would she really be able to cope with another woman in the house she had run on her own for so long? Although are you still running the household, she reminded herself, you spend more time away from the farm than on it!

While Tracy left to powder her nose Tom went and paid for the meal. Walking back towards the shop where Tracy worked Tom mentioned that he'd enjoyed Tracy's company and grabbing her arm he stopped in the middle of the footpath to say, "We should meet like this more often and I don't mean just for a meal."

Tracy blushed knowing full well what Tom was driving at. Softly she replied while looking at the ground, "I can't see why we can't if you really want to go down that path?"

Grabbing Tracy's arm firmly Tom replied, "It sounds a lovely path to go down!"

They didn't move until someone shouted, "Fair go, youse lot, there are others who like using this path you know!"

Without looking who had been shouting they began walking, both lost in their own thoughts, each knew that a change had begun in their relationship.

**

"This is not helping us a lot is it?" Elizabeth's

best loved cow was having a difficult time to drop her calf. "Come on, try again, and keep on pushing!" Elizabeth slowly massaged the cow's stomach knowing full well that it didn't help the cow any but it made her feel better. The cow kept twisting her head to see if anything was happening and Elizabeth kept looking over her shoulder to see if she could spy Ross. He should be here soon. Not that she knew how he could be of any help?

Finally she heard his voice, calling out to him that she was with Daisy, Ross soon arrived at her side. With a glance he took in the situation. Asking his wife how long the cow had been acting like she was, he wasn't too happy with the information Elizabeth gave him. While washing his right arm and making it slippery with soap he told his wife to stroke the cow's head.

"What will that do?"

"Absolutely nothing dear apart from keeping you out of my way as I have to take some drastic action to remedy this poor cow's situation."

Then to her amazement he started to insert his arm in to the cow.

"What are you doing? Don't you think she is in enough trouble?"

"Just keep stroking her head dear. I can see by the shape of her stomach that the calf isn't in the right position and I am hoping I can help her because if I can't she is in big trouble."

Elizabeth stared in amazement at her husband, most of his arm had disappeared and his face was red with exertion as the cow's contractions squeezed his arm preventing him from finding the calf's legs. Making soothing noises the animal relaxed and yes there he had something. Carefully Ross attempted to place the leg in the correct position. Right that was one leg, now for the other. He was in luck the calf was cooperating. Soon he had the legs in the position he felt was the right one. Asking his wife for the piece of rope he had brought with him that was now hanging over the fence, telling her to soak it in the soapy water. He withdrew his arm shaking it lightly to let the circulation restore. "Thanks love," he said. As he took the wet rope from his wife's hands he adroitly made a noose and smiling at Elizabeth he said, "If I can tie this rope around the calf's legs we'll have a chance that it will survive."

Holding the noose in his hand he gently inserted his arm back into the cow who had finally understood that Ross was trying to help her.

"Pull the rope gently until the slack is taken up," Ross ordered softly to Elizabeth.

His wife did what she was told. Slowly Ross withdrew his arm. Washing the soap from the end of the rope and his arm he grabbed the end of the rope and twirled it around his hands to give him a better grip. Looking straight into his wife's eyes as if to draw extra energy from her he said as he started to pull,

"Let's hope this works dear!"

Sweat broke out on Ross' face as he began to pull on the rope. Slowly the rope began to move. The cow mooed and began to help. Elizabeth saw two tied together hooves appear. Everything seemed to stop but suddenly the whole calf slid out to land on the floor of the stall. It was surrounded by a blue coloured membrane filled with liquid which helped prevent the calf hurting itself when it fell to the ground.

"Isn't it big? No wonder the poor cow had trouble," Elizabeth breathed.

The calf's water bed burst and the cow did not hesitate to begin licking her baby to free it from the skin it was surrounded by. "It is this action of licking the calf that the mother will be able from now on to select her calf from any other," Ross explained.

Elizabeth noticed that the umbilical broke without any help from Ross who was waiting for the afterbirth to appear. There it was, now at least the two animals had a good chance to survive. With tears in her eyes Elizabeth moved to stand next to Ross so they could better share the miracle of birth both had witnessed. The calf attempted to stand on its long fragile legs and after some hesitant stumbles wobbled over to his mother's supply of milk to partake of the colostrums which is so important for newborn calves.

"Who can't believe there is a God when you see something as glorious as the 'creation of a new life' unfold before your eyes?"

Elizabeth softly whispered in awe to Ross while holding his hand. She turned to him, "Where did you learn to assist cows giving birth?"

"You'll be surprised what we drovers had to do at times!"

Ross smiled down at his wife. Then Ross became practical again.

"I'll leave it to you when you decide to separate the calf from its mother, however if you want to start using her to supply us with milk I suggest you don't wait too long."

Elizabeth nodded her head sadly. "It seems a shame to separate them so quickly. They have only just met. I'll give them a couple of days."

"Now, now, farmer's wives don't make sentimental decisions. People on the land are practical! Isn't that what the city-slickers say about us?"

"That's enough Ross; can you see a city from here? How will they ever discover that we have a soft nature also?"

"I'll never win this argument! I am going in to have a bath."

Watching the cow and her suckling calf a while longer. Thinking how lucky she was to have a husband who was tough but gentle at the same time. Well, standing here isn't going to get other jobs done and she followed Ross into their home.

— CHAPTER TEN —

"I found out that McGregor is wondering aloud at times to all and sundry how come you and I are doing so much better than he is?"

Tom and Ross were sitting comfortably in Ross' lounge where they had retired to after enjoying Elizabeth's roast lamb which she had been preparing during most of the morning.

"Is he now?" Ross answered vacantly staring at nothing through the window he was sitting close to. "How did you come to hear this?"

"I stopped by to see Tracy and she happened to mention it. The reason it came up was that her Father was wondering how come I am doing so well when I started with nothing and he had the proceeds of the sale of his farm behind him."

Ross cleared his throat.

"The trouble is Tom there are always people who think they've been unfairly treated. What the man can't see is that he is ever so much better off than before. It doesn't matter where you are or what trade you are in there will always be some who do better. To make themselves feel they are not losers these people start to resort to spreading rumours. I don't see how we can stop this from happening."

Raising his arm to stop Tom from interrupting him Ross continued,

"Do you feel that we are drawing attention to ourselves Tom? You know the reason why we do better than most. I didn't think we were spending money to the amount that it was drawing attention to outsiders? Maybe we should hold back for a while and let the others catch up? Surely McGregor can't say he is suffering? His crops and cattle must reap the same rewards as ours unless he is doing something wrong."

Ross had fallen silent and was staring into space again. Tom suggested,

"Why don't we hold back with our expansion? We should only purchase the essential items we need to run our business efficiently for the next few years. At least we won't be giving them any new food for thought to chew on. It is a pity that we have to put the hall and the church on the backburner though, but even with whatever funds the locals donated to the cost they would've soon worked out that most of the finance had to come from here."

"It's sad Tom that we have to hold back on the church, but you can do things too fast and maybe the valley isn't ready for it yet. After all, our large hayshed has served us well, we'll just have to use it a mite longer. We can still help with donations further afield though, there is no need to stop that, I am sure there are hundreds of good causes out there that need financing. The trouble is we don't know how big our resources are and for how long they'll be ours. Anyone could come along at anytime to stumble on them just like you did. Or the gold could just peter out. I think your idea is right, maybe this is a good time to act as if we didn't have the gold and find out how profitable the farms really are. However I am inclined that we should still collect the gold and hold it in a safe place, at least we'll have a nest egg if times should become harder." Ross was staring out through the window again.

The sound of two flies was the only noise in the room as they circled around the flypaper which was hanging down from the light fitting. The flies were probably wondering why their mates remained silently clinging to the paper. However neither one went to investigate to discover what the attraction of the paper was.

No more could be discussed as Elizabeth opened the door carrying a wriggling Alf in her arms and Tom's brother and sister clinging to her skirts.

"Sorry to interrupt, but I feel you two have had enough time together," she said cheerfully. "I thought it was time you met up with your relations before they forget who you are!"

"Let's have them then!" Ross shouted, as he watched Elizabeth place Alf on the floor from whence he crawled directly to Tom while Tom's brother and sister ran towards 'Uncle Ross' to sit on his knee and beleaguer him with questions.

Tom gave a glance towards Elizabeth who laughing aloud spread her arm out.

"Well Tom, you should be able to tell from this tableau which child misses whom the most?"

Tom decided there and then that he would spend more time with his siblings!

The two flies were still circling the flypaper but their sound was lost among the noise the children made.

Walking home with Terry and Mavis chattering about the good times they'd had with Aunty Elizabeth while Tom had been away, they saw an old man sitting on a rock at the side of the track. Terry and Mavis hung back as they did when they came across a stranger. The old man raised his head in a tired manner as the sound of footsteps reached his ears.

"Albert!" Tom exclaimed in a happy voice. "What are you sitting down here for? Why aren't you resting at our farm?"

Of all the swagmen that came to visit the farm Albert was one of the few who Tom had any respect for. Most swagmen when they called in expected a handout with a bed for doing nothing in return; others told a good story and relied on the sympathy that created, while some had quick fingers with which they soon filled their pockets. This lot usually travelled with others so that you never knew who was to blame.

Albert was an educated man who at some time in his life had struck hard times but then had grown to love the daily travelling so much he decided to make it a career.

Tom could see that Albert wasn't his usual chipper self so he sent Terry running home to organise one of the hands to return with a horse and cart.

While Terry was gone Tom and Mavis attempted to make the old man comfortable - leaning over Albert, Mavis pinched her nose and made the comment, "Gee you smell!"

"Mavis," Tom reprimanded her, "you don't say things like that." Mavis looked nonplussed. "I wasn't telling a lie Tom, he does smell."

Tom began to apologise to Albert who waved his hand to stop him talking.

"She's right Tom I do smell." Facing Mavis he said, "I promise that as soon as we arrive at your homestead I'll have a bath."

Mavis crinkled her nose attractively as they smiled at each other.

"Never be frightened to tell the truth my child,"

Albert included Tom in his glance.

"If everyone spoke the truth there would be a lot less misunderstanding in the world - it is frightening at times what good manners can lead to."

Terry came up to them proudly driving the cart.

"I thought I asked you to request a hand to come back with the cart?"

Terry looked defiant at Tom.

"I know you did but I wanted to let you know that I am old enough to do some things myself!" Tom studied his little brother and noticed that Terry wasn't as small as he pictured him in his mind.

"You are right! I keep thinking of you two as little kids but you aren't that small anymore are you. Sorry about that mate, you've done a great job. We might have to find work to do around the farm to keep you occupied, earn your meal so to speak. There's no such thing as a free meal you know."

"Hang on a minute, there is no need to overdo it; we are not all that old!" Terry and Mavis said together.

The three stood looking at each other with big smiles on their faces.

"Sorry to interrupt," spoke Albert, "what about helping me into the cart?"

Pouring the last of his cuppa which consisted of strong black tea laced with milk and a generous amount of sugar fortified with brandy (medicinal purposes only) down his throat Albert stood up.

"Ah that feels better! I think I've recovered enough to go and have my bath, which should please not only me but Mavis as well."

Mavis got up from her chair to lead Albert in the direction of the bathroom, telling the visitor that she'd placed extra towels in the room for his use.

"You are looking after me too well little lady, you'll spoil me and I might not want to leave!"

In a grown up voice Mavis replied,

"Don't worry, this treatment won't last. The longer you stay the more you'll have to do yourself!"

"I knew it, nothing good lasts forever!" Albert grumbled with a twinkle in his eyes.

When Albert returned from doing his ablutions he found the house empty. Deciding to lay down on the bunk in his room, which in reality was an enclosure of one corner on the veranda and rest his eyelids for a moment he soon succumbed to a deep sleep.

Coming back into the house Tom wondered where Albert had gone but soon found him by the snores which emanated from the sleep out. No good disturbing him now he must need the rest or he would've been awake.

Mavis and Terry were playing outside in the shade of the house so he sat down to enjoy the peace and quiet.

It didn't take long before his thoughts centred on Tracy.

Now that he and Tracy had an understanding he shouldn't delay the talk he was going to have with her Father for too long. McGregor shouldn't have too many objections surely, because Tracy was interested in him. However Tom decided not to overplay his hand as you never knew how a Father would react when it came to losing a daughter, even if she only had moved to the abutting farm.

Tom couldn't wait for the day that he would meet up with Tracy again, maybe they could take the kids and have a picnic up the valley; climb the escarpment so they'd be able to see the whole valley.

Closing his eyes Tom said a small prayer of thanks that his dream was finally becoming reality. Tom had always known that Tracy was destined to be his partner for life; it was a pity it had taken Tracy so long to realise it. Tom's thought drifted to other areas.

What could he and Ross do to make it look like they were more efficient than their neighbours? The only solution Tom could come up with was they should be doing something no one else was into.

No good going into engineering; they were too far away from every one for that and there weren't enough people in the valley to make it pay. Perhaps they should see if they could cultivate a different crop? Now there was an idea! Tobacco came to his mind. Only the other day he had been reading that a study had been done and it had been discovered that the inhabitants of the commonwealth were heavy smokers. The article stated that 3 lb. per head of tobacco was used which was twice the consumption used in the United Kingdom. The climate was ideal in the valley and no one else was cultivating it in the area. Yes, this idea could be a goer! Tom couldn't wait to discuss it with Ross, but listening to the clock chimes he realised it was time to organise a meal for his family.

The clock chimes must've woken Albert as footsteps were coming from the sleep out direction. Soon Albert came through the door yawning and stretching his lean frame.

"Best sleep I've had for weeks!" Was his opening statement!

Tom knew from past experience that Albert was ready for a chat.

"Come into the kitchen mate and we'll be able to speak as I am getting tea ready."

While Tom was busy banging pots about Albert took his makings out to fill the cherry wood pipe. Albert had tried briars, meerschaums, corncobs and once even a German porcelain bowl but as far as he was concerned cherry woods suited him the best. Soon the kitchen was filled with the pleasant aroma of fresh tobacco smoke. Although Tom never had any inclination to take up a pipe he liked the smell of a freshly lit pipe. To make conversation he queried, "Have you ever tried the readymade cigarettes

Albert? They seem to becoming more popular?" Before Tom could say anymore Albert interrupted him abruptly.

"Real men smoke cigars or a pipe, that's all I'll say about the matter."

Tom blissfully ignored Albert and carried on with the subject.

"I believe that since cigarettes are available in nicely presented packages, women have taken to smoking. The article mentioned that quite fifty percent of the 'Best People' in Melbourne are smoking albeit only in their boudoirs and the Railways Commissioners are said to have ordered designs for ladies smoking carriages."

"Women should stick to being Mothers and forget about competing with men."

It sounded as if Albert had his own ideas about what was right in society. Tom noticed that happened often when people only had their own company.

"How about calling the kids, we are nearly ready," Tom suggested.

The youngsters had been put to bed and the two adults were sitting in chairs facing each other. Their talk could now turn to serious matters, not that their discussion would interfere or alter any of the politician's decisions but it gave the men a feeling that they were donating their small amount of expertise to the better good.

"Do you feel any different since we have become

a Commonwealth?" Tom asked.

"I haven't noticed much difference in the attitudes of the people I meet every day, but when I read through a newspaper I find that the articles are more slanted towards us maintaining a racial homogeneity. The population hasn't increased much from when it was 3,750,000 in 1901which consisted of 95 per cent British and 99 per cent white."

Albert sucked deeply on his pipe as if to give him time to think.

"As my honourable friend Alfred Deakin stated, 'The unity of Australia is nothing if it does not imply a united race'. You and I know that he was referring to us being made from the same cast. I personally find it difficult to believe that with a land as large and as empty of people as it is now how it is possible to be able to keep it that way. There are a lot of people on earth and we both know they aren't all the same colour and I'm sure they would like to live here, if they knew how to get here."

Tom shook his head in sympathy.

"I tend to agree with you Albert, I treat people much the same as they treat me. If they treat me kindly I respond kindly if they want to treat me rough I'll give them the same. Somehow I can't see their colour or religion affecting my attitude much."

"That's because you think a little deeper Tom. But there are a lot of people who are reacting emotionally because that is a lot easier to do than to hold your breath. Count to ten, then give an answer. I feel that at this stage we're more British than the British, the 'New Chums' arriving from Britain have no trouble blending in with us, it is the land that they are not used to, that is what makes them homesick not the people."

Tom nodded his head in agreement; he'd met a few of the 'New Chums' as the established locals called them, and discovered they were pleasant to work with but they had no idea on how changeable and hard this country was to live in.

To change the subject he asked Albert if on his travels he'd come across any tobacco growers?

Albert perked up; here was a subject dear to his heart.

"Let me think!" he said slowly. "I did come across an area not that long ago." He stopped to think rubbing his chin with the palm of his hand.

"That's right; I was in the Oven's valley when I noticed the tobacco plants growing. It is a beautiful sight you know. The plants are in long rows about a yard apart and their dark green colour blended in gracefully with the paddocks next door." Albert looked up at Tom.

"Are you thinking of cultivating tobacco?"

"I could be!" Tom replied. "Another crop I'm thinking of is walnuts. I've read up on them and I feel that this area has the right conditions to sustain them. Our winters are cold for long enough but fortunately we only have frost occasionally, and our summer weather warms up our valley so that the crop ripens early. We have plenty of water at hand and once the trees are established we can let the cattle in to eat the grass so we don't have to mow." Albert studied Tom's excited face.

"You have done your homework. Don't forget to contact the tobacco company to make sure they know you want to be a supplier."

"We are nowhere at that stage yet, but thank you for reminding me. Anyway it's becoming late and tomorrow arrives early, I think I'd better be off to bed. You can stay up if you like but for me it's time to go!"

Stepping quietly from the house Tom noticed that Albert was sitting on the bottom step. "I didn't expect to see you so early in the morning mate. That rest you had yesterday afternoon must've been just what you needed as when we first saw you I thought we had to measure you for your pine box."

Albert smiled wistfully.

"You weren't the only one who thought I was ready for my box. I am hoping that being tired is all there is to it. As I am becoming older I find it harder each day to walk the distance I set myself."

Swivelling his head round he continues saying, "You wouldn't need a handyman around, would you? Since I've been staying with you I have a real hankering to settle in the one spot for a while. Maybe

I am not well. I've never felt as tired before as I've been during the last three months. You don't have to pay me anything of course; just to be able to kip and eat regularly will be enough payment for me."

Tom observed the pleading look in Albert's face; he could see that the swagman desperately wanted him to say yes.

"Okay mate, we have a deal, you can start right now. There's some fencing to be repaired in the bottom paddock and as I was on my way there you can join me."

"Sure boss; I'm your man! I'm with you all the way!"

Tom and Albert had never spoken about which specific duties had to be done so he could never select the particular day from when he noticed that his lifestyle changed, only that one day it came to him that he was living in an organised home which ran like a well oiled machine. The children's days were organised and to some extent he felt even he had been gently nudged into a different pattern of life. Tom could not get over how much more was achieved in a day. At first he thought it was the extra pair of hands but then he noticed that the whole day had been planned, at times around his own suggestions, but a lot of times the creative ideas came from Albert who modestly declined that he had partaken in any of the decision making.

Tom wasn't going to make an argument about it

and he enjoyed the extra time he could spend with his siblings. Mavis and Terry glorified in all the attention they were receiving from both adults around them and Elizabeth blessed Albert as she had more time to share with her own family. As Tom hadn't seen Tracy for a few months he suggested they should take a weekend away from the farm and see Albury.

Late Friday afternoon they arrived at Elizabeth's Mother's place who tactfully acted as if it was an everyday occurrence that a cartload of people stayed at her place. After each one was settled and messages from Elizabeth had been exchanged Tom asked to be excused as he wanted to let Tracy know he was in town. With an indulgent smile Mrs. Mainwaring let him depart.

As Tom turned round the corner he could see Tracy talking to a woman as she was locking the shop's door. Creeping up behind her and as Tracy straightened he said,

"Hello, I couldn't have timed it any better."

"What are you doing here? You never mentioned that you were coming into town in your last letter," Tracy exclaimed, letting Tom give her a hug turning her face slightly so that the kiss meant for her lips ended up on her cheek.

Tom's heart sank; each time they'd been apart she would treat him coolly for the first hour or so, eventually she seemed to warm towards him to become passionate as they had to part again. His

Tracy was a problem at times!

Telling her that his brother and sister had come down with him didn't seem to upset her too much as she commented,

"We must take them somewhere nice. They don't come to town that often and at their age a visit to Albury should be a memorable occasion!"

Tracey noticed that faint lines crept around Tom's eyes as he smiled at her suggestion.

"Why don't we take them for a walk around town tonight after tea? It doesn't become dark until well after nine and we could have an ice cone from the new Ice Cream Parlour to finish off the evening.'

"Great idea love, you are even making me feel excited in anticipation!"

Chatting about everything and nothing they walked to Mrs. Mainwaring's place.

When the idea of having a walk after tea was broached Albert and Mrs. Mainwaring wanted to come along too. They returned from inspecting the railway station with its extraordinary long platform and large turn tables on which the locomotives turned to face the return journey home as each state had a different gauge track which slightly delayed the journey from Sydney to Melbourne. Meandering towards the Ice Cream Parlour there was a crowd listening to a small band whose players wore a drab dark uniform. As soon as the band stopped playing one of its members started to preach to the crowd about the evil of drink and how they should turn to the Lord to save them. Each time he mentioned a relevant point his supporters shouted, "Praise the Lord!" while the drummer enthusiastically banged his drum.

When Tom asked what the little band was about Albert soon enlightened him.

"There's more and more of them harassing the poor drinkers. In some towns they visit the hotels so often that the poor publican can't make a living! Police fine them and even place them in gaol, but they keep coming back to spoil the working men's drinking time." In a lower voice he continued, "I will admit that women folk and their children suffer as there is very little money left to feed the rest of the family when (father has poured his wages down his throat) with little or no consideration for his family. Personally I don't think the 'Salvation Army' as I believe they named their organisation will last, most 'do-gooders' disappear quickly from the scene, but who knows, they seem very determined in what they are preaching. One editor of the local paper wrote that the Army had invaded the country from England 'just like the foxes and rabbits' had done and would most likely spread and be as big a pest."

A young girl came near to hand over a news letter which she was giving out. She was wearing a uniform type of dress with a bonnet to match that had a large bow on it. Tom noticed her kind eyes and the smile she gave to each person as she handed them a pamphlet by what he now knew was called the 'War Cry'.

Some young drunken bystanders began to shout back at the preacher so the band cleverly began playing a popular hymn which soon drowned out the hecklers who when realising they were being ignored, entered the pub instead.

Moving on, with the band music fading in the distance, Mavis and Terry grew excited when the Ice Cream Parlour came in sight. The meeting with the 'quaint' group was forgotten as more important decisions were to be made.

There were so many choices that it took nearly the remaining part of the evening to decide what each person was going to have.

Their small group had grown silent as they contentedly tasted their ice creams. Stopping in front of the Cinematograph to check which 'coming attraction' would be worth seeing they noticed that the small group of 'Salvationists' busily chatting amongst themselves stepped past them seemingly on their way home.

Tom stated, "How about I take Tracy to her place as we are not far from where she lives and I'll meet you at home?"

After opening the gate, nearly ready to step onto the veranda the front door swung suddenly open and an angry voice demanded, "What took you so long

I've been worried sick..." Seeing that Tracy was accompanied by Tom and that they were standing close together the voice stopped abruptly.

"Sorry!" James said in what Tom thought as a surprised but hurt voice.

Saying nothing else James stepped backwards and slammed the door shut.

Tom looked enquiringly at Tracy, who had gone pale as she replied,

"Oh dear, I forgot he was coming today! Sorry Tom, but I'd better go in and apologise." Without any further ado she opened the door to step inside.

Flabbergasted Tom stood still to let what happened soak in. In the past James never had much to say to him but to be treated like this was completely unexpected.

"You are home a lot earlier than I expected?" Mrs. Mainwaring queried. All Tom said was, "Yes, James had arrived unexpectedly, so I came home early."

Albert and Mrs. Mainwaring studied Tom's face and he realised his voice must've sounded different.

"James seems to visit his sister frequently! It is nice to know they get on so well with each other," Mrs. Mainwaring stated in a kind manner.

"Does he?" Tom asked surprised, as he thought that James would've been too busy helping his Father out on the farm and Kathleen never mentioned it.

"O yes, many a times have I seen them

wandering about town, usually with their heads close together, seemingly in a world on their own."

Changing the subject, Albert said, "I don't care what you two are going to do but I'm going to retire!"

Both Tom and Mrs. Mainwaring thought this was a good idea and soon the lights were extinguished and everyone except Tom was asleep.

"Why do I care so much for Tracy? It isn't that she treats me lovingly! But in the end that's what I'm hoping she will do." Tom tossed and turned trying to fall asleep but the same thoughts kept turning like a windmill in his mind. Thinking back to when he first met Tracy; even then she had treated him with disdain. Had he really won her over since that time?

He hoped he had but deep down he knew that he loved her a lot more than Tracy ever loved him. So why did she establish a closer relationship with him? Was it because she thought he was well off? But a girl with her looks could pick any suitor she'd like! Turning over again Tom murmured,

"Dear Father in heaven please gather Tracy to your bosom so that she can see me through Christian eyes."

Maybe that was the reason why Tracy treated him like she did. She felt uncomfortable about him being a Christian?

Clearly he heard the voice in his head.

She will never be for you, my son!

Tom reared straight up, his heart pumping -

surely he had misunderstood what he'd just heard. No, he cried deeply within his heart; God would never interfere with the love a man had for the woman he had selected to be the mother of his children. What if the words he had heard were true though? Breaking out in a cold sweat Tom threw the blankets away from him to kneel down at the side of his bed.

Praying desperately to God and pleading with Him at the same time, Tom eventually capitulated tiredly, "I don't understand Lord, and I hope you'll change your mind, but if it is your will all I can do is follow it."

As the false dawn was heralding that daytime was near, Tom finally fell asleep.

— CHAPTER ELEVEN —

"It's a long time since we've done anything like this together," remarked Ross to Elizabeth as they ambled past the ornamental pond with its ornate fountain towards the grandiose domed Exhibition Buildings. Built for the Great Exhibition in 1880 it was still used for trade fairs and many other functions that attracted crowds. The three of them, as Elizabeth refused to leave young Alf behind in the care of Albert, had come to Melbourne for Ross to discuss the possibility of supplying tobacco companies with home grown tobacco.

"Yes, it was nice of Tom to suggest that you approach the companies and use the time in Melbourne as a holiday at the same time. It was after all his idea that we should look at cultivating tobacco." Ross smiled, before answering.

"Tom can come up with a new idea, that's for sure. Just before we left he also suggested I look at the cost of walnut trees. He'd read somewhere that we are located ideally to cultivate them. The beauty of it is that the cattle can graze in the same paddocks once the trees are established, which saves us the trouble of having to scythe the grass."

They walked in silence keeping their eyes on Alf who was busy chasing pigeons that were settled on the green lawns. Looking up at Ross Elizabeth opened the conversation again.

"Didn't you think he looked rather tired and depressed when he and his siblings returned from Albury? To me he didn't look like the normal Tom at all. Very quiet and withdrawn he seemed. Has he said anything at all about Tracy to you? The love of his life she is and at times I wonder about that girl, don't you?" Elizabeth grasped Ross's arm tighter.

"No dear, Tom only mentioned the business venture to me. At times I think you worry more about him than his own Mother did. A real mother hen you are at times when it comes to Tom."

"I suppose I am, but I would love to see him settle down. Tom is a real family man; you can tell that by the way he looks after his brother and sisters."

"Talking about his sister, when are we meeting her?"

"Tom! You'd forget your head if it wasn't screwed on. Kathleen is meeting us on her way home from college in our rooms at the Windsor this evening. You wanted it that way so we didn't have to bother hiring a babysitter for Junior."

"You are a darling. I suppose we should begin to

walk back to the Windsor so we can be organised to meet the Grand Kathleen."

"Don't you get too uppity young man, Kathleen has organised some free seats for us at her college performance. It sounds like it is going to be a great night; I believe they expect Mr. Musgrove to be there. Kathleen informed me that Mr. Musgrove is planning to provide Melbourne and Sydney with yearly seasons to cater for the Australian theatre-goers. Opera is becoming more popular each year and that's why Mr. Musgrove and Mr. J. C. Williamson are on the lookout for local talent."

Ross had to admit that the operatic evening was a great success. The students entertained the audience by singing arias from Lohengrin and Tanhauser in English. Kathleen appeared often on stage and someone sitting next to Elizabeth was overheard to comment that this young singer was destined for a great career in opera. After the performance was over Ross and Elizabeth were waiting in the foyer to congratulate Kathleen on her performance when Ross noticed that she was speaking to a young girl who had been sitting a few rows in front of him. Somehow the girl looked familiar but as she had her back towards Ross it was hard for him to see her. The girl left Kathleen who smiled at Ross and Elizabeth as she strode towards them.

After compliments had been paid to Kathleen, Ross asked who the girl was that she had been chatting with.

"She is a girl who lives in the same boarding house as I am. I asked her to come over and meet you but she had another appointment to attend, so she left straight away."

Another student came to wrap her arms around Kathleen and give an embracing hug cheerfully chattering on about how much she had enjoyed the evening. Kathleen looked embarrassed over the girl's shoulder at Ross and his wife who smiled in answer. The hugger was pushed aside by Kathleen's teacher who informed her that he had been approached by not only Mr. Musgrove but also the esteemed Mr. J. C. Williamson who asked to be informed about Kathleen's report at the end of year results.

Kathleen was over the moon. So much so, that the subject of her flatmate wasn't raised again.

During the next few days fleeting thoughts of the girl came to Ross' mind but as he was too busy to do any following up she was soon forgotten. Elizabeth was glad that they would soon be returning home. It was nice to be in the hub of civilization but the smells, dust and flies that accompanied it was becoming tiresome. She even commented to Ross that,

"Melbourne must be a very popular city as five million flies wouldn't be wrong!"

One day when Elizabeth was trying to cross Spring Street holding a hanky in front of her mouth a dowager smiled at her and said, "It's pretty grim isn't it? However think yourself lucky there's not a blustery 'Northerly' blowing because I do believe it lifts the top layer from the street into the air and the dust enters everywhere." Fortunately the staff at the Windsor excelled in their service so she never had to worry about the cleanliness of her garments.

"How do the people living in the suburbs keep their clothes clean and dry in the winter time?" the thought often entered her mind. Surely not everyone had the superb cleaning facilities that her hotel possessed?

Once again she realised how fortunate she and Ross had been. Many young squatter families began with a bark hut, 1000 sheep and a small orchard, with the wife having a baby in the first year and after five years of surviving drought and many other obstacles plus an increased family they would most likely still be residing in the same hut they started in.

Elizabeth felt guilty at times at how financial they seem to be. Ross didn't seem to mind how much money was spent, as long as it wasn't wasted on trivial items. When she wondered aloud if they should be at the Windsor he remarked, "We can only spend the money once dear, and you can't take it with you, can you? At the moment we have it. When times become tough we'll have to do without. Enjoy yourself dear, while we can, after all we don't do this often!"

And Elizabeth had enjoyed herself, walking through interesting arcades and popping into the different shops that were hidden in there was sheer bliss. As welcome to the lonely homestead the itinerant hawker was, he could never carry the variety of goods available in the city. Being able to attend a church service which for many years now they'd done without, was another blessing. At home the people in the neighbourhood used their largest room or their barn to meet and worship together. Here in Melbourne you could choose from a variety of proper built churches that had not only a priest or minister leading the service but there was also a large congregation attending combined with a choir singing to the accompanied organ music which at times sounded so nice you thought you had died and gone to heaven.

However Elizabeth secretly yearned to be back home on the farm. It was a pity that young Alf wasn't old enough to remember his stay in Melbourne although with God's help in a few years from now they might be able to visit the city again. That evening Ross came home with the news that they might have to extend their stay in Melbourne due to him having to wait for the final word of a Director who was visiting Sydney and would not be back for another three days. Seeing Elizabeth's face drop Ross suggested, "Why don't you and junior travel to Albury and stay with your Mother until I come and then we'll travel home together."

Elizabeth thought this a great idea; there was no great hardship in travelling on a train, you only had to get on and off at the right places.

The decision was made and the next day saw Ross saying farewell to his wife and son at Spencer Street Station.

When Elizabeth and Alf couldn't see Ross anymore they stopped waving and returned to their seats. She missed Ross already and could smell his shaving soap that she must have picked up when they kissed each other. A lingering kiss it had been, it told her how much he regretted to say goodbye to her. Unknowingly Elizabeth let her tongue moisten her lips.

She looked around the carriage. They were fortunate that there was only one other passenger in their carriage. The elderly man was looking through the pages of 'The Bulletin' he had purchased at the station before entering the train.

Once the train passed through Fawkner leaving a plume of black smoke in its trail, the man closed his magazine to stare at the country side wheeling past.

"I am hungry Mummy; can I have something to eat please?"

Elizabeth nodded yes and stood up to pick the hamper from the rail above her head. The elderly man rose and offered to take it down for her. Thanking him Elizabeth opened the hamper and while rescuing a sandwich for Alf she thought it would be bad manners not to offer the gentleman something to eat.

While Alf was engaged in demolishing his food, Elizabeth and the man were making small talk.

"That's a well behaved boy you have Madam, you and your husband must be awfully proud of him! He reminds me a lot of when my son was his age."

The man had a wistful expression on his face.

"We are, although he has his moments you know?"

The man smiled saying, "Haven't they all?"

Elizabeth thought that he reminded her of someone when he smiled.

"Are you going far?"

"Only as far as Albury, after that I am not sure what will happen?"

The man turned towards Alf.

"What's your name son?"

"Alf is my name sir!" replied the boy proudly. "I don't like junior much."

"His father calls him junior at times," Elizabeth explained.

"He's named after his great grandfather. My husband had a lot of respect for his grandfather."

The man smiled at the boy.

"Do you know that my name is Alf too and I was also named after my father?"

Conspiringly the boy looked at the elderly man.

"I've got another name as well," Alf piped up in a smug voice.

Elizabeth sat watching the two of them. It always amazed her that the old and the young could get on so well with each other.

She observed the man's face grow white and his hand covering his chest when young Alf blurted out the name Smith.

Without realising how come she knew Elizabeth whispered hoarsely, "You are Ross's Father aren't you?"

Alf looked mystified at the response that his name had caused.

"Fancy that; you must've missed seeing your son by only a few minutes. He was waving us goodbye while you sat only a few feet away from him." Elizabeth turned to her young son to say, "I want you to be a very good boy while the gentleman and I have a talk." Smiling gently Elizabeth looked towards the man who slowly began to put his thoughts together again.

Moving nearer to him she stated emotionally, "I do believe we have a lot to speak about, don't you?"

Weakly the man nodded his head before he began to speak.

"Fifty five years it has taken me to admit for the first time in my life that everything I called wrong in my life was my own fault."

Elizabeth was going to say it couldn't be

completely his fault when her Father-in-law raised his hand to prevent her saying anymore. It was rather funny how the word Father-in-law sounded so natural to her.

Never had she expected to ever have any need for the title. Now, here she was sitting next to him.

"Look, it was my fault. Ever since I was old enough to know that my Father's property would become mine one day, I couldn't wait for time to move quickly enough. It is only about a year ago that it entered my mind that it could not have been anybody else's, but my own fault. My greed has ruined the relationship with my Father, my wife and my children. You, Elizabeth, you don't mind if I call you by your name?"

Elizabeth shook her head.

"Elizabeth, you pointed out that my son had a fondness for his grandfather? Well as soon as I discovered that Ross went to my Father more than he came to see me I set about making sure my Father was living in a place away from the farm. It took me a few years but by the time Ross was ten I had succeeded. It broke my Father's heart to leave the place he had built, but I ignored that and by sending Ross to a boarding school prevented both of them from finding out that it was I who had organised the shoddy deal. As low as I was sinking I still wanted Ross to think well of me. As Ross grew up he learned more about how a property should be run, and there came a time when I realised that he knew more than I did, especially when it came to the latest up to date farming developments."

The old man raised his head which had been sunk on his chest as he stared at the carriage floor while narrating the story to face Elizabeth.

"This was not going to be! No one was going to be above me. My wife was a beautiful spirited girl when I met her, but within a few years I had been able to subdue her to such a stage that she moved more like a zombie than a living person. It made me sad to see her like that but my sadness soon turned to arrogance and anger so I treated her like the witless moron I had turned her into. That was another of my faults - as soon as I had degraded a person to the level I wanted to see them in I became angry at the spineless creatures they were. For years we continued to exist in that mode and it wasn't until a few years ago just after my wife died, that my daughter rebelled and disappeared to God knows where. My anger and to my disgust my weakness for the bottle made me carry on blaming everyone else but myself. The employees I had working for me left me; there is only old Clarence left now, who is looking after the place while I am gone. When I realised one night this was all that was left, the thought entered my mind it could have been me who had created this horrible situation. That is when I made up my mind to set out and find my children. It was a big step to take, but as the farm couldn't become much worse, I actually thought it might fare better if I left, so the decision wasn't that hard to make. For a year I've been searching, probably in all the wrong places, but it wasn't until this week that I found out that a property owner named Ross Smith was located east of Albury."

He found Elizabeth's eyes peering into his. "Thank heavens we met up, it seems like the Big Fellow up there had a hand in this and although I haven't met Ross at least I know he is happy with a wife and son."

Elizabeth sat silently crying, then noticed that Alf had propped himself up against his Grandfather's arm and had dropped off to sleep while the old man was unconsciously stroking the child's back.

"Ross very seldom spoke about his past, which indicated to me how hurt he was. When he did eventually speak it was about his Mother and his younger sister, he used to wonder at times when we were in bed before we fell asleep if Jessica was married or not. He'll be upset when he discovers that his Mother has passed away, he really missed her."

Elizabeth turned towards her father-in-law with some anger in her.

"It isn't for me to criticise your actions sir, we are not allowed to judge, but I think you do realise now that your behaviour has altered many lives, not always for the best."

"I sure have." Alfred said humbly.

"We'll have to design a plan to get it all back on track, right?"

"Right!" he answered as they smiled at each other.

***

Whether you worked for a squatter who owned a large run or were a 'free selector' with a small farm of your own Albert realised that you had to be versatile. Milking Elizabeth's cow while they were away in Melbourne, gave them the good fortune of having the use of the extra milk. It also gave Albert the opportunity to serve up some different dishes, which were gratefully appreciated by Tom's family. So far, apart from assisting in running the household he had also helped with blacksmithing, repair a wagon, make new iron hinges for a gate and some saddlery work.

Albert didn't classify himself as a bushman but during his years on the road he had picked up some skills which helped him to earn a crust. It was one of the reasons why he was welcome at the many properties he called on.

Heaving the bucket of milk onto the kitchen table Albert gave a sigh of relief. He must be getting old. A few years ago he could've carried two buckets but now he began to puff before he was halfway home toting only one bucket. That's why he was so happy to be with Tom. Albert considered himself to be very lucky that he had ended up in a situation like he was in at this time of his life. He was also grateful for the sum of money Tom gave him each week. When Albert refused the offer Tom made him take it as he believed no one should ever be without some cash in his pocket. Acknowledging the wisdom of this Albert accepted his pay.

Life wasn't only hard for the elderly on the land - even in the cities people had their difficulties. Albert knew only too well that one out of every thirteen children born died before it reached its first birthday. Illness was feared by every parent, especially when for no reason, they could think of, diseases like diphtheria, typhoid or whooping cough could strike out of nowhere.

Albert believed that cleanliness whether personal or in living conditions stopped diseases regaining the upper hand and so he was fanatical to keep himself and his surroundings clean. Which was detrimental to Mavis and Terry's feelings, as they didn't appreciate the soapy water entering their eyes?

Albert also observed on his travels that quackery flourished among people who were ignorant of disease. There was never a shortage of unscrupulous men and women who adopted bogus titles to peddle a range of bogus cure-alls which in many cases hastened death among the patients rather than curing them. It was horrifying to Albert that sick people became gullible and accepted any 'cure' that promised improvement.

Once Albert's thoughts were centred on how men treated each other he couldn't control his thinking on the matter. Fortunately he was in the kitchen on his own and so could give vent to his feelings. If he was annoyed at the fake healers he despised the quacks who practised the pulling or filling of teeth even more. At least to become a doctor you had to study and pass tests but anyone could become a dentist. All you required to pull or fill teeth were a pair of forceps and heaps of self-confidence. You could ignore the pain and blood of your patients once the shilling you charged for each extraction was in your pocket. Yes, Albert smiled cynically, dentistry was a lucrative business. A Royal Commission should be created to look into quackery; that might open a few eyes!

Deciding to make himself a 'cuppa' Albert sat down to reflect further into the past. Well, did he remember that day in January 1900 when the wife of a sick man begged him to visit her ailing husband? Meeting the doctor coming out from the front door of his patients premises, Albert enquired how the patient was. The reply coming from the doctor was a curt, "He has bubonic plague" which stopped Albert in his tracks.

What to do? He knew he had made a pledge to God during his training as a minister, to always look after his flock. But did that apply to a sickness that could grow into plague proportions? Couldn't he help mankind more if he was alive and healthy?

Without any further ado Albert made a decision that he would regret for the rest of his life. He turned from the house and walked away. At this stage Albert wasn't sure that he had stopped running yet? Having learned that over 300 cases of 'black death' were reported, of which a third died, it still hadn't left Albert feeling any better over what he knew was a cowardly decision. In his mind he knew that God forgives a repentant sinner his sins, but was Albert ready to forgive his own sins?

Glancing through the kitchen window Albert saw Tom busy removing a stump from his favourite paddock. According to Albert's thinking there was no need to remove the tree. The tree gave character and shade to its surroundings but no, Tom decided that he didn't want it there. The way Tom attacked the stump it seemed to Albert that Tom was really trying to work out a problem that had nothing to do with the tree but more about something that was inside Tom. The stump was large enough but not that large that a chain and a horse couldn't have removed it in an instant. But no, Tom was tackling the stump in a manner that required a lot of effort and should burn up a lot of frustration. Tom hadn't shown much contentment since the visit to Albury and Albert was sure that this workout had something to do with what had occurred during that trip.

***

Elizabeth stood with young Alf impatiently waiting for the train to arrive from Melbourne. Finally it heralded its arrival by blowing the whistle and surrounding the area with steam and smoke. One of the first people to appear from the mist was Ross who had to drop his bags as his son nearly bowled him over in the excitement of seeing his Father again. Greeting his wife with a long hard kiss they walked away from the station - Ross toting Alf and one bag, with Elizabeth carrying the other. Before Elizabeth had a chance to ask if his business deals had come to fruition Alf began to squirm and yell out,

"Pop, Pop." Ross uncertain about what was happening, lost hold of his son who raced across the busy street and narrowly missed being run over by a single brougham, driven by a foppish young blood who was too busy chatting to the young miss sitting next to him. Ross yelled for Alf to come back while Elizabeth held her hand over her mouth to prevent screaming.

When Ross and his wife managed to cross the street Ross saw that an old man was holding his son by the hand. Walking towards the man to thank him Ross stopped dead when he realised who was holding his son's hand. Elizabeth standing looking at the two men who made no effort to move to each other said nervously,

"It is your Father, Ross that Alf ran to?" Slowly Ross came to.

"I know it is my Father dear." Without turning to his wife, he added, "What I can't understand is how come you and Alf know who he is?"

"Well dear," Elizabeth said light heartedly although her heart was beating in her throat, "we found him sitting in our carriage when we came up from town. It all sort of just happened, didn't it father-in-law."

The father-in-law didn't reply; he was as frozen as his son. Wetting his lips nervously with his tongue and clasping young Alf in a firmer hold to his chest he eventually came out with, "You are looking well Ross and from what I have seen so far you've selected a wonderful wife and have a clever son."

The clever son felt he was becoming squashed so began to squirm vigorously in attempting to free himself from the tight hold he was in.

"Why are you here?"

Elizabeth went towards her father-in-law and took Alf from him. Slowly he released the child hesitating to let go as a barrier would be removed and nothing would be between him and his son.

"Alfie and I will walk on ahead so that the two of you can speak."

As the two walked away you could hear Alf tell his Mother in an indignant voice, "My name is Alf! Don't call me Alfie!"

The men smiled at each other, both of them saying almost together, "He has a lot of you in him." This helped break the tension between the two of them as they walked alongside each other to follow Elizabeth.

"Son, you are going to find this hard to believe, but I've been looking for you and your sister." Ross looked up with a start. "Yes Ross, Jessica ran away just over a year ago and I haven't heard anything from her since then. I wish I could give you some good news but your Mother passed away." Ross stopped walking. "It wasn't long after the funeral that Jessica packed her belongings and left the district."

Hoarsely Ross asked, "How did Mum die?" A silence hung in the air.

Hesitantly his Father replied,

"Mainly because of my neglect, I suppose. After you left your Mother withdrew from her daily chores more each day until the time came that she never even left her room. My sarcastic comments didn't help her any and in my arrogance to prove how retarded she was I never noticed when she moved from thinking herself unwell to actually becoming ill. Yes Ross, I have created a lot of suffering for others during my life."

Ross heard the note of distress in his Father's voice. Much as he had disliked the person walking next to him, a tiny speck of respect entered his heart for the direct and honest manner in which his Father

187

had spoken. Surely what his Father was going through could not be easy?

"Every day after you had gone your Mother asked if a letter had come from you? Especially during the last days of her existence her mind was full of you. I tell you now son that her love for you really annoyed me! So much so, that I never even let her know that the letters you had written had been destroyed by me to make sure they would never be read." Ross quickly glanced at his Father.

"Much as it hurts to tell you this now, you must understand I have to relate it as it happened not as I think you would like to hear it, not even on her last day on her deathbed did I tell her or Jessica that you had written quite often to them.

"I curse myself now because if only I had mentioned to both of them that you had so often tried to contact them, your Mother would've died a happier person and your sister might've remained at home."

Ross noticed his Father's hand groping in his trouser pocket to come up with a handkerchief into which he had a long blow, wiping his eyes unobtrusively at the same time. Ross noted that Elizabeth was trying to get his attention, she was discretely pointing towards a shop window. With his mind full of what his Father had told him it took Ross a while to realise they were passing Tracy's shop or at least the shop where she served. Looking to see why

Elizabeth had made the fuss he observed Tracy and her brother standing face to face not noticing anyone around them and perceiving the finger pointing that James was doing at his sister, he assumed they were arguing. Ross raised his eyebrows to let Elizabeth know that he had seen the brother and sister. A light drizzle had started and Ross said to his Father that they'd better move a bit faster before the rain really set in. In a way Ross thought it was fortunate that it had begun to rain. Because of the faster walking his Father fell silent giving Ross some time to think about everything he had just learned?

Ross was thinking as his feet automatically avoided the small puddles forming on the footpath. Innocent bystanders would see this small group of people rushing home and assume that here was a family united in what they were doing. Not being able to discern to realise that the old man was heartbroken with grief and the son completely bowled over at seeing a Father who was nothing like the man he had walked away from so many years ago.

By the fuss Elizabeth's Mother made of his Father Ross could see his Father had been a regular visitor since his arrival in Albury. A tiny spurt of hurt came inside him, didn't they realise what damage this man had done to him and his family? It was all very well for his Father to say that he had dealt out a nasty hand and he was now very sorry about what he had done to his family but that didn't help Ross and his sister Jessica very much right now. The more Ross thought about the current situation the angrier he became. So much so that felt he had to leave the room as he couldn't breathe.

"I have to go out for a while!" Ross blurted! Suddenly the room became silent and everyone looked at him. Ross felt embarrassed.

"Where do you have to go to, it's still raining?" Elizabeth queried? Ross faced her directly and told her, "I feel I need some time and space to clear my head. So much happened so fast I feel as if I'm bowled over."

A softness of understanding appeared over Elizabeth's face.

"I'll come with you dear, if I'm welcome that is?"

Returning her smile Ross answered simply, "You are welcome!"

Warmth returned to his heart. He was so fortunate to have Elizabeth for his wife.

They walked close together sheltering under the umbrella held firmly in Ross' hand, their shoes crunching the gravel of the path on the bank of the Murray River. The smell of wet grass mingled with the mind cleansing eucalyptus aroma coming from the overhanging moist leaves pervading the air. The deep black water of the river slid silently past on its long journey to the ocean. Apart from the continual sound of rain falling; all was still.

Elizabeth walked in silence, she was enjoying the

walk. Walking in the rain without becoming seriously wet is one of the nicest sensations weather can bestow on mankind. She was also wondering when Ross was going to break his silence. Knowing him as she did, she knew the time wasn't far away for him to begin sharing his thoughts and feelings with her. Elizabeth was right!

"What do you think dear, should we invite him to come home with us tomorrow or do we shake hands and leave him to go his own way?"

Elizabeth realised that her husband hadn't forgiven his Father for the way he'd behaved in the past.

Ross spoke again,

"I mean, he still has to find Jessica. He shouldn't waste too much time. We both know that the longer you wait the harder it is to locate a person."

"Are you trying to convince me or yourself Ross Smith?"

Ross glanced guiltily at his wife. "You know what I mean,' Ross mumbled.

"I leave the decision with you as always Ross but don't you think your Father is trying hard to turn over a new leaf. I know I don't know him as well as you do but I believe and feel he is sincere in his actions!"

"Right then, it looks like he's coming with us."

Ross straightened his shoulders as if a load had slid from his back.

"We'd better return home love, they must be wondering where we are?"

As they changed direction they noticed another couple walking as one, heads close together completely unaware there were other people on the planet.

Elizabeth whispered, "Did you recognise them Ross, am I reading more into this than I think I am seeing?"

With clenched teeth Ross replied, "I certainly wished we had never come across them, it isn't normal. I feel sick in my stomach."

The rain had cleared overnight but the sky was still covered in cloud. Once their carriage had turned off the main road Ross had to negotiate the ruts that represented the track home with some care. It must've rained more here as the track was downright sodden. At times it paid him to leave the track and make a new one as the wheels sank deep into the mire.

A rider hurried past them his hat pulled well down over his face, clods of dirt springing up in the air as the soft mud left the steel shod hooves.

"Someone's in a hurry," Ross' Father commented.

Elizabeth and Ross didn't answer him as they glanced at each other. Both of them had no trouble recognising their neighbour's son.

Coming round the last bend Elizabeth sat up to

enjoy the pleasure of seeing their home. It might've been a dull cloudy day but somehow someone had helped in leaving a hole in the clouds for a golden shaft of sunlight to pierce its way through the gloom exposing the homestead in a golden surround of light. Turning to her father-in-law Elizabeth said, "Welcome to our home."

— *CHAPTER TWELVE* —

Slowing down, her ears cocked, Kathleen could hear the footsteps slowing down behind her. She was right, there was someone following her. For the last couple of days Kathleen had a suspicion that there was someone tailing her. Hiding behind a tree she waited to see what would happen. Not that she had any idea of what she could do once whoever it was that was watching accosted her. Letting a few minutes go by Kathleen slowly poked her head round the bole of the tree. Suddenly a stale tobacco overladen with beer breath wafted into her face.

"Gotcha miss," Kathleen ran away but a hand grabbed her coat stopping her midstride, nearly pulling her off her feet.

"Leave me alone you brute! How dare you treat me like this?"

Kathleen was resisting the rough looking man's advances by squirming and wriggling, she also got in a few good kicks that connected sharply against her attackers shin.

"Stand still you silly woman, stop fighting so that I can speak to you. My boss wants to know if you are the sheila that was living with DeVilliers in Albury."

"What does Mark have to do with this?" Kathleen said in amazement. Then instantly blamed herself for giving the game away.

"Right deary, so the boss was right, you are the woman. He wants me to tell you that he would like to speak with you..."

Suddenly the man crumpled to the footpath. Stunned Kathleen looked round to see Jason standing next to her with a smile on his dial.

"What are you doing here?"

"Saving you for that important singing career you are always raving on about."

"What do you mean, saving me, I was in no danger, the man was only talking to me." Kathleen spat the words out like a cat hissing at a dog. How come that buffoon was here anyway?

"Why did you try to run away from him then? Why did he have a hold on your coat? You can't fool me dear, I saved you!"

Glaring at him Kathleen thought, "Why does he get on my goat so easily?" Smiling at Jason she gave in saying, "Okay you saved me!" Pointing down to the collapsed man on the path Kathleen sweetly asked, "What are you going to do about him?"

"He'll be right in another few minutes."

Kathleen interrupted him. "You mean to say you

know exactly when a person recovers after you clock him one? Do you hit people that often?"

Jason smiled at her wickedly, "I only hit them when they attack my favourite friends and as I have so many friends that need my protection I have, even if I do say it myself, gained quite a bit of experience." The thug on the path began to move.

"There you are, the little sense he has is returning. Let us find out what your friend really wanted from you."

Kathleen was also interested to hear what this had been about. Anxiously she leaned over the man and asked him why he needed to speak to her? The thug glanced over his shoulder and shrank when he noticed Jason.

He asked Kathleen,

"Did that bloke clobber me?" Before Kathleen could reply Jason answered,

"No my good friend, I was coming down the footpath and saw a limb fall down from the tree. I called out to warn you but the branch hit you before I could get the words out." Kathleen glared at Jason, who only shrugged his shoulders as if to say, what else can I say?

The man looked around him to spot the branch but Jason forestalled any further questions by saying, "I threw it over the fence. We don't want to see anyone else hurt by it now, do we?"

Kathleen asked once again! "Why did you want

to speak to me?"

The man shook his head trying to regain his thoughts.

"My boss wants to meet up with you."

Kathleen studied him before saying,

"I can't understand why he would want to see me? I only sang for DeVilliers, I don't know anything about the man. I only worked there."

Shrugging his shoulders the thug stated, "I'm only passing on what the man said, I would listen to him if I were you as he has a nasty streak in him when he doesn't get his way!"

Looking unhappy Kathleen's eyes met Jason's. Realising she was lost for a reply he said to the lackey,

"Tell your boss that if he wants to meet Kathleen he should send her a proper invite so that the lady knows who and where they should meet?"

The ruffian looked relieved, at least he had something positive to tell his master, he only remembered too well what had occurred to his predecessor, you don't get far in life with two broken arms and legs. As he walked away he said over his shoulder, "Right, I'll inform the boss of what you said!"

"Well, that's a nice mess you got me into," Kathleen said with a sarcastic voice.

Jason smiled as he replied,

"You think you would've felt better if Jessie 'Carbuncle' Parker had you picked up by two of his bully boys?" Kathleen lurched to one side, gasping in disbelief.

Two years ago, an eager journalist who wanted a fast rise to fame, had written an editorial about certain characters of the local underworld. Not mentioning any of the gangsters by name in the article he however referred to one character as the 'Carbuncle man'.

As Jessie through no fault of his own, had been born with a rather large lump on his forehead he took the reference personally. Many others who read the article made the same assumption, that it was Jessie to whom the writer was referring. Jessie, right from the day he was born, had an intense dislike for the lump that he could see each time he stood in front of a mirror. So when Jessie read the article he wasn't concerned about the amount of truth that was presented to the public. To tell the truth Jessie was very proud of his misdeeds that had been aired in print. He considered that it gave him more status among his confederates. What most concerned him was that now the public knew about his disfigurement! Jessie Parker always thought of himself as being a man of action, although at times without him realising it, it was mainly re-action that usually drove him to most of his decision making.

Once again re-action set in; vengeance shall be mine, was one of Jessie's favoured quotations - within a week the journalist went missing. Despite the whole police force actively knocking on suspects' doors not a trace of him was found. Jessie swaggered openly through town because he had a watertight alibi so the police were helpless and could not detain him.

Two months later, some fishermen discovered parts of the journalist when they brought their nets in and the only other parts the police divers obtained were the cement boots that had held the poor man to the bottom of the Yarra River. Ever since then the word 'Carbuncle' was whispered around town and definitely never mentioned within Jessie Parker's hearing.

"Are you talking about Jessie Parker 'king' of the underworld?"

"Sure am, he is the only one I know who organised the removal of Mark DeVilliers, much as I dislike the man and as much as I would like to have the credit of placing him in gaol, I'll always be grateful to him for what he did to DeVilliers."

Slowly the two of them walked in the direction of Kathleen's home.

"I hope you won't mind me walking you home but as I saved your life I feel I am now responsible for you. Therefore I better spend more time with you so you won't encounter any more situations which you might not be able to handle."

Confidently Jason reached for Kathleen's arm.

"What do you mean by situations I won't be able to handle? Let me tell you right now Jason, I've handled life very well without having had you looking after me."

Kathleen was so uptight that it had never entered her consciousness that the two of them were walking arm in arm along the footpath.

"That's true Kathleen, but now that you are mixing with a certain low grade individual you will need protection and at this stage I feel I suit the bill perfectly."

"You, did you say you fit the bill perfectly?"

"Yes I did! I can fight, I have contacts and I can tell porkies without blushing. Also I'm handsome and you find me desirable..."

Kathleen tried to interrupt but Jason ignored her. "I know what you are trying to tell me but all the same what I'm saying is true. Secretly, deep inside yourself you know that you want to be closer to me. Ever since you've met me in Albury I've been in your mind. You attempted to forget me in many different ways but always I come back, especially late at night when you have trouble going to sleep."

"Wow," Kathleen thought, "did this guy have an ego!"

"Call me vain, call me an egotist, and I know I told you I could tell lies but you do know I'm not lying now?" Jason continued earnestly.

Kathleen didn't answer; it had finally penetrated that she was walking hip to hip with Jason. It felt very comfortable, as she was nearing her home Kathleen began to walk a little slower so that the nice feeling of having the protection of Jason's company could be extended. Jason ceased talking when he realised that Kathleen wasn't arguing with him anymore and concentrated on keeping in step with each other instead.

Words weren't always necessary in certain situations and this seemed to be one of them. He opened the gate so that Kathleen could enter her front yard or at least enter the yard of the premises where she resided. For no reason she could think of Kathleen was loathe in letting go of his arm, she wanted this mood to continue a while longer. Maybe Jason was right? Mayhap she was the girl for him? The last fifteen minutes had been very compatible. Pity he had opened the gate... Just hang on? Her suspicions were raised. Stepping away from Jason she asked in a cold tone, "Jason, how did you know which gate to open?"

Jason took a while to answer the point raised. His mind had been on other things - for instance, should he give Kathleen a goodnight peck on her cheek or would that be too forward on their first walk home? Perhaps a long lingering handshake instead would suffice better?

"Come on Jason, I demand an answer! How did you know which gate to open?"

Even in the small amount of light available from the gas light on the corner of the street Kathleen could see the flush rise on Jason's face. Jason pulled his shoulders back.

"You probably won't approve of my answer Kathleen but I've been secretly following you home whenever I was free from work as long as you've been living in Melbourne."

Kathleen gasped in surprise.

"Ever since we met in Albury and knowing the people that you've been associating with I felt that I had to keep an eye on you as I suspected that eventually they'd want to contact you. I am glad that I did check on you as tonight could've been a lot different than it turned out."

Softly Kathleen asked, "How did you find out I was in town?"

"O that was by pure chance. Tom and I walked into each other in Russel Street. Of course when he stayed at my parent's place he told them the reason he was in town was to see you settled into your flat so you could attend the college to study your singing."

Jason was wise enough not to tell her that Tom had asked him to keep an eye on his sister.

"Once I knew which college you attended I had only to hang around until I saw you come out the door one night and since that time I've been following you home at every opportunity possible."

Kathleen was lost for words. If she hadn't been approached by that smelly individual Jason would've still been secretly following her? Not knowing whether to be pleased or angry she shrugged her shoulders saying, "What will you do now? I mean I know you are there now!"

"Sadly there is little we can do until your admirer Jessie Parker contacts you. If he sees you with me it won't take him long to discover that I am a detective and that could be the end for you and for me. Parker doesn't hesitate to protect himself at all costs if he thinks his life is threatened. And I am a threat to him that's for sure."

Fear replaced the anger that Kathleen had felt initially.

"Jason, what are we going to do?"

Kathleen searched for Jason's hand. She needed some comfort.

"I'll have to place you under heavier protection. We don't know at this stage why Parker wants to see you? Until we find that out we can't really do much. Before I can say anymore I'll have to speak with my superiors, for all I know they might see this as an opportunity to place Parker behind bars, who knows what they'll dream up, they've been waiting a long time to get their hands on him. For once we'll be aware of where he'll be, that is, if you'll co-operate with us of course?" Jason looked at Kathleen enquiringly.

"The problem is we would have to make sure that he'll never find out that you were a plant. This whole thing could be a bit tricky. I'll have to think about it, I would hate to see you hurt, especially now we know each other better. Anyway before I go I would just like to tell you that you sounded great on the night of your concert, as far as I'm concerned you were the best of them all!"

"I didn't see you there." Kathleen was pleased to hear he had attended the concert.

"I even spoke with you!"

"You never did Jason, you are having me on, I would've recognised you."

"Just goes to show how good some of my disguises are, although your brother Tom didn't take long to see through the one I used in Albury! There have been many times I walked with you in a crowd, but I'll admit talking with you like this has a lot more appeal." Jason took hold of her hand to raise it to his lips after which he wished Kathleen a goodnight.

Kathleen shivered slightly clasping her hand protectively where his lips had kissed her as she watched Jason stride away. Jason had been nearly right when he stated that she thought about him at night. There had been the occasional times when he had entered her mind. Tonight however she knew it would take her some time before she'd fall asleep.

Two days later a crippled man sidled up to Kathleen as she left college, apologising as he bumped into her he slipped a note into her hand. Astonished at what was happening she saw the man give her a sly wink before he hobbled away. Surreptitiously placing the note into her pocket Kathleen hurried home, her heart beating fast. Knowing it was Jason who had given her the note she couldn't wait to see what it was all about.

After she read she sat still in her room staring into space. Who would've thought that Jason the man obsessed with his job, had a romantic streak in him? Kathleen admitted to herself that Jason was affecting her feelings more than she was willing to admit to.

Looking at all the facts in a practical way she realised that this relationship couldn't work. Here she was a potential singer whose career was just starting to look promising and there was Jason who wanted a career in the police force. She'd be travelling to different opera houses throughout the world and he would, let's admit it, be stuck in Melbourne with the occasional trip to a Victorian country town. What did they have in common?

Kathleen drew a deep breath.

A knock on the door made her hide the note in her reticule.

"Come on Kathleen, open the door, I know you are in there?" Jessica's voice came impatiently from the other side of the door. Kathleen opened the door to let her in.

"What have you been up to? I haven't been able to catch up with you for weeks?"

"Oh, I don't know, time just seems to disappear at the moment."

"You are not wrong there. We are so busy at work that at times I think a week consists of only four or five days instead of the seven it's supposed to have." Jessica studied her friend intently.

"There's more to it though, isn't there? Do I detect a frown, something I've never seen on your face before? Come on Kathy you can tell me, we are both existentialist people, when we feel, we act! You know that a problem shared is a problem halved."

Kathleen looked at Jessica with an innocent look.

"Honestly Jess, there is nothing wrong!"

"That's good then." Jessica turned sideways to study Kathleen's reaction through the mirror which was hanging in a convenient place for her when she made her next comment.

"Well I'm glad it isn't the chap that brought you home the other night then. It seemed to take a while before he departed."

Kathleen's face could not hide the shock she felt. Here she'd thought that no one had seen her that night but trust Jessica to know all about it.

"How did you find out about him?"

"I just happened to glance out of my window before I retired and saw him open the gate for you."

"You mean you were spying on me?"

"No, I wouldn't call it spying. I would call it watching over you." Jessica smiled sweetly. "That's the words you used when you were spying on Gloria and her suitor a few months ago."

Kathleen shrugged her shoulders in a defeatist manner.

"Let's forget this discussion, sit down, I need your advice."

"Now you're talking. That's the Kathy I know."

Jessica bounced unto the edge of the bed to sit close to Kathleen.

"You've heard me speak about Jason, you know Tom's friend, well, unknown to me he's been looking after my welfare ever since I've moved here."

Jessica's face was a question mark. "What do you mean your welfare?"

"The club where I sang in Albury had a rather shady reputation. Not that it mattered or concerned me a lot because all I needed was a place where I could sing. The owner of the club let it be known that if any one gave me a tough time he would return the action a hundred fold. Now Mark might've done a lot of shady deals in his lifetime but when he promised to give somebody a tough time everyone knew he would follow through. The other night a man harassed me and that was when Jason made his appearance to rescue me. Jason knocked the man unconscious and when he came to we discovered that the man was just a bit overzealous in presenting his masters message to me."

Kathleen paused as she relived the event.

"What did his master want?" Jessica wanted to know.

"The message was that his master wanted to know if I would see him."

"You mean he wants to take you out?" Jessica's eyes were shining.

"Jason and I don't really know what he wants to see me about. I am a bit frightened actually because he is the man who organised the killing of Mark, (you know the owner of the place where I sang) because Mark was a bit slow in paying what he owed the man."

"Doesn't sound like he's a catch, does he?" Jessica stated.

"I wish I'd never heard of the man, its driving me crazy not knowing what he wants to see me about. Does he assume I know something about DeVilliers deals and if he does think like that, why has it taken him so long to contact me?"

Jessica had expected a long discussion about Jason; instead she discovered that the Melbourne underworld was after her friend.

"Why don't you go and visit Tom for a while, it might all blow over if they can't locate you?" Jessica had a lot of faith in Tom; deep in her heart she knew he'd solve Kathleen's situation somehow

"I thought of that, but there are a few rehearsals coming up and I have a good chance to obtain the leading part in a new show. I've waited long enough to be in this position. I must say it is dashed inconvenient that this should occur right now. I just wish I knew why Jessie Parker wants to see me?"

"Did you say Jessie Parker as in Carbuncle Parker?" Jessica's eyes were as round as saucers; she also had trouble closing her mouth. "Gosh when you get involved you go for the best don't you. Or in this case, it is the worst."

Dash it all, in her anger Kathleen realised she had said too much. Jason wouldn't like this at all! In alarm Kathleen turned towards Jessica.

"Never repeat any of this, will you? We'll both be in trouble if they find out," Kathleen cried out in a plaintive voice. Jessica didn't have any intention to find out who 'they' were; secretly she wished that she had stayed in her own room.

"Kathy what does Jason intend to do? He is a detective after all; he should know how to handle situations like these, surely?"

Kathleen had given up on being secretive, and it was nice to be able to share the horrible news with someone close.

"He's waiting for his superiors to give him instructions. It is alright for these men to sit in a room and make decisions but it is me that is in the front line. I should have protection right now, these senior police have no idea what a young frail little girl goes through in times like these."

"Hang on a minute?" Jessica laughed nervously. "From which play did you borrow those dramatic lines?"

Kathleen stared at her, slowly her face cleared.

"You are right that was a bit melodramatic, it felt good though, I've always wondered why writers wrote those trite lines and now I know why!"

Jessica's eyes locked unto Kathleen's.

"I think that you should suggest to Jason that we need at least three handsome young detectives staying in this house to give us the protection we need."

"Why should there be three of them?" Kathleen asked in wonder.

"Do you expect Gloria to stay in her room if there are only two of them?"

***

Two days later a large shiny black Station Brougham with its powerful motor throbbing pulled up alongside the footpath Kathleen was walking on, her heart began to beat faster. Only a gangster would be proud of owning a car that size. She knew no one else who could afford a vehicle of that quality that would have a reason to stop for her. Ignoring the car Kathleen kept on walking hoping it would drive away. The vehicle kept pace with her. Her wish was granted, the car took off only to stop further down the road. The driver leapt from his seat to open a door for his passenger. A large cumbersome person stepped from the car. Even at the distance Kathleen was away from the car she could recognise the deformity on his forehead. Reaching back into the car Jessie Parker came out with a bouquet of flowers in his hand. Walking over to the footpath the large man stood waiting for Kathleen to come nearer.

Taking a deep breath Kathleen drew upon everything she had learned at college, she would have to play a part here - that was the only way she would be able to cope with this situation.

Smiling she looked into the man's pockmarked face.

"Hello, do I know you? Are those flowers for me?" Kathleen said in a sweet voice. Not expecting so much sweetness Jessie Parker dumbly nodded his head. Then remembering he was supposed to be in charge he swept his hat from his head and with a stiff bow presented the bouquet to Kathleen.

Taking the flowers from him she simpered and fluttered her eyelashes at him.

"Oh you dear man, this is the nicest thing that's happened to me. I'm sure I don't know what I've done to deserve this?" Thinking to herself, (here I'm talking to the king of the underworld and he is acting like a country oaf) are all men simple when a pretty girl speaks to them?

Growing more confident as she recognised Jessie Parker's discomfort Kathleen stood smiling in front of him.

Jessie Parker shook his head as if to blow the cobwebs away that prevented him from thinking.

Finally Jessie cleared his throat and spoke.

"Miss Matheson, would you be willing to give me the pleasure of your company? I have to ask a favour of you? With your permission we could discuss this matter as I drive you home."

Kathleen glanced over to the car; she could understand why some people called it a horseless carriage. Apart from the size and shape of the wheels and the additional place where they kept the engine there wasn't much difference at all. Stepping hesitantly inside Kathleen was impressed with the comfort and room that was available. There was much less swaying as the seats were closer to the ground and the new designed shock absorbing springs plus pneumatic tyres made it a completely different ride. Jessie could see how impressed Kathleen was so while she was enjoying the drive he broached the matter which was close to his heart.

"Miss Matheson, the favour I would like to ask is if you would be available to sing for my Mother on her eightieth birthday. My Mother heard you sing during the college concert and fell in love with your professional approach and the quality of your voice."

Kathleen's heart rose - is that all he wanted? Here she had expected him to accuse her of holding unto Mark DeVilliers money, and all he wanted was for her to sing at his Mother's birthday. A nervous giggle of relief escaped which she caught in just enough time to change into a cough. Jessie Parker was looking at her expectantly

"Of course I'll sing for your Mother, how can I refuse her when she said all these nice remarks about me?"

Jessie's face was all smiles. "My car and driver will pick you up and drop you home again." Handing Kathleen a card he stated, "This has all the information on it even the times when my driver will call on you and the approximate time you'll be driven home again." Jessie glanced outside as the car had stopped. He continued, "We are here, I'm glad we have everything sorted out."

Inwardly Kathleen panicked.

"How did you know where to stop?" Jessie had the grace to blush.

"Sorry Miss Matheson, a man in my position has to play it safe. I've had someone watching your movements for some time. I hope you won't change your mind? My Mother is really looking forward to seeing and hearing your voice again."

"No Mr. Parker, once I give my word I stick to the promises I make." Thinking to herself, "I wonder how many more people have been following me?" As Jessie helped Kathleen to step down he stopped and studied her house making the smug comment,

"I was right, one of my boys said we should check to see if you had the rest of DeVilliers loot but when I learned where you were boarding I knew you were unaware of Mark's dealings. Let's admit it dear, if you had money you wouldn't want to live in a boarding house like this, would you now?"

Kathleen had recovered enough to say,

"You are right. If I had money I definitely wouldn't live here!"

Thank heavens she had followed her younger brother Tom's advice. If she had followed her own inclinations her career could have been over before it had started. Making sure that Jessie Parker realised how much she had to struggle due to her lacking finance, Kathleen ensured that the little gate wobbled, squeaked and scraped over the ground. Shrugging her shoulders she made a face saying, "See what having a load of money will get you?"

Jessie had a good belly laugh as he climbed into his luxurious vehicle.

— CHAPTER THIRTEEN —

Walking back from the gate after saying goodbye to Ross and his family, Tom was thinking how much better Ross was getting on with his Father. The first time that Tom had seen the two together was the day they'd returned from the time spent in Melbourne. Hearing a voice calling out to him he changed his direction towards it.

"I am glad I caught you!" McGregor called out puffing and red in the face.

Tom returned the greeting wondering what the man was calling on him for.

"Young James informed me that Tracy will be home for the weekend and he should know as he seems to be spending more time in Albury than at the farm lately. He's so often away I'm thinking he's found himself a lady friend. Of course I'm only assuming this as James never shares anything about himself. Very secretive the boy is and I have a feeling he isn't very interested in farming although I'm hoping that once he settles down he might be able to deduce there is a good living to be made here."

Tom made a noncommittal reply because as soon as he heard James' name something froze deep inside him. After discussing the conditions of their cattle and the state the country was in their communication petered out and McGregor said he'd better return home.

Meandering back to his homestead Tom felt the nip that was in the air to indicate the seasons were ready to change. The dust which had blown into the air during the day created the elements required to make the perfect sunset. At times Tom wished he had purchased one of the box cameras that were becoming so popular with amateur photographers so he could record the spectacular sunset this evening provided.

During his stay in Melbourne he had seen the result of the Lumiere Autochrome process and was very impressed by it. However the images were dense and difficult to see when projected unto a screen. Also the equipment required to develop your photographs was cumbersome and needed a special darkroom, most keen enthusiasts soon discovered they weren't appreciated at home when they took over the bathroom or laundry to use as a makeshift darkroom to do their developing.

Knowing how popular the magic lantern slides evenings were Tom had no doubt someone would soon improve the quality of homemade slides to gain the same quality as the slides produced by Messrs. Rakers and Rouse. They advertised a range of slides that illustrated the Paris Exhibition, a Passion play and the Boer War. Many an entertaining evening was held at home by people watching slides then continuing on by singing around a piano. It wasn't often there wasn't a reasonably talented singer available who was only too willing to demonstrate his ability to sing a solo, upsetting some of the other singers who thought they should be singing. The sun had well and truly set now and Tom softly chuckled in his beard as he remembered the overheard comments regarding the show-off soloist.

Mid Saturday morning a pounding on the front door heralded the arrival of Tracy. Terry who opened the door squealed with delight as he saw Tracy saying with a high pitched excited voice,

"It's about time you got here we've been waiting all morning for you. Tom promised that we would go horse-riding if that was alright with you?"

A look of relief flooded Tracy's features but she soon composed herself.

"Well, don't you look a picture?" Tom smiled while giving Tracy a hug and a kiss that nearly made it to her cheek.

"I couldn't help overhearing that Terry spilt the beans, are you in agreement to ride along the valley with us?"

With a serious look Tracy answered,

"Only if you can guarantee perfect weather and keep your siblings in order." Tracy ruffled Terry's hair fondly. Terry put up with it patiently because being a child he knew how fond grown-ups are in teasing children.

Albert finished packing their lunch at the same time as Tom brought the horses round from the stable. Instead of riding in the valley Tom decided to follow the higher track to obtain a better view when they reached the escarpments. Most of the track was easy to follow but at times it decided to hide and a new route had to be found. Since it had been only a few days ago that a thunderstorm had swept over the valley, the smell of moist earth and eucalyptus surrounded them especially when fresh leaves were crushed under the horses hooves. Every so often small streams to the enjoyment of Terry and Mavis, had to be crossed and all had to be alert for the occasional snake which was soaking up the sun on a rock and didn't like to be disturbed. Although there had been little time for Tom to ride alongside Tracy he could see that she was enjoying the outing. Her face was flushed with the exertion of keeping her mount under control.

Near lunch time they arrived at a place which Tom and Ross had named the Rockies, because of the outcrop of rocks and boulders which gave the impression that they had been stacked by a crazy man. The trees for some reason had withdrawn some distance away from the escarpment which made it an ideal resting place to have a picnic. Some of the rocks became handy tables while others were the right size to sit on. Meanwhile you could gaze along the valley and absorb the sight at your leisure.

As Ross' property was nearest to them it gave you the best view, also as Tracy commented, "If you wanted to know how many heads of beef you had this would be the place to count them."

Terry and Mavis were first to finish their food and Terry was eager to explore the area. "Come on Mavis; let's leave the old couple while we investigate the rocks. You never know a bushranger might've left his stash and we could just be lucky enough to find it?"

"Just be careful you two, some of these boulders look very slippery," Tracy called out in a concerned voice.

"They won't worry me!" Terry yelled confidently. "I'm as surefooted as a mountain goat!" To prove his point he jumped from the boulder he was standing on to a smaller lichen covered rock. Unfortunately the lichen still held enough moisture to reduce the friction and Terry's shoes kept moving, neatly depositing him flat on his back with his head missing the offending rock by inches.

"Well Terry that should prove something," Tom said after seeing that Terry's pride was hurt more than his body.

"Prove what?" Terry asked, slowly getting up from his humiliating position.

"How many mountain goats have you come across?"

Tom smiled at the others.

"As far as I know, none, but that could be because these mountains around here aren't high enough," Terry stated, slowly massaging his posterior.

"That could well be true Terry; however another reason could be that they are not as sure footed as you thought they were."

"You mean the goats have all slipped down crevasses?"

"Exactly Terry and that's just where you might end up if you aren't more careful."

More sedate now after his little mishap Terry walked away with his trusty little slave following him.

"They do get on well with each other don't they?" Tracy stated wistfully watching the two children go round a large boulder.

"Good they've gone now we can have some time on our own!"

Tom grasped Tracy closer to him trying not to notice that Tracy was avoiding him.

"Tom I think the time has come that we should have a serious discussion!" Tracy spoke but made sure there was no eye contact involved. Acting light hearted but fearing the worst Tom said, "Give it to me dear! I've always been interested in serious discussions."

Softly Tracy murmured, "I don't think you'll like what you are going to hear." Without giving Tom time to interrupt she continued,

"Dear Tom, you know that I would never..."

A scream from Mavis brought her to a halt. Tom was already on his feet running towards where he thought the sound had originated.

It didn't take him long to see what was wrong. Terry was standing on a rock that was partly protruding from the escarpment. He stepped back towards Mavis when he saw Tom running up.

"What's going on here? Terry, why do you have to upset your sister all the time?" Tom asked unkindly although he was relieved nothing disastrous had occurred.

Tracy went to place her arm around Mavis who was still sobbing uncontrollably.

"Come now dear, it is all over. Terry is off the rock."

Tracy was holding Mavis tightly to her skirt while stroking her hand gently over the child's small back.

"I saw the rock move and I thought Terry was going over the edge!" The child said sobbing her heart out.

Tracy studied the rock from which Terry had

stepped and couldn't see anything indicating the rock had moved.

The two walked over to where Tom and Terry were standing.

"Mavis told me she saw the rock move while you were on it. Did you feel anything at all Terry?" Terry looked mystified.

"Not a thing, when I stood on the rock I was so impressed with the view that I jumped up and down with joy."

Terry looked over at Tracy, saying, "You can even see your Father's farm from there."

Before they could stop him Terry ran over to the rock, stood on it, turned round and came back to them.

"See, it is as solid as a house!" Terry turned towards his sister, "See Mavis it was all in your imagination." Mavis didn't look convinced.

"I know what I saw Terry, the rock definitely moved!"

Tracy grabbed hold of Terry's arm. "Let it go Terry, it is only because Mavis loves you so much that she is concerned." Tracy smiled at Mavis.

"There is nothing wrong in loving your brother you know!"

The way Tracy said this made a cold feeling pass through Tom's heart.

"Terry! Did you say you could see our farm from that outcrop? Terry confirmed his answer by nodding his head. "I would love to see it myself."

Walking towards the rock the others followed her.

"Do you think you should Tracy, I'm sure I saw it move?" Mavis said in a concerned way.

"Don't worry about it Mavis, I will only take a quick look and step back."

Coming near the rock they stopped. Tracy looked at them took a deep breath and stepped on the rock.

"You have to stand at the end before you can see it properly," Terry advised. Tracy took another hesitant step and leaned over to gain a better view.

The three of them felt the soil rise under their feet as the rock lifted majestically from the soil which had been holding it for centuries.

Tracy turned round to face Tom who stood frozen stiff as he tried to work out what he could do to save her. A look of horror passed over Tracy's features to be replaced with a smile of contentment.

"Sorry Tom, I do love you but this will solve all my problems!"

Tom screamed a low cry of anguish which tore from his throat.

"Come back Tracy, come back, we can solve whatever is wrong."

Tracy made no attempt to save herself. In slow motion the rock slid from its position and when it was on an angle where there was nothing left for

Tracy's shoes to hold on to she let herself fall back, eyes locked with Tom's and with that funny smile of relief still on her face Tracy disappeared from his sight." Terry and Mavis stood stock-still as if in a trance, wide eyed opened mouth, neither could believe what they had just seen.

Whirling about Tom cried, "Follow me."

Without looking to see if they followed him Tom went to where the horses were grazing. He had mounted his horse and was well on the way before Terry and Mavis could think.

Sanity returned to Terry's mind. Bundling everything in a large tablecloth he tied it on the horse which had brought Tracy up.

"Come on sis, follow me and I will try to see which way Tom went to enter the valley. The way he took off, it seemed he knew of a way to get down to Tracy. Fortunately Tom's tracks were easy to follow and soon the two were on the valley floor seeing Tom's horse standing alone.

Tom was cradling Tracy's head on his lap when he realised that Tracy was moving. A surge of hope rushed through him. Tracy was trying to tell him something. Lowering his head near Tracy's face he tried to understand what she was attempting to say.

"Oh dear Tom, I've made such a mesh of your life." Blood trickled from Tracy's mouth and her breathing was laboured. "I was hoping you would never find out but somehow I think you will and I hope you will remember me kindly. I did love you Tom, and I am ever so sorry that I could never show you how..."

A spasm shook her body as a small whimper indicating the pain she was in escaped her lips. Somehow Tom recognised a difference in the body of the woman he loved. The essence of life had departed from Tracy's body.

"No God, don't do this to me please," he pleaded.

Rocking Tracy in his arms Tom cried about what could've been. Suddenly everything went peaceful around him; it was so quiet he could hear the grass grow. Once again he heard the comforting words in his head.

Be still; I'll be with you always.

Tom raised his head to heaven saying,

"Lord this is so hard but you know I'll follow your way!"

"Who are you speaking to?"

Tom's head swivelled round to see that Mavis was standing next to him.

"I was speaking to God my dear."

Before he could say anymore Mavis said,

"I hope you asked him to check all the other rocks on earth as I don't think he placed the one that Tracy stood on too firmly in the ground when he made the world."

Tom smiled sadly at Mavis, thanking God for sending an innocent little girl to shake him out of his melancholy. Mavis stood looking at him expecting an answer.

"I don't know if we can really blame God for making the rock fall down he did have a lot to do on the day he made the earth. I suppose we have to be careful also." Mavis was satisfied with Tom's reply.

Studying Tracy she blurted out.

"I didn't think you could look so nice when you are dead, she looks happier now than when she was alive." Mavis might've been blunt in her ignorance but when Tom looked down he saw what she meant. Tracy looked very peaceful.

Noticing that Terry was holding the horses he lifted Tracy, walked over to his mount that was nervous and trampled the ground when he could smell the blood on Tracy. Tom calmed him by speaking gently in his ear then climbed on with Tracy in his arms.

"Let's take Tracy home kids."

When they neared the Smith's farm Tom instructed Terry to call in and ask Ross and Elizabeth to come directly to the McGregor's place also to call in at home and inform Albert of what had taken place. Terry knowing he had an important job to do rode away with a serious expression, wondering which was the best way to relay the bad news to the others. Tom kept on with Mavis stoically trailing behind.

Slowly Tom rode up to the front door, it didn't

take long before the barking dogs brought McGregor out. He was having a respite from cleaning the stables which was the reason he happened to be inside. As he saw Tom sitting on the horse carrying his daughter McGregor took a step backward then rushed forward to see how bad the situation was. Tom's tear stained face expressed the lot, there was no need for any words.

"Good heavens, my puir wee little girrl," was all McGregor said as Tom handed Tracy over to him. McGregor carried Tracy inside to lay her on her bed, then stood back to look at her. Tom dismounted, having trouble moving after holding Tracy for so long, he eventually followed McGregor inside.

As James stepped round the corner of the barn he noticed two horses in front of the veranda, one of which had a small girl sitting in the saddle. He recognised her as Tom's younger sister so wandered over to find out the reason she was there. He heard the words,

"Tracy was standing on the edge of a cliff and fell down a long way, James rushed inside. As he ran into the room he heard Tom's words.

"The last words Tracy said were that she loved me."

Pushing Tom and his Father aside James screamed,

"Tracy would never utter anything like that to you, arrogant fool that you are." Placing his arms on

Tracy's shoulders he shook her and told her not be silly and get up. Tom tried to restrain him but James turned around and punched Tom in the face saying once again that Tracy would never have told Tom she loved him as she was in love with him.

"Ignore what he says Tom, the wee laddie is besotted with grief, he doesna know what he's saying."

McGregor's northern accent showed the stress he was under.

Once again James turned his anger against Tom.

"Why didn't you protect my sister? Knowing you, you most likely pushed her off the cliff when she told you that she was going to leave you for me."

Tom was too astonished to reply. He still felt sorry for James, the suffering at the loss of his sister that James must obviously be going through; all the same some of the things James was saying didn't make any sense.

James had thrown himself over Tracy's body, moaning aloud that she shouldn't have left him behind.

"We made a pact remember Tracy. We made a pact and you've let me down. You know you were the only woman I ever wanted."

Tom glanced over to McGregor who was staring with horror at his son. Ignoring Tom, McGregor walked over to his son, lifted him from the bed and yelled at him.

"Be gone from here and don't bother to come back until you've recovered.

"How dare you speak about your sister in that horrible manner when the puir wee girrl can't defend herself?"

Shaking himself loose James tried to speak but he was in such a state his mouth was covered with froth. Frustrated he dropped his arms looked at his sister for a while then stormed from the room.

Ross and Elizabeth entered the room with concerned eyes as they had been surprised at how rudely James had pushed them out of his way as he passed them. After offering McGregor their condolences Elizabeth pushed the men from the room so that she could prepare Tracy.

Elizabeth studied the girl pensively, "What a waste of a young life," she sighed; then she knew she had to be practical.

"Ah well, this won't get the work done?"

Slowly she undressed the body and using the water from a carafe which was placed on the dressing table originally ready to be used next morning she began slowly to wash the body.

Suddenly she froze, no, it could not possibly be, but all the signs were there.

Tracy McGregor was or to be more accurate had been in the family way!

Elizabeth wondered if Tom knew.

Mavis had become bored with sitting on her

horse; everyone so far had ignored her. Mr. and Mrs Smith had nodded to her but that was all. When the younger brother rushed past he spewed out all types of rude words. Most of them she had never heard before but they sounded rude and as she didn't like James a lot - she assumed he would use rude words anyway. Mavis tied the horses to the veranda post. Slowly Mavis ventured inside. Hearing the men's voices she moved towards the sound. Tom saw her standing in the doorway. He raised himself from the chair; lifting Mavis up in his arms he carried her back to where he had been sitting.

"Good heavens, I've completely forgotten you were outside. Did you tie the horses securely?" Mavis nodded contentedly, sitting on Tom's lap was sheer heaven, he felt so strong and safe.

"I wonder where young James has gone. Mebbe I was a bit too hard on him but it broke my heart to hear what he was saying about his puir sister. Makes you wonder what grief will do to different people, doesn't it?"

Tom didn't bother to reply.

"He was very angry when he rushed past me," Mavis commented drily.

"He was using words which weren't very nice and he was still using them when he went into the stable after coming from the shed carrying a heavy rope."

The three men looked at each other, "Oh heavens

no?" McGregor breathed. Tom stood Mavis on the floor and the three men rushed away, leaving Mavis wondering what she had said to cause such a fracas.

When the three men entered the stable they noticed the kicked over chair on the floor. James' legs and body were rotating slowly. Tom grabbed hold of James' legs lifting him up while Ross positioned the chair and attempted to undo the knot. McGregor just stood there wringing his hands completely in shock.

The knot became undone and Tom laid James carefully on the ground. Ross felt for a pulse but alas there was none. Ross tried to revive the heart as he had heard that at times this remedy could be effective but after a while he knew he had to stop. While Ross still on his knees, was wiping the sweat off his face Tom noticed a sheet of paper with writing on it. Picking it up from the floor he read,

NOW YOU HAVE THE PROOF TRACY BELONGED TO ME!

WE'LL BE TOGETHER FOR EVER!

Slowly Tom crumbled the paper and stuck it in his pocket.

"What did you find there?" Ross queried.

"Oh, just a piece of paper, that's all, it was nothing important!"

Tom decided that McGregor had suffered enough. Ross studied Tom's face but decided to let it go. James was carried to his room on a ladder. McGregor a broken man, led the way. As they walked past the open kitchen door Tom saw the astonished expression on his younger sister's face.

No child should have to go through a day like today and here the little tyke had to cope with a double-dose, this was the thought that went through Tom's head. When the men left the room they noticed that Mavis was bringing Albert and Terry up to date. In a subdued voice Mavis related the facts as she knew them and Albert observed that the young girl's outlook on life had matured greatly since he bade her farewell earlier in the day. When Albert looked round the room he felt the pain of each person as if he was hit by a sledge hammer. No parent should ever have to deal with the trauma of knowing his or her children died before them.

A tired and strained Elizabeth entered the room; Ross made a chair available so she could sit next to him. All eyes in the room were on her and quietly she said, "They are both prepared."

Silence hung like a heavy curtain over the room. Sitting upright on his chair Albert said simply, "It is now time for us to let God enter this company! Let us pray!"

Slowly heads were lowered, eyes closed and Albert prayed with a soft calm voice asking the Supreme Being to come and take over!

CHAPTER FOURTEEN

Holding the letter in her lap Kathleen stared into space, wondering if Tom was still going through the agony he was obviously in when he penned the letter. Tom was uppermost in Kathleen's mind, she knew how much he had loved or possibly still loved Tracy, who as far as Kathleen knew was the only girl that Tom had ever shown any interest in.

Only meeting Tracy twice hadn't given Kathleen much time to become better acquainted. She would love to have been at the farm right now so that she could give support to Tom; after all that was what being a family was all about.

Much as Kathleen wanted to be at the farm there were other duties calling on her - Jessie Parker's Mother was celebrating her birthday on Friday night and Kathleen was pretty sure that if she didn't attend 'Nice Guy Parker' would become 'Nasty Guy Parker' in a very short time. She was going to be chauffeured to the party in Jessie's car and had been informed she could stay as long as she liked before being taken home again.

That was the part that Kathleen was concerned about. Who would be in the car with her on the way home? Once her duties were fulfilled would 'Carbuncle' still treat her with the respect he had shown her. Kathleen slapped her wrist to remind herself not to call Jessie by that name.

During the get together with Jason, although in her mind Kathleen always called them 'furtive meetings' because they had to be sure no one was around before they could talk, she had given him all the details about the evening of the party. Jason never informed her of what he had planned for that night.

"The least you know the better off you are!" Jason stated in a firm manner.

"Even if Parker only has the faintest suspicion that you were involved his anger would know no limit."

Kathleen shivered with apprehension. How had her life become so complicated? She realised she should never have become involved with Mark DeVilliers. Knowing him and what she had done after his death made it all so dangerous. But the drive to sing was so strong that at the time it felt like a compliment when Mark invited her to sing at what he called 'one' of his clubs.

Banishing the negative feelings which were invading her, she began to think of the time when her studies would be finished and she could seriously begin to concentrate on being an opera singer, preferably one who was actually singing in an opera instead of wishing to be in one. Having held back some of Mark's money after his death, "and let us not fool ourselves," Kathleen thought, "I did not keep all of it, Pat and Mick didn't complain too much when I handed some of it over to them. But yes, the money has been helpful for my career. Through attending the college I've met people who are not only in the right place but who also have the contacts you need to advance. If only Jessie Parker's Mother had stayed at home the night the concert was on; none of this would've happened." Despondently Kathleen stood up; it felt as if she was carrying the weight of the whole world on her shoulders.

At times like this when Kathleen felt low, she wished she was back at the farm away from what Tom called the rat race; however life is very seldom the way you want it to be so you cope the best way you can. Maybe Jessica is in her room, she might like a cup of tea. Better still, I'll knock on her door and if she is in she might like to make a cup for me? It would be silly of me to be making a cup for Jessica if she's not in. It sounded like a reasonable excuse anyway.

***

The chauffeur brought the immaculately kept Brougham to a stop. With the engine stopped Kathleen could hear the strains of band music coming from the building. There were plenty of other cars parked in the courtyard Kathleen noticed as she emerged from the car with the assistance of the driver. Raising her gown with one hand Kathleen elegantly moved towards the entrance. Jessie Parker spoke as he strode to Kathleen.

"You look a picture my dear, the dress fits you to perfection and I'm sure if I could span your waist with my hands, my fingers would overlap.

Once inside Kathleen released the dress letting the material trail behind her. Seeing her reflection in a mirror Kathleen remembered what she had been taught in college.

Actresses don't walk, they glide towards their destination!

Well tonight Kathleen felt she had to act like she never had acted before so it was the perfect night to put what she had been taught into practice.

Jessie took Kathleen direct to his Mother. He lowered his head to speak into the ear of the person conversing with his Mother. The lady looked, swung her head round as if stung by a bee, and hurriedly vacated her seat. Seeing the frown on his Mother's face he forestalled her by saying,

"Dearest Mother, I've only interrupted your discussions because I want to alert your attention to the 'present' which has taken me quite some effort to obtain and receive her consent to come down to meet you at your birthday party."

Mrs. Parker looked confused as if she didn't have a clue to what her son was going on about. With a flourish Jessie flung out his arm in Kathleen's direction.

"Dear Mother, without further ado, I have the pleasure of introducing you to the one and only Kathleen Matheson!"

To Jessie's chagrin his Mother's face looked even vaguer. Leaning over her the son whispered into his Mother's ear,

"The opera singer you wanted so desperately Mother, the opera singer!"

His Mother's face cleared.

"Why didn't you say so in the first place dear Jessie? Stand aside, let the girl sit down so I can converse with her."

Softly apologising about his Mother's forgetfulness Jessie offered Kathleen the seat next to his Mother who was all smiles as she spoke.

"Oh that poor boy of mine, I hope you can forgive him. He is ever so shy when he meets a nice looking girl and has no ideal whatsoever of how to treat them."

Kathleen was thinking what does she mean 'no ideal'?

"It is his upbringing of course. At times I think I

was too gentle with him as he has such a kind nature and an abhorrence of violence."

"Doesn't this lady read the newspapers?" Kathleen thought, keeping a noncommittal expression on her face?

"I must tell you my dear that the night I attended your performance I was just blown away when I heard your voice. 'Emily,' I said to myself; 'you've just heard the voice of an angel!' Even a nightingale couldn't produce a nicer or a sweeter sound."

"That's very nice of you to say so Mrs. Parker," Kathleen said warmly.

"And while I have the opportunity may I congratulate you on your birthday?"

"Oh you are such a sweet person, not only are you talented but you also have a sweet nature. Don't you think it was a great ideal of mine to invite you to sing for me tonight?" There was that word 'ideal' again? The penny dropped. Jessie's Mother mixed up her words. The old lady probably had been drinking too much and the word idea was pronounced as ideal!

Mrs. Parker moved uncomfortably on her seat.

"Is there anything wrong?"

Kathleen asked concerned. It would be just her luck for the lady to keel over while she was sitting next to her. Looking round the room she noticed a lot of the visitors seemed to have minders hovering around them.

"No dear, there is nothing really wrong!"

Jessie's Mother moved closer to Kathleen's ear.

"The wine I'm drinking is giving me wind which is upsetting for an old malady I have. To please my son I've been partaking of the wine he is so fond of and my haemophillioids are giving me merry hell, I do hope you'll pardon my language."

Kathleen smiled demurely thinking, "You nearly have that word correct lady." All the same, Jessie's Mother may be putting on airs but she wasn't such a bad old stick. At least Kathleen felt a lot more at ease then when she had first entered the room. The old lady was silent for a moment as if deep in thought, once again she wriggled on her seat. The inconvenience she was in must be taking its toll because suddenly she blurted out, "Look after yourself while you are still young, my dear, because it isn't easy to start doing it when you are older, I can tell you that much. You don't want to end up looking like me do you?"

"You look great; I can hardly see any wrinkles on your face at all!" Kathleen lied.

"The reason you can't see any is probably because I'm sitting on them!" the old lady replied. Not being able to stop herself, Kathleen burst out laughing – it was so spontaneous that Jessie's Mother joined her.

It didn't take long however for a grimace to appear on the old lady's face. Kathleen asked what was wrong.

"It's me bleeding piles love, they are giving me whoopee." Totally forgetting she was supposed to be a lady.

"Would you like for me to sing a song, it might take your mind of them," Kathleen suggested.

"Yes that's a good ideal. I'd love to hear you sing again I was so impressed with your spittaco. Your teachers must be ever so pleased with you."

Kathleen's eyes glazed over for some seconds then she realised that this lady might not know how to pronounce some words but she knew her subject. After all, how many people would know that spiccato is a term used for indicating that every note has to have its distinct sound. "I'd better be careful when I sing," was her last thought, because suddenly on an order by his Mother, Jessie by using a spoon on his cup brought the room to silence.

"Thank you everyone for being here, but my Mother has indicated to me that she now wishes to hear the magnificent voice of Kathleen Matheson."

Indicating by sweeping his arm in the direction of a small dais, Kathleen knew that that is where he wanted her to stand to give her repertoire. Before she began Kathleen cleared her voice saying, "I feel it is an honour for me to stand here on this grand occasion and I hope you will approve of what I have selected to sing." Kathleen smiled at Mrs. Parker who looked as formidable as Royalty the way she sat on her chair.

"The aria I'm going to sing is taken from Verdi's opera Otello!"

Ignoring the type of people in the room Kathleen threw everything she had into the aria and when she was halfway through she could see she had an audience that would eat out of her hand.

The applause when it came was thunderous, there was shouting, cheering even some whistling and one galoot lifted the flowers from a vase and threw them at Kathleen's feet.

There was so much noise that it took awhile to sink in that the police had entered the room blowing their whistles and shouting,

"THIS IS A RAID! NO ONE IS TO LEAVE THE ROOM!"

Mrs. Parker was so offended by this uncouth behaviour that she tipped the table over in her haste to express her indignation. Kathleen was also overwhelmed at the suddenness of their appearance; she stood frozen on her dais. Then Mrs. Parker let out such a roar of indignation even the police stopped what they were doing.

"Who do you horrible bully-boys think you are to come and interrupt my birthday party? Remove yourselves from here at once before I set my Jessie on to you."

One policeman pointed out in a loud voice that her dear little son would find it hard to help his Mother as he was cuff linked to a sergeant.

"Cuff linked, cuff linked to a sergeant?" Stepping through the mess her upturned table had caused she moved towards the sergeant. In her eagerness to get to him the angry old lady stepped on a blob of cream, her feet shot up in the air landing with a solid thud on her derriere.

A fleeting thought entered Kathleen's mind, wow, that won't help her piles, when an eager detective grabbed her arm saying to his comrades.

"Here is one of Jessie's tarts, make sure she doesn't get away!" After handing her over to another copper, he walked to Mrs. Parker to help lift her from the floor. The old lady gave him such a tough time by belting him with her walking stick that in the end two policemen placed handcuffs on her. Escorting the protesting lady from the hall she was placed in the vans with the others.

Where was Jason? Not seeing anyone she recognised Kathleen began to wonder what was going to happen to her. Soon the remainder of the 'partygoers' were shunted towards the divvy vans who were waiting for them outside. Kathleen's protestations were simply ignored by the police. It didn't matter how often she claimed she was innocent and had only been there to give entertainment the answer was always the same.

"Yes dear, you thugs always say you are innocent but if you really were you would not have been here tonight would you?"

Frustrated, Kathleen plonked herself down on the wooden bench, never in a million years had she expected to be treated like this. Complaining bitterly until locked in a cell and then there was no one other than Mrs. Parker to complain to. The birthday girl had also fallen silent. The other women, placed in the cell next to them, were not known to Kathleen – they sat patiently talking to each other giving the impression that they had been through it all before.

"Why did they place me in a cell, Mrs. Parker? Surely the police must know that I'm an innocent bystander."

"Don't worry about it anymore dear, everyone knows you don't need a large brain to become a copper. Eventually when they recover from the excitement of placing us all in the cells they'll work out that we were innocent bystanders. This is definitely one birthday party I'll never forget."

The old lady made herself as comfortable as she could and soon her head drooped against the wall beginning to snore like the clappers.

Two ladies had been taken away for questioning and an hour later the cell door opened and Mrs. Parker and Kathleen were informed it was their turn and to follow the two policemen.

Each were placed in a separate cubicle and after a minute Jason entered.

"What took you so long?" were Kathleen's first words to Jason?

"There was a spy in your cell, she would've informed Jessie so we played it safe and treated you the same as the others. I'm sorry love but you should know that with tonight's episode we have made a large impact in cleaning up our town."

"Are they really that bad? I was having a great time until you and your friends broke up the party." Kathleen fumed when she remembered how she had been treated.

"Well I've come to take you home now."

"Why would I let you take me home? For all I know there are people out there watching us? At this stage I'd rather go home with Jessie's Mother!"

"Good thinking Kathy, you just might make a policeman's wife yet?"

Kathleen gave Jason a (pigs might fly) look. Jason returned her look with an innocent smile.

"We'll time it so that you and Carbuncle's mum will meet accidently at the front entrance, you can play it from there. Oh, I forgot to tell you that the commissioner was very impressed at how coolly you acted all night; he wants to meet you soon to give you his personal thanks. I must say Kathy, I kept my eye on you all evening and you certainly impressed me."

"You watched me all night? I never even saw a policeman let alone you."

"Thank you for the compliment, it means we are improving our undercover operations each time. The boys will be pleased!" Jason said in a pleased voice as he opened the door.

Giving Kathleen a wink he suddenly shouted in an angry voice.

"You can go Miss Matheson. Just remember we don't want to see you in here again. If I were you I'd be more careful with the company I'd keep."

Mrs. Parker heard the last words as she came from her cubicle.

"The man is dead right dear; even I don't want to be seen dead in this place. To be seen surrounded by policemen would definitely ruin our reputation." Kathleen smiled at her friend.

"Don't take it to heart Mrs. Parker. He's only shouting at me because I refused his offer to take me home. I told him I'd rather walk than be seen with a nark like him."

Holding the old lady's hand Kathleen continued, "I think the two of us can organise our own way home, don't you?"

"Of course, you are a girl after my own heart. I am pretty sure that Jessie's car is parked not far away."

And so it turned out to be, also the newspaper photographer who took the picture of the ladies as they exited the police headquarters ensured that for the rest of Kathleen's life there was that question on how deeply she was involved with the underworld?

— CHAPTER FIFTEEN —

"What are you doing?"Mavis asked her brother in an 'I'm ever so bored' voice. Terry who was busy making channels at the bank of the sandy shore so the water from the creek would flow through them ignored his sister.

"What are you doing?" Mavis said in a more strident voice.

"Are you blind, can't you see what I'm doing?" Terry still ignored his sister as he was fascinated in seeing the sand particles being picked up by the flowing water which in effect made the little channel deeper and wider without him having to do any work.

Totally absorbed in his scientific project he didn't hear Mavis creep up closer.

"If you aren't going to speak to me I'll tell Tom you are playing in the creek?"

"Tell him what you like!" Terry spoke confidently. "Tom isn't at home anyway so how are you going to tell him?"

Mavis had to ponder how to retort to that answer, finally coming up with,

"I'll tell Albert and he'll tell Tom, so there you are!"

"Good heavens, I am surrounded by a pack of dobbers!" Terry exclaimed.

"All the same little sister, have you given any thought that someone might ask where you were? Look around you dear. Aren't you standing in the same creek bed as I am?" Shocked Mavis looked around. Terry was right! Why couldn't she be his age, at least she'd be just as clever. Despondently she replied, "You are right as usual, and since I am here I might as well help you in what you are doing, if you'll ever tell me what you are doing?"

"Can't you see that I'm making new channels for the water to run in?"

"So what, after all what is so important about water following a new track, when it is in the same creek bed?"

Terry didn't bother replying to Mavis' female logic; after all, thinking along that vein didn't create earth shattering discoveries. Once again letting the water enter a newly dug channel he shouted excitedly to his sister,

"Watch this sis! See how the water moves the loose and irregular heaped sand along and then when it has smoothed its path the water just flows through without taking anymore sand with it. I wonder why it does that!"

Mavis didn't know why water behaved like that either but that didn't stop her from coming up with an answer.

"Well Terry it would have to behave like that wouldn't it?"

Mavis had an expression on her face which showed that you had to be a fool if you didn't know why.

"Alright Mavis I'll give in, why does it do it?"

"If it didn't behave like that you silly boy, the water would just keep eroding more and more soil away until it was so deep that the whole world would break apart and then there would be nothing to hold it together!"

Terry looked stunned, could his little sister be right? What she'd said did make sense in a certain way. Well even if she was right he would never admit it so changing direction he threw himself at his sister pushing her into the moist sand.

"Who gave you permission to call me a silly boy?" Terry said tickling Mavis ferociously who screamed and giggled excitedly, both of them forgetting all about the scientific experiment that was being trampled underfoot.

Ambling slowly back home they noticed that Albert was attempting to snare the cow they called the 'race-horse'.

For some reason after giving birth to a still-born

calf the 'race-horse' refused to let herself be milked. It didn't matter what technique you used in attempting to withdraw the milk from her, but one thing was guaranteed, eventually the bucket with whatever amount of milk in it would end up flying through the air. At this stage not a drop of milk from the cow had been used at the breakfast table.

Not only was the cow hard to catch, but once you had your hands on the rope which hung continually around her neck, there was no guarantee you would be able to entice her to enter the bail so you could attempt to milk her. (Attempt), being the operative word? One time, as Albert narrated his story at teatime he had the cow bailed up. To be on the safe side he'd tied each leg to a post so that there was no chance of him being hurt. Albert had sat himself down on the milking stool placing the bucket between his legs, resting his head against the side of the cow's convenient spot where you receive the warning in advance when she decides to send you flying by kicking out with the rear leg.

Everything seemed to be going fine, even the milk was rhythmically squirting into the bucket. Albert had collected enough of the creamy substance that froth began to appear on the milk. This is a sure sign that the operation is working like it should. Already planning what he was going to use the milk for, Albert pulled his hands away from the teats barely in time as the cow decided to settle herself down and her whole udder disappeared into the bucket. Under the pressure of the udder the excessive milk squirted from the side of the bucket covering Albert and the surrounding area. Giving in, Albert untied the cow. As she rose she stately backed away from the bail with the bucket swinging under her. Once free the cow turned to eye Albert and with a mischievous look sent the bucket flying by kicking it. Almost as if to say, "No one will ever use my milk I'll see to that." All those around the table had a good laugh.

Just as it appeared to Terry and Mavis that Albert was in total control, leading the cow to the bails the animal decided to run at Albert who hastily jumped sideways. The cow kept running and Albert not being agile enough to regain his balance, was pulled off his feet. Hanging on to the rope he slid past the children yelling out,

"She won't get away from me this time!"

Alas, once again Albert was proved wrong because the cow showed why she was named the 'race-horse'. Aiming directly for the barb wire fence she took a dive through it seemingly coming out unhurt at the other side.

Albert didn't think he was going to be so lucky so only just in time let go of the rope. The cow had won again; or had she?

Early next day Albert used Terry and Mavis in herding the cow to the bails. The battle hadn't been that hard and the kids were wondering what the 'race-horse' had planned for today. The animal was calmly eating the allotment of bran that had been set in front of her in the trough. The only one who was upset in this serene setting was Albert.

Muttering to himself he walked back to the house instead of the dairy shed where he normally kept the bucket. Terry and Mavis wondered what was going on. Albert returned carrying a shotgun in his arms. The children were horrified.

"Isn't that a bit drastic Sir?" Terry asked. Albert growled fiercely.

"If you can't pull your weight on this farm you are not needed! This animal refuses to cooperate so if she won't let us share her milk, we'll see how she'll act if we are going to eat her instead?"

Both kids looked even more horrified.

"But Sir, how can she react after you've shot her?"

"That's her problem! Don't you think we've given her enough rope in the past to mend her way?"

Meanwhile the cow stood there calmly and unknowingly enjoying what was turning out to be her last meal. Standing in front of her Albert pointed the muzzle of the weapon at the cow's head. Mavis covered her ears tightly closing her eyes. Terry looked on fascinated.

"Don't look at me like that?" Albert cried out with frustration at the cow.

Her nose covered in bran, her large brown eyes steadily aimed at Albert the cow calmly went on chewing. Mavis peeped through one eye to see what was causing the delay. Turning away from the animal Albert agitatedly walked in a circle. Making up his mind Albert approached the cow again, aimed the gun and pulled the trigger.

Mavis opened her eyes in shock as she heard the loud blast seeing Albert standing in front of the munching animal with the gun aimed at the sky. A raven who happened to be flying overhead unfortunately copped the full blast dissolving instantly into an explosion of feathers which slowly drifted down among the trio.

"You missed!" Terry whispered, blowing a feather away from the corner of his mouth. To regain his self confidence Albert spoke hoarsely,

"I only tried to frighten the silly animal!" Albert opened the bails to release the cow. Mavis walked to the still chewing beast, giving it a hug and crooning.

"You poor little animal, see all the upset you've caused. We only want to release you from your milk you know. You'll feel so much better for it!"

The cow refused to move, her long tongue aiming for the corners of the crib to ensure she ate every last morsel.

Terry came back with a bucket he'd picked up from the dairy.

"Surely you're not going to try to milk her

Terry?" Albert asked, raising his eyebrows heavenwards.

"I'll give it a try Sir; somehow I receive the impression that there has been a change of attitude. Don't ask me what it is but I feel I have to attempt to milk her. We'll soon find out if I'm right."

The cow moved obligingly over so that Terry could get near the stool, placing the bucket and holding on to it with one hand he gingerly began tugging on a teat with his other. Mavis went and gave the docile cow some more bran all the while talking calmly to the animal. Albert stood and watched what was going on in amazement.

"I am seeing this, but I don't think I believe it?"

Gaining more confidence Terry placed the bucket on the ground so he could work with both hands.

"That's it!" Terry cried after a while, handing a full bucket of creamy milk to Albert. With a cheeky grin on his face he said to Albert,

"It looks like we'll have some milk tonight Sir, unless you drop the bucket on the way to the house."

"Don't you worry about this milk son; I've been waiting a long time for this."

Mavis gave the cow an extra hug saying aloud, "Looks like we finally scored our own milker. No more long trips to carry milk from Ross' place."

Releasing the bails again the three walked towards the house, stopping halfway to watch the animal slowly back away from the crib.

"Was it because I frightened her with the gun?" Albert wondered aloud.

"No it was the way I cuddled her!" Mavis called out.

"You are both wrong, it was the gentle way I milked her!" Terry stated.

"Whichever it was," Albert said gleefully, "we have our first bucket full of milk."

Terry ran back to pick up the gun which had been leaning against a post where Albert had left it saying over his shoulder, "Maybe it was the poor raven who made a difference? Yes, let us give the raven the credit; at least it didn't die in vain!"

***

The reason for Tom not being at the farm was that he hadn't been able to settle down after the funeral of Tracy and James. For some reason known only to himself, McGregor had selected a location for their resting place that was in full view of Tom's residence. Each time Tom came outside the first thing he would see were the two bare patches of earth. At times McGregor would stand near them at other times there would be some flowers left on each grave. Somehow the graves being so close and with what he knew about the two resting (for want of a better word) in them Tom found it difficult to obtain closure. So one evening when he called on Ross and Elizabeth making sure that Alf would be in bed before he got there, Tom mentioned his dilemma. Elizabeth didn't hesitate in giving advice.

"I'm ever so glad you brought the subject to our attention. Ever since McGregor made that spot a cemetery I've thought how thoughtless a location it was. I mean you'd think the man would've had some respect for your feelings knowing the relationship between you and his daughter."

Both Elizabeth and Ross noticed the wry grimace that appeared for a split second on Tom's face. They looked at each other before Ross said, "Tom that was a funny expression you made. Is there something you know that we don't?"

Tom stared at them for a moment before replying.

"Tracy was on the verge of telling me something that according to her I wouldn't want to hear. We never did finish that conversation as Mavis interrupted us by screaming when she thought she saw the rock move when Terry was standing on it. What I will never forget is when Tracy stood on the rock and it moved she never made any attempt to move back to solid ground. Once her panic had subsided she actually smiled and said she was sorry to me but this would solve her situation."

Tom was staring at his friends with tears in his eyes, reliving the whole episode again,

"For the remainder of the day her words and expression kept coming back to me wondering what it meant. However later in the day the puzzle solved itself."

Ross broke into the conversation.

"You never did show me what was written on the note you found, did you Tom?"

"You are right Ross, the reason I didn't was because that wasn't the right time to show it to you. However if you promise not to tell McGregor about what is on the note I can show it to you both."

Dragging the note, which he had placed there before he left home, reluctantly from his vest pocket Tom handed it over to his friend. Elizabeth moved over so she could read the note at the same time.

Together they raised their faces from the paper to Tom with Elizabeth commenting to Ross, "Well that confirms the suspicion we had!"

"What do you mean confirm your suspicions?" Tom queried in a puzzled voice.

"Not long ago when we were in Albury we saw the two of them walking together in the rain near the river. They were so involved with each other they never noticed we were there also."

Once again they sat and gazed at each other.

"Your Mother mentioned some time ago that they used to walk regularly together. I never took much notice; they were brother and sister after all. It did make me wonder when I saw how James lost his temper when I dropped Tracy off at her home and he hadn't realised that I was in town. Ever since I wondered why he was so upset? After I read the note I didn't have to wonder anymore."

Hesitant Elizabeth raised her head mouthing something to Ross who gave her the go ahead.

"Tom, I don't know how to say this kindly so I'll just say it. Many a secret has been shared tonight so I feel this is the time to bring this matter up!"

Tom looked enquiringly at her with a (sure there can't be much more) expression.

"Did you know Tracy was going to have a baby?"

The look on Tom's face showed he had never heard this information before. Letting the news sink in he stated,

"No this is the first time I heard Tracy was going to have a child. I suppose you discovered that when you prepared her for the funeral?"

Elizabeth nodded her head in agreement.

"At one time I thought I knew everything there was to know about Tracy, but now I know that I never knew her at all."

With a twisted grimace he continued, "The only thing I do know is we all know more about McGregor's offspring than the poor man does himself." Tom studied them both while taking a deep breath.

"There is no need to emphasize that none of us will ever enlighten the man to how sick his family really was, is there?"

Ross and Elizabeth agreed wholeheartedly.

"Now I can really understand why you are feeling so depressed about seeing the grave sites," Elizabeth said with a sympathetic voice.

"Why don't you plant a row of trees near there?" Ross suggested.

"Why not, that is a great idea!"

Elizabeth confirmed in an enthusiastic manner.

Tom ignored them both. Staring into space he went over everything he had learned tonight again. He made up his mind.

"Having some time all to myself sounds just great to me at the moment. Elizabeth you will check on the kids when they come for their schooling won't you? I feel I really need to be surrounded by nature so that the nasty taste in my mouth can be purified." Tom looked towards Ross. "A trip right up the valley sounds like the right medicine for me and I'll check up on that other little matter at the same time."

Ross' wife's ears pricked up.

"What other little matter could there possibly be up there in the middle of nowhere that you would have to look into for us?"

Ross looked rather uncomfortable but Tom smiling openly stated,

"Why not tell her now Ross? So many secrets have been shared tonight why not share one more. You'll have to tell Elizabeth some time."

"At times I don't like you as much as at other times Tom. This is one of those times I wish you had gone home early." Ross looked none too pleased.

"Don't you dare speak to Tom like that Ross Smith; I have a feeling that what I am going to hear I am not going to like!" Elizabeth's forehead creased as she frowned.

"Oh no dear, I think the news you'll hear you'll like, what I think you won't like is the time it has taken to apprise you of the news. I know I should've told you earlier but somehow it never was the right time and I wish I wasn't in this position now as you know that I don't like to hurt you."

Elizabeth sank back into her chair not knowing what to expect.

"Stop waffling Ross, just tell her," Tom said sternly, then faced Elizabeth.

"Part of this is my fault too, so don't blame it all on Ross!"

"I just wish I knew what the two of you are waffling on about," Elizabeth shouted, becoming exasperated.

"Liz dear, you know how at times you asked me how come we could buy so many things in the short time we've been on the land?" Elizabeth nodded.

"I gave you many reasons, most of which I knew you didn't believe?"Elizabeth nodded her head again wondering what was going to come next. Ross gave a nervous cough glancing quickly over to Tom who was signalling for him to continue.

"Well, after Tom and I finished our first small home we decided we'd been surrounded long enough by the smell of cow-dung and needed some fresh air so we went to explore the property. It was the best thing we ever did wasn't it Tom?"

"For heaven's sake Ross, you are going about this the right way to make me angry, just tell me what you should've told me years ago!"

"On the second morning I slipped and fell off a log to land on a heap of gold nuggets!" Tom chortled loudly not being able to hold the information back any longer.

"You mean like...?" Elizabeth couldn't find the right words.

"You are perfectly right dear, not only did Tom find a load of gold we also found the lode or seam where it came from!"

Elizabeth swivelled her head from Tom to Ross to see if they were pulling her leg, but the smug looks on their faces revealed they were telling the truth.

"Ross Smith, you surprise me. Many a time I thought that I had married a bank robber. At other times I convinced myself that you were too nice a person so you couldn't possibly be one of them. Always there was something nagging at me. Then when your Father came I realised you came from a moneyed family. This put my heart at ease and now you tell me we own a gold mine!"

"Hang on dear, who mentioned a gold mine? We found a source of nuggets that's all. It hasn't been easy you know trying to live so that no one would become suspicious. Even so some people in the valley wonder how come Tom and I did so well in such a short time. That was the reason why Tom and I decided to say nothing. We still don't know how big the seam is anyway and do you want a quarter of our population to begin digging in all directions on our land?"

Elizabeth stared at both the men pensively.

"Don't worry Ross; what you are saying makes a lot of sense. Of course I don't want the valley flooded with miners all they'll do is wreck the area. And while I admire the two of you for holding onto this secret for such a long time I have also to admit that there is some hurt deep inside me which tells me that you felt you couldn't trust me. That part really hurts me Ross Smith!"

Ross glanced at Tom, "I just hate it when she calls me Ross Smith!"

Ross stood up and walked over to his wife, lifting her up from her chair he held her tightly in his arms while looking deep into her eyes.

"You will never know how hard it was to keep it to myself dear, believe me, there's been many a night I watched you sleeping next to me and I wanted to waken you so I could tell you. But you know when I promise something I hold to it and I did promise the same as Tom promised that we wouldn't share it with anyone."

Tom decided it was time for him to leave the room and let the two of them sort out what he thought at heart was only a mild situation.

"I'll go and make some more tea. I think we could all do with a drink!"

Ross and Elizabeth never heard him leave the room. Later that night while holding each other closely in their conjugal bed Elizabeth mentioned softly to Ross, "Tom took the news that Tracy was going to have a baby very well, didn't he?"

Ross flat on his back stared sombrely at the ceiling before replying,

"Knowing Tom, and knowing how long he has kept his thoughts to himself, I feel he was so disillusioned about Tracy that nothing else he would learn would make much difference any more. A person can forgive only so much, someone who is in love can forgive the other person a lot more, as long as you love them and have respect for each other you can still have a satisfactory relationship. Once you lose that respect however it doesn't take long for the love which had remained to fly out of the window and then some very hard decisions have to be made."

There was silence in the room as each was absorbed into their own thoughts.

"It was a good decision Tom made to go away for some time. It is hard for him to make a clean break when he has to view those graves each day, don't you agree?"

Elizabeth received no answer from her husband. Raising herself slightly she noticed his regular breathing, and studying Ross's face with the light from the moon entering the bedroom window, Elizabeth observed the faint lines which represented life's difficulties appearing on her husband's face. The lines on her own face softened with love. Knowing she was a lucky woman to have a man like Ross she slowly sank back into her favourite position and fell asleep with a smile on her face.

***

When Tom nearly reached his home he noticed a reddish glow in the sky. Wondering who would light a fire so late at night he decided to direct his feet towards the source. Suddenly he realised that the flames were coming from the McGregor farm. Hastening his steps he rushed towards the shed hoping to arrive in time to assist in saving the shed which he now could clearly see briskly burning in the dark. Arriving at the fiercely burning barn he could see that McGregor was standing with his arms folded across his chest watching the flames.

"What's wrong with you, why aren't you trying to stop the fire?" Tom shouted.

McGregor stood there, standing very still, with a

sad smile on his unshaven face.

"Why should I extinguish the fire when I've only just lit it?"

"You did what?" Tom shouted, not believing he had heard correctly.

A spiral of sparks flew upwards as a beam collapsed on a wall taking it down with it. In a way it was beautiful to behold the fire as it lit up the surrounding area with its red and orange colours mixing to all types of shades depending on the ferocity with which the flames devoured everything in its path. Everyone in the district must've been asleep as apart from the light from the fire the rest of the world was in darkness. There was nothing else to do now but to watch the barn burn down to the ground. In a way it reminded Tom this is how you feel when you see a large ship give in to the battle of an overpowering storm and slowly the ship that looked so large and secure sinks deeper and further into the ocean.

"I couldna luik at the barn any longer; each time I walked past I could picture my wee lad." McGregor turned towards Tom.

"If this doesna clear my mind I might have to walk away from the place. It would hurt but there are some pains in life a man canna cope with."

On and on went McGregor pouring all his grieve and feelings of guilt out to Tom, who stood next to the man not saying much if anything at all but bursting with a similar pain deep inside his heart.

The sun was beginning its journey over the hills highlighting the mist mixed with the smoke that floated like a thin white curtain over the paddocks. The charred remaining stumps you could see were hardly recognisable as the solid poles that had held the barn safe against the strong hard winter winds. Here and there a few wisps of smoke rising nearly vertical, curled heavenwards. A strong sour and acrid smell lingered in the air leaving a nasty taste in the mouth. A stranger reviewing the scene would've found it difficult to recognise what he was seeing as the remains or leftovers of the solid well used barn that it had been. Sounds from neighbouring properties were intruding into McGregor's thoughts and he slowly emerged from the stupor into which he had sunk after the outburst about his children. He noticed Tom sitting next to him.

"Tom; you are still here then? Pardon me for being so uncivil to you."

"Don't worry about it McGregor, you gave me time to do some soul searching also. I loved your daughter a lot and most of my future plans had Tracy included. I am finding it hard to cope with the Lord's decision..."

McGregor interrupted Tom.

"It's funny you should say that, I've been asking Him the same question myself, at this stage I can't see the benefit of His actions but Albert tells me that the

Lord works in wondrous ways and only good will come from it!" McGregor sat shaking his head as if it was all too hard to believe.

"The hardest time is when you are on your own, I can cope well as long as there is someone nearby but the night is one long black time for me."

Tom knew what McGregor was saying and a saying his Father used sprang into his mind. When his Father was sick Tom found it hard to sleep at night.

That's when he discovered that the lack of light illuminated all his worries making them loom larger than ever. Bringing this to his Father's attention one day his Father mentioned some lines he remembered one of his friends used.

When your friends have gone,
And you are on your own.
When there is no one left.
And you are totally bereft.
That's when it pays to have faith in the Lord.

"Your Father must have been a wise man," McGregor commented.

"I still miss him, that's for sure and I wish he was with me right now as I am sure I could use his advice," Tom replied with great fervour.

Tom noticed that McGregor was sitting straighter and when he spoke there was hardly any sign of the burr that came out when he was stressed.

Standing up he shook hands with McGregor informing him that he had to be on his way as he wanted to check up on a few matters with Albert before he was off.

"You are leaving?" McGregor queried.

"Yes, I decided that I require some time on my own so that I can work out which way to go in my life. I am hoping to be back within a week?" Tom said rather stiffly.

McGregor watched Tom walk away thinking to himself that through the passing away of his daughter he had lost the opportunity of having a son-in-law that he liked.

— *CHAPTER SIXTEEN* —

Deciding to leave early the next day Tom felt required to catch up on some badly needed sleep. With the capable hands of Albert in ccntrol Tom knew that there was nothing for him to be concerned about. He had also asked Albert to keep ar. eye on McGregor mentioning in passing that if the burning of the barn hadn't brought any closure the farm could well be placed on the market. Idly Albert had enquired how much the farm would be worth, Tom carelessly answered, "I would be surprised if it reaches 2000 pounds. The place has been neglected and with the barn gone some one could probably pick it up for less."

Tom was too busy to notice that Albert remained standing thinking for some time before he realised what he was doing, Albert swivelled his head to see if he had been noticed. Noting he was on his own Albert went on with his job.

***

Cleaning the remains of his meal by washing the enamel plate and mug with sand from the creek Tom slowly stood up after making sure they were both clean.

Packing his belongings in his saddlebags Tom observed that the ears of his horse were in the alert position facing the direction away from the creek. As far as Tom could see there was nothing there but his horse neighed softly and Tom was sure he could hear a reply coming from the scrub. Ensuring his horse and packhorse were secure Tom stepped carefully over to where he thought the noise had come from. Something was definitely there; he could hear distinct sounds coming from the area.

Ears alert, eyes wide open, he drew closer pushing branches apart that closed together behind him so that it was hard to see where he had been. His feet shot from underneath him and it was only Tom's quick action by grabbing hold of a nearby branch that saved him from falling into a depression. Pulling himself up with his arms his feet blindly searching for a hold Tom eventually got into a position where he could see. To his surprise he found himself looking down at a young black stallion who was staring back at him.

Talking softly to the horse Tom glanced around to see how the animal had got there, but nowhere was there an obvious spot how he had entered.

"You fell in here the same way I nearly did -

didn't you?"

Tom whispered calmly to the horse not wanting to frighten it. The animal had been there for some time and would've most likely died there but for Tom coming on the scene.

"Hang in there mate! I'll come back with some rope and a tomahawk and we'll see if we can release you from your predicament."

Slowly Tom worked his way back, the horse staring after him as if to say he had full confidence in him. Remembering the black stallion he had seen on his first trip into the valley Tom realised that this animal had to be one of the offspring of the magnificent stallion he had seen then. Not only collecting the rope and a tomahawk Tom also grabbed some chaff and oats plus a bottle of water. Returning he noticed the disturbance of the soil showing there had been horses in the area earlier, Tom surmised that they would've waited for the young stallion to come out but eventually they had to move on.

"The quickest way to get in is if I make a path that'll be wide enough for both of us to walk out on," Tom thought. No sooner than the thought had been expressed Tom began hacking in a systematic way and it didn't take too long before he was standing at the edge of the depression. Removing his hat, turning it upside down and filling it with good green wheaten chaff and oats, Tom held it in front of the horse.

At first the animal nervously retreated as far as it could go, it didn't like the smell of human associated with the smell of grain. Eyes rolling, nostrils flaring the beast tried to cope with the new element. Not having had a decent meal for nigh on three days the smell of food began to have an effect. Speaking in a soft quiet tone Tom told the animal how wise he would be if he ate the chaff. Slowly the horse's head drew nearer to Tom's hat, eyes alert, and ready to pounce away at the first hint of danger. He couldn't resist any longer, snatching a quick mouthful and backing away the animal began to chew. Tom kept on speaking in the same soothing voice. The horse came back for another mouthful. This tasted good especially after the fast he'd had. Being young and inexperienced in the way of men he stayed near the hat and continued eating uninterrupted. The horse reared its head when Tom's other hand began to stroke the animal's forehead, but soon filling his stomach became number one priority. It didn't take long before the hat was empty and the animal eagerly followed the empty hat as Tom pulled his hand back. Taking the rope Tom made a noose, when he had finished he cleared the path by throwing the heavier branches gently into the hole.

Filling his hat with water this time, he called the animal over and it didn't take long for him to smell the water. Tom had fed the horse with chaff and oats first as he knew it would welcome a drink of water afterwards. While drinking Tom managed to slowly place the rope around the animals' neck.

As a young boy Tom had used a similar method to entice sparrows and magpies and he was hoping that it would work for horses also. Food being the universal enticer! Talking continuously to the animal, all the while stroking its neck gently and tightening the noose Tom felt he was in a position to attempt to guide the horse out of the depression. Placing the hat back on his head Tom could now use both his hands. However things were moving a bit too fast for the horse as it had not only discovered the rope around its neck but also a collection of saplings and branches that altered its floor space. Neighing shrilly while swinging its head left and right the stallion complained about his new conditions. Tom decided to tie his end of the rope to a tree and give the animal some time to become used to his new surroundings. Collecting the tomahawk he returned to his camp sitting down to study the matter at hand. What was he going to do with the young horse if he could get it out of the pit? Or even worse, what if he couldn't remove it from the pit?

At the moment it acted in a very sedate manner but that could be because it had been starved for food. It would be a nice horse to own though once it had been cleaned and fed it would look like the thoroughbred it was. Taking some more wheat chaff and oats Tom went back. By the marks on the animal's neck Tom could see it had been resisting the rope but was now standing breathing deeply as if waiting for the next move. Holding the hat in front of him Tom made sure the colt would know that there was more food available. The horse grabbed a small mouthful. Tom moved slowly back making soothing sounds. To follow the hat the horse had to stand on the branches which moved under the animal's weight. Panicking but greedy for more food the horse persevered. Now came the difficult part, Tom placed his hat on the ground far enough away from the depression but close enough so that the horse could see it. For the animal to receive more food the stallion had to climb the edge. Grabbing hold of the rope Tom hummed as he gave it a gentle tug.

"Come on boy, you can do it! Come on now, you want some more tucker don't you?"

The stallion stared at Tom as if trying to work out what was required of him. Looking around the depression Tom realised that there was now more clearance than earlier on. The young colt had tried to climb out before but lack of space had prevented him from succeeding. Whether it was the food and the water or most likely the logs and branches under his feet that made the difference but by suddenly tensing his muscles the stallion leapt from the depression like a cork leaving a champagne bottle, to stop in front of Tom's hat. Tom was sure the horse had given him a wink before lowering his head to begin eating. Once he had a mouthful he raised his head as if to say, "What did you expect me to do"?

Tom could not restrain himself any longer; walking close to the horse he stroked its neck and adjusted the noose. The stallion let him, contentedly continuing to eat. Tom sensed a bond had been created between the two of them. Untying the rope and picking up his hat Tom began to walk toward his camp. Making sure that he could get to what little food remained in the hat the young stallion followed Tom, only looking up when the other two horses neighed a greeting.

Leading it towards the creek Tom used a wet rag to wipe the animal clean while it was busy drinking. It was pure joy for Tom to run his hands over the animal's flanks. Deciding to remain at the same spot for another night as this would give the small group the opportunity to get to know each other better before moving on the next morning, the remainder of the day was spent letting the horses graze and Tom making a more comfortable halter to replace the noose around the stallion's neck.

Not once did the animal make any moves to run away, once he even playfully knocked Tom's hat from his head as if asking for more food. That night while watching the stars shining like diamonds attached to a dark blue velvet sheet hanging over him, Tom realised that not once that day had Tracy entered his mind.

"Bless you Lord, for sending me the young stallion to distract me; I'm sure you had a hand in today's work?" Before falling asleep Tom was sure he heard the words.

Remember dear son, I'll be with you always.

***

Charging into the room Mavis didn't realise Albert was sitting at the table until she was halfway into the room. With an irritated look on his face Albert looked up but his features softened as he recognised it was Mavis who had entered the room in such a rush. "Sorry Sir, I didn't know anyone was in here!" Mavis apologised knowing full well Albert's dislike of people (especial children) running wildly through the house. Mavis knew the man at the table had a soft spot for her on which she capitalised quite often. Standing next to him Mavis noted the sheet of paper in front of Albert which had a lot of figures scrawled on it. Looking up at Albert she smiled and said,

"Are you trying to work out how rich you are Sir?"

Albert returned her smile answering, "I wish it was so dear, but so far the figures are only telling me how poor I am!"

Mavis pulled a sad face but then it lighted up.

"Ask Tom for an increase in wages that'll make

your figures look better?"

"It's a bit late for that Mavis; I should've saved the money I had when I was younger. If I had that sum with the interest added from a bank I might've had three times the amount I have now."

All this information went beyond Mavis' capacity to understand, but somehow she felt she wanted to help Albert, he had after all always treated her nicely.

"If you really need some more money Sir, you can have what I have saved in my piggy bank." Albert smiled down on her.

"That is the best offer I've had for a long time, young lady, I might just have to resort to that when I find out exactly how much money I require."

The big beaming smile reflected the happiness in Mavis' expression knowing that she'd been able to help in Albert's financial situation.

***

Travelling with the younger horse didn't bring the problems Tom had anticipated. At times he wondered if the horse had been trained by a previous owner, but it didn't matter how thorough a check Tom made, there were no marks on the animal that would indicate this had taken place. Apart from wanting to play at times the stallion followed the group demurely. After the midday meal Tom added a longer rope to the halter, it didn't take long before the animal was trotting in a circle and obeying Tom's instructions. Tom couldn't believe how easy it was to train the young stallion. No other horse that Tom had ever trained was as obedient or understood the instructions that it was given as fast as this young animal did. The stallion had to be very clever! Nothing that Tom tried did the animal balk at. Tom felt that if he threw a saddle on the horse's back he would be able to mount the horse and ride away. The animal was too young otherwise Tom would try it but why ruin a high quality colt of this standard by being impatient? It was unbelievable? Tom was sure none of what he had seen was normal but who was he to look a gift horse in the mouth? Studying the animal once again Tom knew he had come across a gifted horse indeed!

There must be one frustrated wombat dwelling in what Ross and Tom thought of as their goldmine. The hole in the cliff wall was still well hidden, so well hidden in fact that Tom had wandered past the spot when searching for it. Fortunately the log was still there to span the creek but the young saplings had grown into trees. If the increased flow of water which occurred after heavy rains banned the wombat from living in what he assumed to be his quarters it also had to remove the dirt the increased flow brought down with it. Standing on the log Tom could hear the animal grunting with the effort of having to clear the hole from its contents of rocks and gold so that it could regain his living quarters. Tom could understand the frustration the animal went through but it made life very comfortable for whoever was there to collect the nuggets at his leisure. There couldn't be too many locations around where the pickings were so easy.

Once again the pickings were about the same as the last time when Ross had been to visit the mine. Not being able to spend the gold too fast so as not to raise any suspicion Ross and Tom had to store it at home. Both felt that was a better place than leaving it where nature or the wombat placed it. More and more people were roaming the country and so far they had been very fortunate in that no one else had stumbled across it. The discolouration in the water flow created by the wombat disturbing the soil as it cleaned its nest could well lead to someone wanting to satisfy their curiosity.

Placing the nuggets into small bags Tom carried them to his camp which was away from the mine. It was heavy work toting the bags but at least his feet left less marks than bringing the horses to the source. As soon as he arrived at the camp he stored the bags inside the saddlebags. Facing the cliffs while doing that job Tom hadn't heard the sound of the large black stallion that had stolen up behind him. It had been the snickering sound from his own animals that alerted Tom there was something different about the camp. Tom noticed the animal had aged since the last time he had seen it.

It still held the power of leadership in its stance but his black shiny hair was sprinkled with grey here and there, however that didn't take anything away from the strength that oozed from the animal. Realising he was in trouble Tom could see the stallion was slowly but deliberate stepping towards him. Keeping his eyes in contact with the horse's eyes Tom could see the meanness reflecting in them.

Tom was in trouble! There was nowhere for him to go. The animal wasn't going to thank him for freeing his offspring. No this stallion was going to punish Tom for placing a halter around the young colt's neck so that he could be taken away from the valley and the herd with whom he had been running.

"Please dear God in heaven help me," Tom pleaded desperately.

Confidently the powerful stallion came nearer, not expecting any opposition. To make himself look taller Tom waved his arms above his head. In response the animal stood on his hind legs neighing shrilly while slashing the air viciously with his front hooves. Without knowing he was doing it Tom stepped back, the beast looked awesome. Catching the heel of his boot in the high grass Tom lost his balance and fell over backwards.

The stallion realised his opponent was defenceless so rushed in for the kill. Tom closed his eyes in anticipation; there was no room or time to do anything. Hooves hitting the ground making a sound similar to that of a drum being played penetrated his mind. Expecting to be trampled into a broken heap of bones Tom remained on the ground, eyes closed, waiting for the inevitable. Nothing happened! The noise came from somewhere to the left of him. Slowly opening one eye Tom noticed to his amazement the young colt had tackled the stallion.

That must've been the sound he had heard. The young horse had run into the old stallion pushing him away from Tom. This was something that had never entered the older horse's mind and it was the reason why the younger horse had regained the upper hand. The old stallion stood still, thinking over the change that had occurred. Each time he tried to get near Tom the younger one attacked him and succeeded in driving him away.

During the pause the young stallion came closer to Tom so he would be in a better position to defend him. Still in shock Tom slowly stood erect, standing next to his saviour Tom stroked the colt's side softly speaking to him.

"You are a brave horse aren't you? If it hadn't been for you being here to save me I would have been a dead man! Don't you worry about your future I'll look after you for the rest of your days?"

Whether the colt understood him or not didn't matter; it let out a soft neigh and moved closer to Tom again. The older stallion could not stand this betrayal any longer, it sickened him to see one of his offspring becoming friendly with a despicable human being, turning round and raising his tail he showed Tom and his offspring what he thought of them.

Angrily he galloped straight through his own watching herd, which understood there had been a challenge for the leadership of some sort, but weren't sure whom to follow. Coming to the conclusion that only a few of the herd were following him the stallion stopped, rearing himself to his full height displaying a load of lean glossy muscles, he neighed aggressively until his herd gathered around him. Taking the whole herd with him the stallion vanished into the distance.

"What a morning, I am fortunate to be still alive?"

Tom whispered aloud to himself. If 'Ebony King' hadn't interfered I would not be here to tell the tale, Tom's thoughts ran on. Deciding that someone who'd saved your life could not remain nameless Tom had named the young colt 'Ebony King', the horse was as black as the ace of spades and had that autocratic manner in which he carried himself.

It was nearly time to return home, Tom realised, but there was one more area he'd felt drawn to and this was as good a time as any to visit it. Noting that the ants were busy building small levees to prevent water from running into their holes Tom deduced that rain would be coming his way in the not too distant future. To survive in the bush you have to learn to read the signs. Many a life had been prolonged when the person could predict what was ahead of him or knew what eatable tucker was available.

Coming closer to the top of the mountain Tom found the air he was breathing becoming quite nippy. Stopping in a clear spot he turned to look backwards and in the far distance noticed a mountain; its peak had to be covered with snow as the reflected sun's rays gave it the illusion that it had been sheeted with solid gold. Checking the sun's location Tom deduced that he was looking at Mount Kosciusko; also with the amount of snow covering the mountain, winter must be only just round the corner.

The air was clean and crisp with a hint of eucalyptus that cleared the passage way for the scented air to enter your lungs. It was the oil exuding from the foliage in very fine vapour that gave the far away hills a blue appearance.

Seemingly endless, the alpine country stretched around Tom who had read somewhere that the ranges were much lower than alpine ranges in other parts of the world. Our ranges lack the sheer escarpments and the high jagged peaks, but never the less they still stand majestic especially in winter when they are covered in snow. Not many people know that there is more snow in the Australian Alps than in the Swiss Alps. Tom vowed that one day he would return to this spot in mid winter so that he could see all the surrounding peaks covered with snow.

Moving along, Tom was awed by the snow gums that towered so high they touched the sky above, even the horses behaved as if the air they breathed was charged with some unknown article of energy.

Suddenly it came to Tom that there was an atmosphere around him that was similar to what he had felt when he had visited a large cathedral. Total peace, that was it, there was complete peace and stillness around him. Dismounting and letting the horses graze Tom went to sit on a nearby rock to let the peace and quiet enter him.

The only sound that reached him was when the horses moved their feet. Tom remembered when he had moved into the valley to live, it had been filled with a peaceful silence but compared to what he felt here he now knew that he had been wrong. His four footed companions had found a new patch of grass and were quietly grazing, even the young colt moved sedately from one patch to another.

Tom had been in places during his travels where the atmosphere had been charged with such evil vibes the hair on his neck had stood on end. Here it was completely different, Tom now knew why some people believed evil and good spirits existed in different locations.

Surely God had created places like these so that mankind would question if there was a Superior Being who controlled the universe and everything in it?

Sitting lost in his thoughts Tom could feel the tension drain from him. Maybe it was the rock that absorbed the tension, or perhaps it floated away to be dispersed into the atmosphere.

Tom didn't care one way or the other. He knew he was at peace with the world and most of all, Tom realised he was at peace with himself. Tom was no longer concerned how James and Tracy had treated him. There was nothing more he could do and both seemed to have paid the absolute penalty for their deed. It was all in the past; now he had to be prepared for the future! But as he sat there he knew that there would be times when their actions would return to haunt him; he realised that he was going to have to take each day one at a time. Tom would try to 'be still' and leave the control of his life in God's powerful guiding hands.

Stepping away from the rock Tom observed that previous visitors had left small 'thank you' gifts near rocks and at the feet of the tall snow gums whose leaves scented the air even as they lay scattered along the ground. As there were no other white people living in the area he knew the gifts had to have been left by the natives who travelled through here, especially during the season when the Bogong moth arrived. Their nutty flavour was well and truly appreciated by the natives who had walked for miles so that they could not only eat the moths but also meet their friends and relations to share the corroborees that eventuated when the fires were lit at night. This was the time for the tribes to meet and greet, create new alliances and at times settle old scores. Piccaninnies who were born since the last gathering were compared and admired while young couples had a chance to discover if they were suited for each other. It was an exciting time in their calendar and definitely not to be missed. Most property owners in or near the hills didn't approve of the natives wandering through their property. They knew full well that a sheep or a yearling would be a nice alternative to feast on while partaking of the Bogong moths. The farmers were also clever enough to realise that at the time the natives were on the move the locals were partial to partaking of someone else's stock also. Often during that period tempers were raised among the community, but seldom was the blame laid where it truly belonged.

The horses were becoming restless as if they wanted to be on their way. Not wanting to use the same track he had used to come up here Tom selected a narrow track that at least in his estimation would lead him in the direction of home. It was a peculiar sensation although Tom found it quite normal as he had never known any different. To find out in which direction home was Tom felt that without his feet leaving the ground or in this case his stirrups his mind's eye could oversee the area from a great height which showed him clearly which way to travel. The view might not show all the obstacles he would have to cross or overcome but at least he always returned home. Tom quite liked the sensation as he felt like an eagle soaring over the countryside while it was happening.

At a calm pace the animals moved through the forest, rays of sunlight penetrating through the foliage above left dappled designs around them. The patterns Tom discovered were a delight to study. Once again it came to Tom, what a beautiful country he lived in. The land on occasion could be stark and lonely and at other times be so dry that you felt it was only waiting for the tiniest spark to set it ablaze. Once lighted it would move like a ferocious uncontrollable beast ready to destroy and pounce on anything or anyone that it could hold in its deadly embrace. Once in its embrace the victim was lost. The heat was so hot that it absorbed the oxygen in the air leaving a product that when it was inhaled, would sear the lungs to not only dry and blister them but also make them unable to be of any practical use.

The victim would collapse and fortunately would be only slightly aware of what was happening. A smaller fire is crueller to its subjects as it doesn't eliminate the air completely and the victim has a small chance to escape but the scars can take a long time to heal if you survive.

But it doesn't matter where you are in this great

land, always there is that feeling of ancient mystery; you perceive the land is very old, there is a sense of timelessness about it. Somehow it sends you a message that states; you may attempt to conquer me, I might even let you discover secrets about me but don't ever think you can tame or own me, as I have ages of experience behind me that you will never catch up on! The original inhabitants were aware of this factor. They looked at the land as an offering from their gods. Fences weren't required, the whole tribe worked as one unit.

The tribes were scattered far enough away from each other that there was no need for tribal wars although at times these did occur especially when food had become scarce due to flooding or drought. If you compared this vast south land to Europe you'd notice that hardly anything had changed while mankind had altered the whole of Europe. Sadly the white men begun to change our land from the day they landed.

As no fences existed, the white man assumed they could possess any area of land they liked. Once they surrounded their property with the horrible restraining wire they defended it, even to their death. It took the original owners a long time to understand that once the white man had his hands on their land there was no returning to the old way.

The white race could not believe that anyone could live on land and leave it the way they found it.

They had been brought up to believe that whatever you inherit each generation had to improve it. Secretly they despised the people who in their eyes had been too lazy to work and utilise the land. A conflict Tom knew that was still active today.

Sitting relaxed while leaning against a sun warmed boulder Tom watched the daylight slowly fade away. The warmth of the day breathed still from large rocks surrounding him with the clean eucalyptus smell permeating the evening breeze. According to Tom this was the perfect part of the day. Some people found the early morning the nicest part but Tom preferred to see the sun setting while inhaling the smells the day had created. In the morning you didn't have time to sit back and watch nature, the reason you rose early was so you could have time to tackle the work that had to be done. In the evening however you could cast your mind back to the achievements of the day and go to sleep with a certain sense of pride.

Ever since the young colt had defended him Tom had let it wander freely. Never once did the animal attempt to run away instead it remained close to Tom often playfully knocking Tom's hat unto the ground. Watching the animal appreciatively Tom noticed it disturbed a magpie that got up and flew away, scolding vehemently. Now there was a bird; most magpies that Tom had seen acted as if they were in charge of any area they lived in. Nothing was too big if the bird thought its area had been invaded. Another magpie came to its assistance and soon the two of them drove Ebony King away from where he had disturbed them.

Once the horse was clear the bird continued to play with a branch, hanging unto it as it sagged under the magpie's own weight making it swing up and down. The other bird waited patiently until he realised that it was time for him to have a go - he flew up to knock his mate from the branch and soon was bouncing merrily up and down. The birds kept busy with this activity for a good fifteen minutes.

The sound of kookaburras laughing in the distance added to the beauty of the evening, the sun rays had finished painting the sky and long fingers of darkness were beginning to take over. Preparing to settle down Tom cleaned the camp so that he could leave early in the morning and arrive at Ross' place in time enough to have a chat before going home.

— CHAPTER SEVENTEEN —

Sitting on his horse Tom had a last look at the valley, the grass which was ready for cutting slowly waved in the soft breeze along the valley floor. Looking towards where the farms were located he could see the fences breaking up the valley floor. Tom felt a pang at the sight. When he had first seen this view he had been overcome at the rawness of the land and was eager to tame the valley. Now when he could see what man had done he wasn't sure if he was sad or happy. Perhaps there was a mixed feeling of both? After all, man had to make a living! When you make a living from the land some things have to change. When you make an omelette you have to break the eggs! Farming was very similar to making an omelette.

From his vantage point you could tell that some farmers were more proud of their work than others. You could tell by the neat way they left the stooks of oats standing straight and evenly spaced behind them as they progressed along the paddock. This was Ross' first attempt to produce his own crop of oats as he didn't like the price he had to pay when they were supplied from the merchant in Albury. From where he stood Tom felt the venture looked successful.

His own crop of tobacco was coming along nicely and he felt proud at seeing the straight dark green rows stand out from the black weed free soil. It was a pity that you had to rotate the crop after about four years. One of the things about tobacco that impressed Tom was that the seeds were so small. It was hard to believe that there were 300,000 or more seeds to an ounce.

From where he was standing it was also hard to believe that the tobacco plant 'Solonacea belonged to the Nightshade family which included the tomato and potato plants. Fortunately Tom was able to purchase the Nicotania tabacum plant which was a flue cured tobacco from America.

Tom's eyes locked onto the paddock which he had selected for his walnut trees. Set alongside his open paddocks the walnut trees were coming along nicely. The trees were too immature to bear a crop as yet but eighty percent had survived the first year and that showed promise. He couldn't wait for them to be tall enough so that his cattle could roam underneath their shady branches during summertime.

He knew he wasn't a true farmer in the sense that some of his neighbours were, but with the competent staff that he was fortunate enough to be able to hire he knew that his property was making more profit than most others in the area.

Staring straight across the valley he could see the scar left behind where the rock had parted from its mates. It surprised Tom that he could study it with so little feeling of pain. Only a week ago he hadn't been able to glance in the direction of the cliff knowing what he would see. Now, since all that had happened to him this week he could look at it without flinching. All he felt was the sadness at the torment that Tracy must have gone through in trying to live a double life.

Kicking his horse softly with his heels to indicate he wanted to move on Tom travelled along the faint path that would take him to see Elizabeth and Ross.

As there was no wind Tom was amazed how clearly the sounds in the valley reached his ear. A cow was mooing to call her calf. In one of the sheds there was the sound of someone chopping firewood, while the shrill voice of a tired Mother was berating her child by telling him if he didn't stop misbehaving his Father would be informed when he arrived home.

Not far to go now before he would reach his friends' farm. Deep in his own thoughts Tom didn't see or hear that Ross had snuck up behind him.

"Ahoy there stranger, asleep are we?" Ross greeted Tom who nearly fell from his saddle at the unexpected sound of a human voice so close.

"Looks like you have done well for yourself, I am glad to see your packhorse is heavily laden and that young colt looks good enough to win a race right now."

The young colt had moved over to Tom as soon as he had seen Ross come galloping towards them. Riding close together Tom shared the week's happenings with his friend. As they neared the homestead Ross informed Tom that he had visitors and although he was welcome to stay as long as he liked he could understand if Tom would want to see his sister Kathleen, who had arrived yesterday with a friend. Together the two mates removed Ross' share of gold from the packhorse filling the empty pockets with some balled up paper. At least everything would look the same to anyone who had noticed Tom arrive. Better to be safe than sorry!

"Right let's go inside to see Elizabeth and the nipper!" Ross laid a hand on Tom's shoulder as they walked close together to the homestead.

"The hands tell me that there are two young ladies staying at your place!" Elizabeth greeted Tom warmly, while young Alf rushed up to cling to his leg.

"By the descriptions our boys gave us we assume it is Kathleen and one of her friends. Probably one of the ones whom we didn't meet when we were in Melbourne as I can't picture her from the description the boys gave me. Anyway it sounds like you'd better ride shotgun tonight as our boys haven't seen single girls for a while and would like to remedy that situation. Consider you've been warned!" Elizabeth smiled. Tom shook his head in mock despair.

"Trust our Kathleen to arrive and upset the peace in the valley. It wouldn't surprise me if she has been drummed out of Melbourne."

"Rumour has it her friend is very attractive!" Elizabeth was warming to her theme.

"The girl is probably one of her flatmates," Tom suggested. "Here is hoping that it isn't Gloria?"

"What is wrong with Gloria?" Elizabeth wanted to know.

"I've only met her a few times and each time I've seen her she had a new boyfriend hanging on her arm. Still, that didn't stop her from giving me an inviting look. I'm hoping she doesn't stay too long as I can see a ranch war happening if she is here."

Elizabeth disappeared into the kitchen. Tom was trying to eat and drink with little success, as Alf was sitting on his lap.

"How come your son is always sitting on my lap, while you are his Father?" Tom looked at Ross. Before Ross could reply Alf came out with,

"I can sit on my Dad's lap anytime but you are my most favourite uncle so I sits on your lap whenever I have a chance!"

"There you have it then! I couldn't have said it any better myself," Ross remarked with a gleeful smile on his dial.

"What are you lot smiling about?" Elizabeth walked in from the kitchen toting another dish of steaming vegetables in front of her.

Ross and Elizabeth knowing that Tom wanted to depart early, had by various questions and actions delayed his departure till it had become late afternoon.

Realising it would be nearly dark, which meant it would be too late for him to show Ebony King off; Tom had ridden quietly and unnoticed into the stables while the others were having their evening meal.

It would be interesting to see how the young colt coped being inside an enclosure but at this stage he had shown no resistance to how he had been treated. Stowing all his equipment at their correct places, Tom had hidden the gold as soon as he entered the stables; Tom glanced around to see if he had forgotten anything. All seemed alright. Giving the colt a last affectionate rub Tom walked away from its stall to leave the building. Stepping through the half lighted open doorway Tom walked direct into someone entering the stable.

"Eek!" A female voice cried out in shock.

However before Tom heard the voice he'd already discovered it was a woman he had collided with. The person's whole body had made contact with his and had sent a feeling of weakness through him. Holding her in his arms to prevent whoever it was from falling over he once again felt the softness of a young girl's hair whose head rested against his chest. Somehow he knew this wasn't his sister Kathleen. Trying to push her away so that he could see the girl's face was made difficult as the young woman seemed incapable of movement. Slowly she raised her head to see who was there.

"Ah, it's you Tom. You gave me such a shock! I thought I was the only one here."

Seeing the young woman was slowly recovering although making no effort to withdraw, Tom hesitantly withdrew his hands. He knew he had seen her before but to his embarrassment couldn't recall her name. Standing there, feeling like a fool with her being so close whilst looking up at him didn't make him feel any smarter. Suddenly his senses returned and he realised that this was the girl he had met fleetingly when he first dropped Kathleen off at the boarding house.

"Jessica?" Tom said haltingly.

"You recalled my name?" Jessica said surprised and pleased. Then realising she was still leaning against Tom she blushed prettily and hastily stepped back. The young colt neighed. Jessica turned her head and noticed the new horse in its stall. Quickly she walked over while chortling.

"Aren't you a pretty horse then? What are you called?"

Jessica was rubbing the animal's forehead.

"His name is Ebony King!" Tom said surprised that the colt was letting anyone else but him touch him. However he could see by the way that Jessica was handling the horse that she knew what she was doing.

"Ooh, I'd love to ride you!"

The horse acted as if he wouldn't mind being ridden by Jessica.

"He's too young to be ridden and he hasn't been broken in yet!" Tom stated churlish. He didn't understand why he was angry with Jessica or was it with Ebony King. Why did the colt take to the girl anyway?

"He's still too small for you to ride, but he would take my weight alright."

Jessica could see by the look on Tom's face that she'd said the wrong thing.

"Not that I would ride him unless I had your permission first."

Tom's face softened, he understood that anyone seeing the colt for the first time would want to ride him.

"We'll see after I've broken him in."

"I could break him in for you? My brother always said that I was the gentlest person he has seen school a horse! Even my Father agreed with him and normally they didn't agree with each other on any subject."

Tom could see that Jessica was desperate to prove to him that she could train Ebony King, but he felt this wasn't the right time to discuss the matter, also as he was hungry, he wanted to be inside the house, so to keep the peace he said,

"We'll talk about it in the morning; I would like to eat something before the table has been totally cleared!"

As Jessica apologised for holding Tom up he could see the hurt in her eyes. Why did he feel so miserable knowing he had hurt the young girl?

Giving Ebony King a last rub behind his ears while he was nuzzling her other arm Jessica withdrew from the stables.

Surrounded by sounds of cricket mating calls Tom and Jessica walked towards the homestead each lost in their own thoughts. Preceding Tom into the kitchen Jessica theatrically announced his arrival.

"Look everyone; see what I came across when I walked into the stable!"

After Tom finished his belated supper which Albert had organised for him, they sat spread around the lounge room answering each other's questions. Jessica was sitting quietly in a deep chair, belonging to the group but not partaking in many of the discussions. Sharing some of the events that happened while he was away Tom noted that each time he glanced towards Jessica he noticed her large sombre brown eyes moving quickly away from his. Kathleen mentioned how close to disaster she had come when Jessie Parker had invited her to sing at his Mother's party but fortunately Jason had been watching over her in the background and to this day 'Carbuncle' still didn't know who had set him up to end up in gaol.

"You see a lot of Jason then, do you?" Tom asked innocently.

Kathleen blushed, brushed the front of her gown and rose from her chair asking, "Anyone interested in another drink?"

Tom smiled, quietly reminding himself to have a talk with his sister when they were on their own. Albert arose from his seat yawning, saying that for a man his age it was time to retire as there would be plenty to do tomorrow, and you two, pointing towards Terry and Mavis should've been in bed an hour ago. Both children complained knowing they wouldn't succeed in staying up any longer especially since Jessica also made tracks to retire.

Lying in bed wide awake Tom could hear every creak the house made as the timbers moved according to the dropping of the temperature outside. Somehow he felt restless and the same conversation went through his mind again and again. Why hadn't he said something different? He could still see the hurt in her eyes.

Turning onto his left side he decided that he would attempt to sleep but once again the memory of how they had collided against each other began to haunt him. Why should she be on his mind anyway? After all he had decided to stay away from any relationship at the moment. He wasn't ready for it and as nice as Jessica was, the faster she returned to Melbourne the better he would like it. He wasn't going to think about her anymore! All the same it was a pity that he had said the words which had brought the hurt to her eyes. For goodness sake go to sleep Tom! He raised his head, was that the back door being opened?

***

Jessica could not stand it any longer in her room, most of the night her eyes had stayed open and finally she decided to go for a walk. Donning her clothes she crept silently from the house ending up at the stables. Ebony King had his head raised in anticipation well before Jessica entered the stables. Feeding him a carrot which she had selected from the vegetable basket in the kitchen, Jessica softly murmured into the colt's ear.

"You were waiting for me, weren't you? You knew I would come back to you! I know you like Tom but you and I have something going for each other, haven't we?" Jessica entered the stall as she was speaking. Once in she let her hands drift over the stallion's flanks. Jessica knew exactly where to touch the horse whose skin rippled in ecstasy.

Grabbing a stiff haired brush Jessica continued the massage with long deft strokes, talking gently to the animal all the while.

"How long have you been here?"

Jessica had not heard Terry enter the stall so absorbed was she in brushing the colt.

"What are you doing here?"

"I could ask you the same question," Terry answered. "I was so interested in seeing the horse after Tom described him last night that I couldn't sleep. However I must've drifted off for a while and something woke me so I thought I might as well come down and meet him on my own. He's beautiful isn't he?"

Terry ran his hand over the horse.

"He's spoilt that's for sure," Jessica replied.

"Well Ebony King, I am becoming tired. Terry, why don't we sit down on the straw in the corner and we can keep an eye on him from there."

Both sat down with their backs against the wall. Jessica placed her arm around Terry so that he could lean comfortable against her. They spoke a while and just before Terry relaxed into sleep he murmured, "You are a lot nicer than Tracy."

Jessica wondered what had made Terry say what he had said. A soft smile appeared around her mouth as she glanced at the young boy; soon she also slowly drifted into slumber. Ebony King patiently stood near seemingly quite content with his lot.

Something woke Jessica. It took a few seconds to work out where she was. Then it came to her, slowly she relaxed against the wall then freezing when she noticed the amused grin on Tom's face as he leaned on the stall's door.

"If only I had brought my camera. The sights you see when you haven't brought your gun. You both must be very tired as I have fed and watered all the horses and neither of you woke up."

Tom was slowly rubbing his hand on Ebony King's forehead.

Jessica stirring woke Terry, who sat up rubbing his eyes wanting to know if he was awake or in the middle of a dream.

"You are finally awake my boy, I won't ask why the two of you had to meet here? Is there something wrong with the bed in your room Terry? You've never complained before?"

Terry, wide awake now looked embarrassed.

"I couldn't sleep so I thought I'd come and have a look at Ebony King." His face brightened. "He sure is a nice looking animal Tom I can't wait to ride him!"

"You'd better get into the queue then Terry because Jessica is way in front of you!"

Jessica looked surprised. Tom turned towards her to explain his words.

"You might not believe this but I was also wide awake most of last night so with your words going around my head most of the night I decided to let you have a go at breaking the colt in."

Ignoring what Jessica was going to say he

continued,

"So the two of you had better hike to the kitchen for your breakfast as I suspect you'd want to start as soon as you can."

The two of them jumped to attention, saluting Tom saying,

"Aye, aye sir!" and ran from the stables.

Tom stayed behind talking to the colt who held his head in a position as if understanding every word.

"It looks like you are going to have a tough time today, I know I looked forward to schooling you but you are big enough to let someone else take over just to please me, aren't you?"

The colt nodded his head and made sounds that sounded suspiciously like 'leave it to me'. Tom shook his head, the more he saw of his horse the more he began to believe that the animal had something of the supernatural about him.

Mavis came running from the house moving her head to see if she could see Terry. Eventually she spotted him sitting on his haunches looking at the ground.

"Terry! Tom is letting Jessica break Ebony King in."

"Amazing!" Terry replied in a vague manner.

"Yes, I thought it was amazing too. I really thought that Tom wouldn't let anyone else near the colt!"

"Yes, I must admit I find it utterly amazing."

Terry muttered as if speaking to himself. Thinking that Terry was taking the Mickey out of her, she came nearer and saw Terry was observing a worm which was desperately trying to wriggle away from him.

"Do you find it amazing that Tom is letting Jessica train his horse or is it amazing that a worm can wriggle?" Mavis said with sarcasm. Terry was always doing things she never could understand or saw any need to do.

"No, what I find amazing is that if you cut a worm in half it automatically grows another head and tail. Most anything else you cut in half dies but a worm lives on."

"You mean you could have a worm that has two tails or two heads?" Mavis asked, finally showing some interest.

"I doubt very much if that would occur," Terry answered seriously.

"After all, the worm wouldn't be able to live for long would it now?"

"You are right; it would either starve or explode if all it could do is eat." Mavis began to giggle.

"Fancy being a worm with two heads and each head is trying to get to a piece of food."

Even Terry could see the funny side of a worm in that position.

"Negotiate and work together would be one of the main items on their list of what to do."

Then shaking his head seriously Terry stated,

"Why bother eating if you haven't a tail. No, I don't think it would ever work."

Raising himself from the ground he looked at his sister.

"I think we'll leave the worms to their own thing and go and see how Jessica is going to tame Tom's horse. Although I have a feeling that Ebony King isn't all that wild. No decent wild horse would let anyone sleep in its stable, surely?"

— CHAPTER EIGHTEEN —

The young wallaby had discovered the fresh plants near the vertical stone by accident. One morning it had meandered into the empty paddock and found the fresh young shoots forming in the newly dug soil.

Near the erect stone there was a container with a variety of plants in it which didn't taste as nice as they looked but the two green bushes which had been planted in the earth really made his taste buds water.

Every second day or so the wallaby hopped over to partake of the luscious addition to his daily food intake. After a few weeks the animal noticed one of the two legged creatures that had taken over the valley was making attempts to drive him away by throwing rocks, so far none of them had come near enough to deter the wallaby from staying away.

Not realising he was desecrating the creature's descendants resting place and because the plants were too succulent to forego the wallaby kept on returning.

Once again the wallaby had given into

temptation. For a few days he had ignored the call to visit the desirable spot but something inside him kept reminding him that the grass should just be the right length and he decided to go over. Sitting on the grave, his mouth full of sweet succulent grass, the animal noticed that the two legged creature was coming his way.

Ears fully alert he kept a wary eye on the creature, wondering why it didn't like him eating from this particular spot. It was not as if he was taking the grass away from the creature's mouth. In fact he wasn't sure what the two legged animal ate as he had never observed them eating anything from their surroundings yet. The creature toted a long stick in his front paws which he slowly raised to point at the wallaby. Sensing something different was going to happen the wallaby tensed his muscles to bounce away when something heavy struck him in the neck and the last thing he saw was the ground rising up at him.

***

The training of Ebony King was coming along slowly but steadily. Not wanting to rush the young colt Jessica kept working with him at a slow pace. The horse was eager to cooperate but Jessica did not move to the next step until the current instruction was fully understood. The kids, not sure what to expect were in fact becoming a bit bored with Jessica's effort as listening to someone whispering soft instructions and tedious stroking is not all that exciting. They in fact had been hoping that there would be lots of bucking and slashing the air by hooves when the colt was protesting against the way he was treated.

There was more excitement in watching Albert plough long straight lines as he guided his team a few paddocks away. Tom noticing that his siblings were disappointed explained that the way Jessica was treating the colt would make it a better horse. "If you treat a horse with violence all you have proved to the animal is that you are the master. It will obey your instructions but only because it fears you. With Jessica's training you gain a friend who'll follow you anywhere and anytime you ask him to do something."

Understanding the sense of what Tom was saying still didn't take the boredom away though. Eyes on Jessica again they noticed that every so often she'd place her whole weight on the colt's back which pranced a bit but relaxed as soon as the girl's body slid away from its back.

Walking towards Terry and Mavis who were sitting on the top rail of the corral, Jessica asked if they could please hand over the saddle. Terry who was sitting next to where the saddle was hanging on the rail handed it over to her and she walked back to the horse that stood waiting while following Jessica's every move. During the training steps it had at occasions glanced over to Tom as if stating, "See how well behaved I am?" Tom could only congratulate himself at how fortunate a find Ebony King had been. Placing the saddle on the ground Jessica let the horse smell the blanket which had come with the saddle. Slowly she placed it on the animal's back, whispering softly to the horse she let it smell the aroma of the saddle and placed it loosely on the blanket. Walking the colt around the corral letting it become accustomed to the extra weight on its back, Jessica gave the instruction to halt which Ebony King instantly obeyed.

Petting the horse excessively Jessica tightened the straps that would hold the saddle in place, making sure she pushed the air from the stomach with her knee ensuring that the straps would remain as tight as could be. Once again she let the colt run led by the long reigns. Jessica was happy with her progress, at no stage had Ebony King shown any resistance to his treatment.

Now to the next step! Feeding the colt another sugar cube and looking towards Tom as if asking for his approval Jessica moved slowly alongside the horse raising her left leg she placed it on the stirrup. Ebony King stood still. Placing all her weight on the one stirrup Jessica waited for the reaction. Ebony remained standing still. Slowly Jessica swung her right leg over the horse ignoring the fact that she showed quite a bit of ankle. Letting herself relax on the saddle while adjusting the annoying skirt she smiled triumphantly at her onlookers. Kathleen and the kids were just ready to cheer when the quietness was interrupted by the sound of a shotgun going off.

The sudden bang must've triggered a distant memory in Ebony King's mind as from a standstill position he moved.

Aiming straight for the corral rails he leapt over them to stampede down the paddock with Jessica hanging on for dear life. The onlookers watched in consternation as Jessica and the horse disappeared into the distance.

Ross was riding in his bottom paddock to check the state of his fences. One of his cows had the bad habit of leaning against the wires, the barbs seemed to have no effect on her and the result always ended up with the fence having to be repaired and the cattle herded back into the paddock they had escaped from. Something moved in the corner of his eye. Turning his head he noticed a girl with flying skirts trailing behind her galloping from Tom's place towards their dividing fence. The sight stirred a memory of his sister riding a horse in South Australia. Ross shook his head. No, this could not be possible? His sister was always in control of her mount and why should she be riding here?

Ross could see the rider was heading for trouble, he also recognised the horse as the new colt Tom had brought home. Wonder what had happened here?

Turning his horse Ross galloped so he could intercept the runaway. Ebony King was ready to jump the fence when he saw the other rider coming at him; he changed direction so suddenly Jessica was thrown from the saddle fortunately clearing the fence but landing heavily on her left shoulder. Ebony King continued to pound alongside the fence eventually slowing down as the panic caused by the gunshot subsided in his mind.

Ross leapt from his steed, striding towards the woman lying on the ground. Kneeling alongside her he began to carefully move her arm. The pain this caused made Jessica open her eyes.

"Hello Ross, what are you doing here?"

Jessica closed her eyes in a faint as if the effort had cost too much energy. Ross stood paralysed. Whatever was his sister doing here? Removing the hair which covered the girl's face he recognised the fact that the unconsciousness girl was definitely his sister Jessica. Ross was so shocked that he couldn't think straight. Abruptly he came to his senses.

Checking to see if he could find a pulse he placed a finger on her neck. He would never forgive himself if on the day when he had found his sister she would be taken away from him due to his negligence. Thank you Lord, there was a pulse, albeit faint, but that could be because his own heart was beating like a drum in his ears.

Tom, breathing heavily from running arrived first, followed soon by his siblings.

"Is Jessica alright?"

This was the first question he asked Ross as he climbed through the fence?

"There are no broken bones that I could find. Why did you let her ride the colt anyway, you knew he hadn't been broken in?" Ross asked in a hurtful voice.

"Because she kept pleading to let her train him, she even told me that her Father and brother agreed she was the best at training horses. Everything was going fine until that fool McGregor fired his shotgun. Ebony King took off like an arrow, clearing the corral rails by at least six inches."

To Tom's surprise Ross declared,

"Yes, she was right in stating that she was better at breaking horses in than my Father and me!"

"Ross, are you saying that Jessica is your missing sister? You won't believe this but she has been living in the same boarding house where Kathleen has rooms. I must admit that I only ever knew her as Jessica, I never did bother to ask for her last name."

Kathleen interrupted saying, "It is probably all my fault! I knew Jessica's last name was Smith but never gave it a thought she could be related to you Ross."

"Excuse me, but can you help me sit up?"

They looked down at Jessica who was attempting

to rise. Feeling sorry that they had been so busy discussing her situation they had forgotten she was there. Tom rushed over to assist her to get up thinking how nice it felt to be able to place his arms around Jessica again. Standing while holding her he kept asking if she was alright.

"If you let me stand on my own feet I might be able to tell, all I can feel now is that my shoulder is giving me whoopee," Jessica replied.

"Sorry, you are right of course," Tom mumbled embarrassed. Carefully he placed Jessica's feet on the ground, who gave a cry of pain.

"What's wrong?" Tom and Ross cried together while the others stood looking concerned.

"My right ankle hurts." Jessica attempted to put some weight on it again but her expression showed the pain she was in.

Tom not being slow witted quickly lifted Jessica up again. Ross checked the ankle but could not find a break.

"Most likely we have a nasty sprain here. Could you place Jessica on my horse and I'll walk her home. There are lots of things we'll have to talk about anyway little sister and this way you can recover your ankle at the same time." Ross felt that he wasn't behaving as a brother should who hadn't seen his sister for years. But everything had happened so suddenly that it seemed his brain hadn't caught up yet.

Sitting unsteadily on the horse Jessica looked down on the small concerned group surrounding her, when her eyes fell on Ebony King who had quietly returned to the place where he had lost his rider.

"Move me closer to the fence," she instructed Tom, "there is someone I must speak to." Tom looked mystified until he saw the colt.

"Don't worry; I'll be having some words with him too,"

Tom warned the colt.

"The poor horse won't need telling off;' said Jessica, "I just want to let him know I am still his friend. Let us admit it, how many horses do you know who return to the place where they've dislodged their rider while being trained?"

When Ebony King observed that Jessica was coming towards the fence he stretched his head to make it easy for her to pat him. After giving his sister some time to console the colt Ross called out to her.

"That's enough Jessica! I think it's time we took you home so that you can rest properly." Ross turned towards Tom.

"We were coming to meet your guest at your place tonight, how about all of you come to my place instead and bring Jessica's things over at the same time."

Looking apologetically at Kathleen he continued,

"I know you will miss my sister but I've missed her a long time. There is so much I want to hear from her and I'm sure Jessica has lots of questions to ask me."

Kathleen hugged Ross over the fence.

"Don't worry about me Ross; it did my heart good to see you finally meet up with each other. I'd be a rich woman if Jessica had given me a pound note each time she mentioned your name. We'll see you tonight, tell Elizabeth we'll bring the sweets, she'll have enough work on her hands having the rest of the meal to organise at this short notice."

Tom climbed through the fence then helped Terry and Mavis.

"Alright let's go home." Looking one last time at Jessica he asked,

"Are you sure you feel alright?"

Jessica smiled sweetly as she looked down at him.

"Don't worry Tom, we Smiths are built from stern stuff, aren't we Ross?"

"We sure are sis. Come on let us get you home."

Ross led the horse homeward while Jessica kept looking towards Tom as long as she possibly could.

"I think she likes you Tom!" Mavis said smiling.

"I am sure she likes him!" Terry stated in a firm manner.

Tom looked at Kathleen in embarrassment. "Not a word from you big sister or I'll tell them about a certain someone in Melbourne."

"Did you hear me say anything?" Kathleen asked innocently.

"Just making sure you won't!" Tom answered gruffly.

"Come on you two slowpokes it's time we went home. We don't want Albert to prepare the meal when we won't be there to eat it, do we?"

To remind Tom he could do with some food Ebony King knocked Tom's hat onto the ground. Good natured Tom rubbed the colt's head and said, "Have patience, your stable isn't far away."

***

Walking slowly with a smile on his face McGregor dragged the wallaby behind him; feeling very satisfied that he had stopped the desecration of his beloved graves.

CHAPTER NINETEEN

Ross lifted Jessica up in his arms to carry her inside. Elizabeth was standing at the sink drying dishes.

"Hello darling, see what I've found in the bottom paddock."

Elizabeth turned round to see her husband arms, full with Jessica.

"Aren't you pleased?" Ross said with a large smile on his face.

"I hope for your sake that she can cook!" Elizabeth stated in a non-committal voice. Ross looked confused for a moment then his features lightened with understanding.

"No, it is nothing like that dear. Can't you see the resemblance?"

Wondering where this conversation was going Jessica kept silent.

"All I can see is that you are holding a strange woman in your arms!"

"You are right dear; however there is a reason for

that."

Alf came running into the kitchen having heard his Father's voice but screamed to a stop when he saw his parent's arms filled with a strange lady.

"Hello son, would you like to meet your aunt Jessica?"

"Jessica! You are Jessica? My missing sister in law?" Elizabeth queried in astonishment.

Jessica nodded too emotional to speak.

"Put the girl down Ross, so that I can greet her properly."

"I would if I could but I can't because my little sister thought she could tame Tom's new colt, but just as Jessica mounted the animal McGregor fired his shotgun for whatever reason making the colt jump clean over the corral rail to eventually deposit her on our property where I discovered her lying unconscious on her back. Phew, that was hard work trying to say all that in one go, but I think I succeeded."

Ross looked quite pleased with himself. Elizabeth looked confused while Jessica had her eyebrows raised to the ceiling.

"Tom, oops, Ross could you please deposit me on a chair." Jessica hoped no one had picked up on her small mistake.

"What do you think dear wife, do you think a certain little girl is smitten with our young neighbour? You know the old saying, what the heart is full of the mouth runneth over with."

"She could do a lot worse," was the short reply Ross received from his wife! "Why don't you place your sister on a chair so that we can see what she looks like?"

"All good things come to an end dear sister. I suppose I'd better do what I'm told; I must admit you are rather heavier than when I last carried you."

After Elizabeth and Alf had given Jessica a hug they placed themselves around the kitchen table. This was also the time that Ross remembered he had invited Tom's family to be at their place for the evening meal instead of the other way round.

"Thank you for letting me know dear, here I thought we were going out but now I find out we are doing the entertaining!" Elizabeth said with a tired voice.

Realising that the long chat with his sister was going to be delayed Ross stood up asking.

"Tell me love, what can I help you with? Would you like me to start preparing the meal while you chat with Jessica?" Elizabeth looked grateful at Ross saying to Jessica,

"Assuming I didn't have to prepare the meal for tonight I spent the time reorganising some cupboards instead." Jessica nodded her head in sympathy.

Her sister-in-law seemed a nice girl and the little boy was adorable, Ross looked a picture of contentment. Something they'd never had at home.

What, did she hear just now? Thinking about the past she'd missed what Elizabeth was saying.

"We met your Father on the train returning from Melbourne when we heard Kathleen sing; somehow we missed you that night otherwise you could've met Ross so much earlier."

"You mean Dad and Ross actually spoke to each other?"

"They sure did! I will admit it took a bit of scheming on my part to bring them together but since your Father did nothing else but talk about the two of you during the journey I felt confident that there had been a change in the man. Not that Ross ever spoke about him much but he was always wondering how you and your Mother fared. He wrote often but never received a reply so after a few years he stopped writing as he assumed that your Dad destroyed his letters."

"Mother's last words were about Ross," Jessica murmured softly.

"Each day she would ask if there had been any mail, but Dad would always answer in the negative."

Jessica's mind wandered away on its own. The man that her sister-in-law mentioned didn't sound at all like her Father. It was hard to believe that someone could change so much? And it was all due to her leaving the property. According to what her Father had told Elizabeth, that once he was on his own he realised how much of a mess he had made of his family. He had even taken time away from the property to seek his family out; something Jessica never had expected her parent to do. Maybe what Elizabeth was saying was all true. To be on the safe side she'd better check with her brother before taking any action.

"O good, they've arrived early, now they can help us organise the meal," Ross shouted from the sink where he stood looking out the window while peeling potatoes.

Elizabeth jumped up from the table to begin her duties saying,

"Good grief, I didn't realise we had spoken for so long, I better give Ross a hand."

Jessica was amazed at her brother's behaviour, she had never met a man who would actually help his wife make the dinner, let alone stand at the sink. She wondered if Tom behaved similarly. Thinking about Tom and knowing how close he was, she'd better rush and make herself presentable.

"You haven't a broom handy so I can use it to lean on, I need it to go and powder my nose?"

Elizabeth opened the broom closet and picked a broom which looked as if it might do the job.

"I bet she wants to go and make herself look pretty for Tom," Ross whispered to his wife.

***

"Terry, you've been sitting staring into space for at least half an hour, what have you been thinking about?"

Mavis was sitting next to Terry leaning against the wall of Ebony King's stall. After watching Jessica and Tom steal furtive glances at each other last night she had been wondering if she would ever meet a handsome boy who would want to be with her and no one else but her. If there was a person like that in the world she hoped he would be like Terry in nature. Someone who shared not only her thoughts and feelings but most of all would listen and heed her advice when it was given. A warm feeling travelled along her spine.

"What did you say?" Terry's mind was slowly drifting back to reality, the thoughts he had been reflecting on had absorbed him completely.

"Aha, you are with us again. Where were you, you seemed to be miles away?"

"I was just thinking about the biblical story that Elizabeth told us a few days ago about how God created Adam, how He moulded Adam from the dust and breathed into Adam's nostrils the breath of life."

"Yes, so what, it sounded like a nice story to me, I feel that when God breathed into Adam's nostrils not only life entered Adam's body but also his soul was created. The only part of the story I didn't like was when God placed a snake in the Garden of Eden. I would've liked the story better if God had left the nasty snake out."

This was a strong statement coming from Mavis as she believed that if it was written in the Holy Bible you could not argue against it. As far as Mavis was concerned the Good Book only held the truth, thus had to be respected.

"I thought it was very nice of God to create mankind to share not only the world but also the beauty of everything that God had created in and around it with Him. Also it was kind of God to realise that it wasn't good for Adam to be alone and that's why He made Eve. This way Adam had a companion with whom he could share his troubles and delights with!"

Mavis liked to see everything nicely paired. To her surprise Terry said,

"Well, that's where my thinking differs from yours."

"What do you mean?" Mavis wondered where Terry's creative mind had taken him now.

"If God knows everything why did it take him a while to realise that Adam was lonely?" Terry had a point there, but Mavis suddenly had an inspiring thought.

"Maybe he delayed the coming of Eve so that Adam would appreciate her more. You know yourself that you appreciate things more when you have to wait for them!"

Terry sat back for some time giving Mavis' reply

some serious consideration. That was why Mavis liked Terry so much; he took her seriously.

"You could be right Mavis." Terry gave his sister a sly grin making Mavis wonder what he was thinking about now.

"You know Mavis; do you know what God should've done?"

Mavis looked at her brother questioningly?

"Instead of making Adam he should've placed two angels in the Garden of Eden and we would've all been able to fly!"

Mavis nodded her head in agreement.

"That would've made a lot of sense Terry; being able to move about with the use of wings might've been a lot easier than walking. But perhaps he didn't want to use them as they had quite a fight among each other when Satan and his mob were at each other's throat."

What Mavis said made sense. Perhaps angels weren't all that friendly with each other? Terry went back to his original question.

"All the same I do wonder why God didn't make Eve at the same time as he created Adam," Terry said with a frown on his forehead.

"God might've had a lot on His mind; He had only just finished creating the universe plus everything else on and in it. You have to be fair Terry, God had been very busy."

Terry admired his little sister; she didn't mind

him using her as a bouncing board for his ideas. She even gave back as good as she got at times.

"But why give Adam a girl like Eve?"

"What do you mean? What was wrong with her?"

Mavis felt a bit slighted, didn't Terry realise that she was a girl also?

"Well, she not only spoke with a snake, she actually took notice of him and heeded his advice. Maybe if God had made Eve from mud like He made Adam she might've acted different?" Terry sighed deeply.

"Anyway, I suppose, this is what we ended up with and there isn't much we can do about it. Personally I feel that God should've thought about it a bit deeper!"

"Terry, that's blasphemy what you just said!" Mavis looked horrified.

"The Bible tells us that God can't do any wrong, He can only do well."

Terry felt sorry that he had upset Mavis, placing his arm around her he said,

"All I meant to say was that God could have acted differently and I find it very confusing to follow why he chose the direction he selected. I can't understand why the first two people God made couldn't adhere to his rules and why one of their children became a murderer by killing his own brother. If it had happened a few generations or a hundred years later you could understand that nastiness had crept in but these were people who actually walked with God. It all occurred too fast for me. That's why I think God should've worked the extra day!"

Mavis stated firmly with a determined look on her face,

"You can't expect God to work on the Sabbath, Terry, especially after he forbade mankind to work on the seventh day."

Terry studied his sister carefully.

"You could work seven days if there were eight days in a week."

He shouted triumphantly.

"I'm sure that wouldn't have been too hard for God to organise. Anyway I think I heard Kathleen calling us, which means the end of this discussion, we'd better move to see what she wants."

Both trailed their hand along Ebony King's forehead as a farewell gesture when leaving the stable. As they walked home Mavis glanced at Terry with a concerned look on her face, she was thinking that at times her brother was a bit too smart. Here was hoping good old Terry wouldn't get off the beaten track too far. Heaven knows where he could end up with the thoughts that entered his head?

**

McGregor was sitting on an empty crate on his veranda surrounded by his faithful dogs, swinging the nearly empty whiskey bottle awkwardly in his hand he lamented mournfully to his canine audience.

"No respect for the dead, that's what's wrong. Out of sight, out of mind, the poor girl's body is hardly cold and that young rake has his eyes on another one already!"

The words tumbled from his mouth much the same as the whiskey spilt from the waving bottle in his hand. The dogs didn't have any notion what their master was muttering about but that didn't prevent them from thumping their tails on the boards and licking their master's hand at times.

McGregor had seen Tom and Jessica ride together and had been rather shocked at the easy camaraderie that seemed to be between them.

"How anyone could act in such an indecent hasty manner to begin courting another woman when the wee little lassie had hardly been dead for a month?"

McGregor wiped his mouth with the back of his unwashed hand clearing away the spilled whiskey which missed his mouth. He discovered that the more he drank the easier it became to forget the niggling thoughts hiding at the back of his mind, which were that his daughter Tracy hadn't always treated Tom fairly. At other occasions the thought came to his mind that perhaps it was his fault his wife had left him and maybe he was the reason why his children had taken their own life. A bitter river of remorse, failure and anger ran through him. At moments when he was reasonably sober he knew he was neglecting the farm which made him feel depressed. The thought of having to do all the chores that needed doing made him tired and drove him to find solace in yet another bottle. Lifting his head well back he raised the bottle to his mouth and let the fiery liquid pour down his throat.

Feeling dizzy McGregor attempted to straighten up but somehow could not find the effort to succeed. The bottle fell on the floor scattering the dogs to make a spreading stain on the wooden slats while McGregor kept falling backwards until the back of his head hit the floor. One dog walked over to lick his owner's face but soon returned to lie down with his mates. Soon the only sound you could hear was McGregor snoring and the buzzing of flies who were circling around the peaceful little group.

***

"Do you think he's dead?" Jessica asked hesitantly.

"With the noise those dogs are making it's hard to tell!" Tom answered.

Jumping from his horse Tom waded through the frantic barking pack of dogs. When he reached McGregor who was still lying in the same prone position as when he had fallen over. That is, flat on his back with arms spread wide apart and his legs poking up in the air at an angle, supported by the box he had sat on. Tom turned to yell in a loud voice at the dogs,

"If you measly flea-bitten mongrels don't quieten down I'll give you something to bark about!"

Not a lot of notice was taken of Tom's loud threats so Tom leaned over to the wall where there was a shotgun resting. Cradling the weapon in his arms Tom checked to see if there was a cartridge up the spout. There was. Good, Tom aimed the gun just over the dog's heads and pulled the trigger.

From where Jessica stood it looked like Tom was going to blast the lot of them to Kingdom come.

Bang! All the dogs stopped barking when they heard the noisy blast. Three seconds later there wasn't a dog in sight. The silence was pure bliss.

"Who is making all the noise?" McGregor croaked, attempting to rise from his position. Falling back he moaned, "Have a care will you, there are horses stampeding through my head."

"Sorry Mr. McGregor." Jessica crouched next to him. "At least we know now that you are still alive. Tom and I weren't sure what we would find when we saw you from a distance."

McGregor never heard a word as he had dropped off to sleep again.

"At least he's alive! I suppose we'd better

organise to take him over to my place." Tom shook his head in dismay at the way his neighbour had let himself go. Weeds sprouted in places which hadn't seen weeds since the farm began, doors were hanging half open at times swinging in the breeze from one hinge only. The place had a real air of neglect about it

"Jessica, could you run up to see if Albert is available to bring the cart down so we can take McGregor home. If there is anyone else with him just give him enough details so that he knows what is required. Thanks love."

While Jessica rode away Tom thought about how easy the 'thanks love' had slipped from his mouth. There was something different about Jessica. Tom knew he wasn't experienced in dealing with girls.

Tracy had been totally different from Jessica. There had been an aloofness that Tom could never feel comfortable with. At times he thought Tracy was stuck up, she had a way of looking down at people that used to embarrass him. Tom recalled a kid that he had attended school with speak about the daughter of the local mayor who was a few years older than them.

"That sheila better be careful, just because she had a private education she shouldn't keep her nose so high in the air that birds will nest in her nostrils."

Jessica had had a good education that was obvious but Tom had never seen her look down at anyone. No, Jessica would make someone a good wife; she'd be a hard worker and would stay with her husband even when times would be hard. Actually Jessica reminded him a lot of Elizabeth, not in looks or appearance but in mannerism, attitude and demeanour. Anyone who was fortunate to end up with a wife similar to Ross' could only end up being contented surely?

Looking down at McGregor again, feet stuck up into the air, drool dribbling down his neck into a dirty shirt; Tom thought it was good that the man couldn't see himself. What was he going to do with him? Taking him home wouldn't solve the problem. What was he going to do about the land? You only had to look around to see McGregor in the state he was in he wouldn't be able to make any clear cut decisions which would resolve any problems. Entering the kitchen Tom realised that laziness and neglect had invaded this domain also. The house smelt, stank actually, nothing had been cleaned, the floor was filthy and needed a good brush. The table was covered with food that should've been stored in a cupboard and the area near the sink was stacked with plates, saucers and cups which had flies walking and buzzing around them. Half empty open jam jars next to a sugar bowl had ants running up and down it with trails leading to and from the outside wall.

Late that night Tom sat alone on the veranda watching the countless stars in the sky. There had been many times in the years since his parents died that Tom wished his Father was still alive. He had desperately missed the man when he was young especially when he was lonely and frightened.

Now that he was able to fend for himself the feeling wasn't that bad, but for some reason or other Tom felt young and vulnerable tonight, he could do with the advice from an older and wiser person.

There, free from any worldly problems was the Southern Cross displayed as clear in the sky as the kite he used to fly when young. It was so low in the sky that the pointers were hidden by the hills surrounding the valley. Tom knew that if he could see the pointers he would've been able to draw a line and then draw another line from the top to the bottom of the kite and south would be where the two lines intersected. His Father had shown him how to do that and Tom had never forgotten. If he waited a few hours longer Tom knew he would be able to see the pointers but as it was becoming late he'd be better to go to bed. Perhaps the answer to his question, whatever the question was, would present itself to him when he was sleeping. It wouldn't be the first time that had occurred during his young life.

***

Waking from his stupor McGregor looked round the room in amazement. Where was he? Everything was tidy and clean, nothing looked like the room he normally slept in? His head was pounding.

From far away the sound that only an angel could make reached his ear. Was he in heaven? No, that would be impossible, with the way his head was aching he assumed that he was nowhere near heaven. Closing his eyes he relaxed to listen as the angel sang.

Somehow the sweet clear sound soothed him making him drift off to sleep.

Not knowing the effect her singing had had on McGregor, Kathleen continued to rock the Osmond Little Marvel Washing Machine from left to right. This action was guaranteed by the manufacturer to suck all the dirt out of clothes which were in the tub. "Typical male," thought Kathleen, why hadn't her brother purchased the 'Ideal' washing machine which had a steel tub plus a built on wringer. What more could a person want?

Of course, if Jessica had still been here, then Kathleen might've been able to give her the menial job of doing the washing. Shrugging her shoulders, Kathleen carried on with her work; at least it gave her time to practice her singing. It wouldn't be long now before her holiday was over and she'd have to return to Melbourne as there was urgent business to attend to.

Kathleen would never forget the moment when the great Melba 'Queen of Covent Garden' had come backstage to seek her out after having heard her singing. The outcome of which was a date to meet at

Melba's home 'Coombe Cottage' a quiet retreat that the star had made for herself in the hills near Lilydale.

"Please visit me; I want to discuss something that would be profitable for both of us," the great star had whispered in Kathleen's ear before departing.

At this stage Kathleen had no idea what the discussion was going to be about, but she was looking forward to it. This could be her big break!

A knocking on the back door brought Kathleen from her reverie. On opening the door she was confronted by a heavily be-whiskered gentleman who when he doffed his cap Kathleen thought she was looking at a large fur ball complete with legs. Pleasant to look at the man it certainly wasn't. The hairy apparition began to offer his services to sharpen all the implements which required being sharp so that a household could run efficiently. Telling the man that his services weren't required didn't make any impression, all he replied was,

"Me sharpen everything real sharp."

Kathleen's retort of, "We sharpen everything real sharp too," met with no success.

Anyone calling at your home in the bush had to be invited inside, given food, drink and was made to feel as comfortable as possible. So it wasn't long before the knife sharpener was sitting at the kitchen table noisily slurping from a mug of strong tea and dunking the homemade biscuits in between sips.

Kathleen moved the large tin of 'Billy Tea' aside

so that she could see her visitor from where she was sitting.

***

After tightening the saddle strap Jessica swung her leg over Ebony King's saddle. Terry was mounted on the horse she had used to ride over to Tom's place. For the last three days the two of them began their ride before the sun rose. To warm up his fine muscles and keep them supple the young stallion stepped high, giving a good imitation of a show pony. It looked like he was showing off, but if he was it was wasted as at that time in the morning there was no one to watch him.

A light mist rose from the fields accentuating the aroma of the tobacco plants growing in the next paddock. Terry was waiting for the time, which was not far away now, that the leaves would be hanging in the drying sheds.

Tom had told him that as the leaves dried their aroma would permeate the air day and night, becoming stronger as the leaves became dryer. They were not supposed to be totally dry of course before they'd be shipped to Melbourne. The consistency had to be just right or mould would set in, spoiling the crop.

Jessica glanced at Terry giving him a nod. Terry understood the signal; this was the part of the morning he really looked forward to. Even the horses seemed to know what was coming as both riders' heels only had to touch the animal flanks for them to lean forward to begin their gallop. The pounding hooves broke the morning stillness. Slowly Ebony King began to pull away.

Terry was frustrated, each morning this occurred. Ebony King was always the faster horse, even if he was too young to race, but somehow, from somewhere he found something inside him that made him drive harder so that he could beat the competitor. Not wanting to burn the young horse out Jessica slowed him down to a walking pace. Terry catching up watched the horse's breath condense into steam as it met the colder morning air. The muscles rippling under the glossy skin indicated how strong the young colt was.

"Wow, what a horse, I wish Tom would let me ride him. Just to sit on him would make you feel like a knight in shining armour."

Jessica laughed. The sound made Terry think of little bells tinkling in the frosty air.

"Well Terry," Jessica smiled, "your wish may well come true."

Terry raised his eyebrows.

"Soon I'll have to return to Melbourne, I can't stay here forever, as much as I'd like to. A visit to Adelaide seems to be on the cards also, Ross told me that as Father isn't well I should go over and speak with him. As you know Tom is still far too heavy to ride Ebony King so why don't we propose to him that you take over my job of training him."

Terry had a grin that went from ear to ear. Suddenly a thought entered his head, without any thought he blurted out,

"If you are going to propose that I ride Ebony King why don't you propose at the same time that Tom marries you, kill two birds with one stone like?"

"Jessica's face went through all sorts of expressions accompanied with a variety of different shades of colour. Terry could not think what he had said should've had such an effect.

"You do want to marry Tom don't you?" he asked in bewilderment.

Taking a deep breath Jessica thought, (from the mouths of babes) how could she answer Terry's simple question?

"Maybe I do or maybe I don't Terry. What I want or don't want, doesn't really count in our society. A lady would never dream of and definitely could never ask a gentleman to marry her. It is simply not done!"Once again Terry thought he had the solution.

"That predicament is easily overcome Jessica. I'll suggest to Tom that he asks you!" Jessica looked even more horrified, however at the same time she admired her sister-in-law for giving Tom's younger brother such a good education. Terry used big words as if he had swallowed a dictionary.

"Don't you ever dare mention any part of this conversation we are having to Tom. I would die of shame. Have you ever thought that Tom might not like to marry me, or that I might have no intention of wanting to marry your brother."

Terry smiled knowingly, thinking, "Who are you trying to fool Miss, remember, it is me you are speaking to."

Secretly Terry wondered why grownups made life so complicated.

"Now look here young man, wipe that smile off your face, I think we have discussed this matter long enough. How about a last run before we return home?"

***

"Do you think I've come up with a great idea then?"

Jessica looked expectantly at Tom, who was idly doodling on the pad in front of him not looking Jessica in the eye as she was standing in front of his desk. Didn't she realise the thin material dress she was wearing wasn't covering her because the light coming in through the window behind her was accentuating her slim but curvy figure.

"To be honest I don't like the idea of Terry riding my horse nor you returning to Melbourne."

Raising his head towards her with a pleading

look in his eyes Tom said hoarsely, "Do you really have to go?"

"You know as well as I Tom that I would like to remain and extend my stay here in the valley, but I have to see my boss so I can tell him I have to return to Adelaide to visit Dad. I'll be fortunate if I have a job to go to after all the time I've had off. Anyway, I feel you under estimate your younger brother, he is a lot more mature than you give him credit for."

Jessica felt on safer grounds when discussing Tom's brother than letting Tom know he was the reason she didn't want to leave.

"You could be right, all the same, Ebony King is a lot of horse for him to control!"

"The horse is young too Tom, I feel that in this case they'll assist each other and work well together. Let's not forget one important point though Tom, Ebony King will always remember that he is your horse, so if you think he'll transfer his affection to someone else you are worrying about something that doesn't exist."

Tom's face lighted up, smilingly he replied,

"These are not my only concerns, but I do value your input greatly and if you say I can trust Terry and Ebony King together then that's the way we'll go!"

Jessica's face pinked slightly as she realised the trust that Tom had just placed in her. She promised herself to have another discussion with Terry to ensure he wouldn't let Tom down. Their meeting was interrupted by the loud voice of McGregor arguing with Albert.

"If you think I am going to clean up my mess while there are servants around you have another thing coming!"

Tom and Jessica left Tom's office to see what the commotion was all about.

Albert's face was red with suppressed anger, while purple lines stood out on McGregor's nose. He looked rather comical standing in the hall dressed in his long nightshirt, red socks and a nightcap that threatened to fall off his head. Wisps of grey hair pointing in any direction from under the cap and a two day beard didn't enhance his appearance.

Kathleen poked her head around the opening of the kitchen door followed by the knife sharpener. Albert grabbed McGregor by the front of his night shirt, saliva leaving his mouth as he spat his words into the bearded face close to him.

"Just because I keep house for Tom doesn't mean that I am your servant McGregor! You made the mess, you clean it up! Comprehendo, savvy, or in plain English, do you understand me."

To emphasise what he was saying Albert tugged the night shirt as each word left his mouth. McGregor stepped slightly back, moving his arm to punch Albert on the nose. As the fist came hurtling at him Albert ducked sideways.

The knife sharpener thought to impress Kathleen

with his prowess in the gentlemen's art of fisticuffs had walked past her to break up the scuffle and thus walked straight into McGregor's fist.

"Ouch!" he squeaked, to crumple gently into a heap as he collapsed onto the floor.

"Who was that man?" McGregor queried, looking down.

"Where did he come from?" Albert asked accusingly.

"Why did you hit the man so hard?"

Kathleen wanted to know from McGregor.

"Don't ask me. I don't know the man; all I wanted to do is give Albert the thrashing he deserves for being rude to me!" He turned back towards Albert.

"Why did you duck anyway? If you had taken your punishment like a man that poor man never would've been hit?"

"You miserable little man, if you weren't a neighbour and would stop drinking long enough so that the small amount of grey matter that hides in your skull could actually start to operate, you might discover what a pitiful creature you are."

The others stopped looking at the crumpled form on the floor to raise their eyes towards Albert in amazement.

"I say old chap," Tom said bombastically.

"That is no way to speak to anyone in this house. We realise the man hasn't behaved like a true gentleman but that is no reason for us to sink to his level?"

McGregor started to smile victoriously when hearing the beginning of Tom's speech but his grin soon faded when it sank in that Tom wasn't paying him a compliment either, perhaps he had overstepped the mark when he tried to hit Albert. He better try to get back into Tom's favour.

"No, no Tom, you are right, I never should've treated Albert the way I did. Please forgive me Albert; you were right I should clean up my own mess."

Now Albert looked uncomfortable, how quickly a situation can change! Holding his hand out he said, "I have a feeling I might've overreacted a bit here. You go and have something to eat while I clean up your room."

"Now Albert, I don't want to hear another word about this matter, I said it was my fault so I will clear up my room, UNDERSTOOD!"

Tom saw that Albert was becoming red in the face again so he changed the subject.

"Kathleen could you organise to remove your gentleman friend from the floor, he doesn't look at all comfortable..."

"I don't know the man from a bar of soap Tom so don't call him my gentleman friend."

Saying this she walked towards the kitchen to return with a large bowl filled with water which she emptied on the man's face. The knife sharpener coughed and spluttered as he came to. Helping the man up, and after drying his hair, Kathleen took him back to his chair at the table promising him another cup of tea and some more homemade cookies.

While all this activity was going on inside the house Mavis had been studying the knife sharpener's vehicle, which she saw consisted of three wheels. One wheel was controlled by a handlebar while a wooden box was slung between the other two wheels. "I could drive this!" Mavis said to herself. Having the three wheels it can't fall over like a two wheeled bike so this should be as easy as drinking water. The little guardian angel sitting on her right shoulder whispered in her ear, "But Mavis this isn't your bike."

This wasn't precisely the information Mavis wanted to hear so ignoring her little friend's words Mavis sat on the saddle, just to see if her feet could reach the pedals. They could.

"See, this vehicle was made for you!"

The black shadow residing on her left shoulder shouted into her ear,

"Go on, there's no one around. You'll never be found out!"

Still ignoring the advice from the right ear Mavis hesitantly pushed a pedal down. The contraption gently moved forward swaying on its springs. A pebble which had been instrumental in preventing the vehicle from rolling forwards rolled aside when the pressure of the front wheel was released making it easier for the bike to move.

The air blew through Mavis' hair, the modern pneumatic tyres smoothed out the bumps on the track. Pedalling faster and faster Mavis had the sensation that she was flying through the air. She thought she heard someone call out her name. Turning her head from side to side she noticed that Terry was watching her, she felt a sudden bump and the handlebars behaved as if they had a mind of their own.

"I've got to stop this thing!" Next minute she realised that she had no idea on how to slow the contraption down. Panicking, looking everywhere but ahead she tried to find something that resembled a gadget that would stop the bike. By the time Mavis realised there was nothing that resembled a brake she found herself surrounded up to her waist in water as the bike ran into the dam. What now? Terry came running up, puffing he said,

"Well that's a nice mess you got yourself into, sis."

Mavis felt this wasn't one of her better moments.

"Just get me out of here Terry, I'm sinking deeper,"

Mavis whimpered, all her bravado had gone. Why hadn't she listened to her guardian angel? The voice on her left shoulder was silent now.

Terry ran back towards the sheds soon appearing

with a horse and some rope. Throwing the rope to Mavis he told her to tie it to her saddle. Obediently she tied the rope to the tube underneath the saddle becoming even wetter during the process. With the help of the horse Terry began to tow the vehicle from the dam but just near the bank the slope proved to be too steep. Mavis felt the bike topple over depositing her halfway on the bank and in the water. Now she was completely wet. Without her weight the vehicle moved easier and soon both were standing on terra firma. Placing the contraption back in its original place with a sharp edged stone cunningly resting against the front wheel Jessica snuck inside to change while Terry returned the horse to its paddock. Jessica hoped the owner wouldn't notice the mud which had stuck to the wheels and pedals or the water that was dripping from the wooden box.

While removing her wet clothes in her room Jessica heard her sister say goodbye to the owner of the bike who with all that had happened to him, was glad to be leaving the premises. The tea and biscuits had been nice, but that was about it.

As the man pushed his bike forward he could sense through the handlebars that the front wheel's tyre had gone flat. Seeing the sharp edged stone he assumed the wheel had struck it when he stopped to get off the bike. Angrily he threw the offending stone away. Studying the matter more closely and pressing down on the tyre only confirmed what he dreaded.

He definitely had a flat tyre! What was wrong with this place? Was it cursed? He began wishing that he'd stayed in bed this morning. Fortunately he was used to having punctures, it was for that reason he kept the required tools hanging from the rear of his saddle in a bag. Had it rained, while he was inside, because the bag felt damp? With a heavy sigh he removed the wheel and began to work. It wasn't long before he could go on his way again.

As the man pedalled his bike along the side of the house so he could make the turn to the driveway, McGregor in his effort to clean the room, had picked up the offending chamber pot. He walked over to the open window and nonchalantly threw the contents out onto the driveway. There, his work for the day was nearly finished! The job hadn't been all that hard.

Blinking his eyes furiously, to clean them from the running liquid, ignoring the smell which clung to his whiskers, the knife sharpener looking more like a fur ball than ever with his moist whiskers clinging to his face, pedalled as if the devil was chasing him.

"I've to get away from here before something disastrous occurs. From now on they can sharpen their own knives, they won't be seeing me again!"

He muttered, as he bounced along the downhill track.

— CHAPTER TWENTY —

Tom was bending over his beloved tobacco plants, checking the underside of the leaves for any pests. Fortunately or unfortunately depending on how you looked at the problem, the tobacco plant attracted the same pest as did the potato and tomato plants. At least he didn't have to cater to a bug he didn't know. Budworm, aphids and hornworms is what he had to look out for. Perhaps he should be growing the other crops also as they required the same fertilizers. No, shaking his head, anyone could grow potatoes or tomatoes but there weren't many areas where you could successfully cultivate tobacco.

A short clearing of the throat interrupted Tom's dreams. Looking up he saw McGregor standing near him with an embarrassing expression on his face.

"How can I help you, McGregor? Sorry, but I was in such deep thought I didn't hear you coming."

"That's fine Tom, I could see you were miles away, but as you were by yourself I thought I'd discuss an idea that's been running around in my head for a few days now."

Tom looked at McGregor with a 'tell me more' look.

"I was wondering if you would like to purchase my property," McGregor blurted out.

"Before you answer however, you'd better listen to the proviso that comes with it though." Tom wondered what else his neighbour was going to say.

"I'm listening old friend; you just took my breath away as I didn't expect to hear what you just proposed."

"The proviso is that I'll sell to you at a good price if you will agree to accept three acres of land at no cost to you." Tom looked mystified, why would anyone give land away for nothing? McGregor continued.

"The reason I'm doing this is that I would like to see a church built where my children's graves are. You think three acres is enough to build a small church, have a parking area and a cemetery?" McGregor asked worriedly.

"Depends on how big a church you'd want to build?"

"Isn't it marvellous how God works?" Tom thought. "Ross and I've wanted to build that church for a while now and here comes the perfect opportunity for it to happen!"

"I am planning ahead here! I can do that now

since you don't let me have anything to drink," McGregor stated looking accusingly at Tom.

"If you don't like my rules you don't have to remain!" Tom replied shortly.

"I'm not complaining Tom, but I will admit I could murder for a drink at times, however with all this going without alcohol, a few ideas have entered my head and to my surprise have actually made sense."

Smiling at Tom, McGregor continued.

"You must remember I am only donating the land. The community would have to find the capital to build the church. I visualised a building that would be able to hold at least a congregation of about a hundred people. In time I would like to see a hall added for social activities and a school so that the children, and remember, there will be more children in a few years time, I'm sure of that, can have a place where they can learn without any interruptions. I know Elizabeth is doing a marvellous job and large as her house is it will never take the place of a good school."

This was the longest Tom had ever heard his neighbour speak. He could feel the enthusiasm the man had for this project.

"If you want all that on your three acres you'd better think again McGregor. The school will require some sheds around it and also a decent size playground would be required. Personally I feel we would require at least five acres if not ten. That way we could plant some trees so there is some where to sit in the shade."

McGregor could see that Tom was becoming quite excited with his idea.

"Do you have any idea what sort of money will be involved with this project of yours, neighbour?" Tom asked.

"No Tom, I just wanted to see if you were interested in my idea?"

"Well, I think it's a brilliant idea. I've always wanted to see a church in the valley, I'm sure that Ross will also want to be part of it but before we say anything to him why don't you and I go to Albury. Once there we can have your farm valued, have the area marked out you think will be required for the church and future school and have it drawn on an official map, that way no one can say there's been any favouritism. At the same time we can have an architect draw up plans for the buildings required and give us a quotation."

McGregor looked amazed.

"Do you think they can do all that on one day?"

"Of course not, but at least we'll get the ball rolling."

Tom punched McGregor on the shoulder.

"By the way, what are you going to do with yourself when all your plans are finalised and there isn't anything else to be done?"

McGregor shrugged his shoulders.

"I would like to be around when the church is officially opened but after that I think I'll go to fresh pastures and see if I can start again! However my dreams could take a few years before they'll eventuate so there's lots of time for anything to happen. At this moment I'm playing it on a day to day basis."

"Good on you, neighbour, I'm glad you are not rushing into anything that you haven't planned properly. Oh no, our peaceful time is over I feel that someone else noticed we are here. This valley is becoming too populated by half."

"That looks like Ross' sister galloping over. I'm sure she won't need to speak to me, so I'll depart."

With this McGregor began to walk back home.

It was nice to see that his neighbour had returned from the negative place that had nearly swamped him. His head brimming with the new ideas Tom leaned over the plants to continue his job. However the bugs could've been as big as elephants and Tom's eyes might be looking, but nothing was registering.

Hearing a horse pull up Tom straightened himself slowly while rubbing his back with both hands. As he walked towards the fence he saw that Jessica was already climbing through the strained barbed wire, not waiting for him to arrive so that he could assist her. With a frantic look on her face she hurled herself at Tom while sobbing.

"Oh Tom, Ross wants me to leave tomorrow, he

had a dream in which Dad kept asking for one of us to come and visit him. He's never had a dream about Dad in his life so he feels that this could be important. I don't want to leave right now Tom. It's not that I don't believe Ross when he says Dad is a changed man, it's just that I remember him as I last saw him and I feel a bit scared in going there on my own."

Jessica fell silent but kept sobbing clinging on to Tom who felt altogether useless as he didn't really know how to handle the situation. He didn't mind Jessica clinging to him and he did keep holding her close which for some reason seemed to work as Jessica's sobs slowly began to dwindle.

"When do you think you'll have to leave us then?"

Tom said softly. Jessica tensed, leaning back slightly she studied him.

"Do you want me to go away then?" She asked in an astonished voice.

"Look love, what I want is not important right now. As far as I'm concerned you can stay here forever. But I think I know you well enough that you'll end up feeling guilty about not visiting your Father and do you want to live with that on your mind for the rest of your life?"

Jessica kept looking at Tom while she replied,

"You are right Tom of course I will have to go. I was just hoping that you would convince me to delay the trip somewhat. I don't want to leave here and did you know you just called me (love)?"

"What else can I call you with the position you are in? To tell the truth, ever since you've been here I thought of you as my love!"

Slowly Jessica lowered her eyes to Tom's lips. Their heads moved tenderly together, then they kissed. When they eventually moved apart Jessica laid her head against Tom's chest.

"You know my love," Tom whispered, "I've been wanting to do that ever since we bumped into each other the night I came home."

"I've wanted to do this when I saw you that first time in Melbourne, you know; when you brought Kathleen to our digs."

"Really?"

"Truly!" Jessica giggled, clutching Tom harder. I hope you don't think I'm a hussy do you Tom?"

"Definitely not Jessica. I think you've shown a lot of restraint and I feel we should remedy that right now."

Tom lowered his head to hers again.

Both of them were sitting on the grass leaning against the fencepost with the horse cropping the grass nearby.

"They tell me we are living in a fast world, steam trains, automobiles and soon there'll be telephones available to every home in the cities."

"What are you referring to Jessica?"

"Dear Tom, half an hour ago we were just two people who knew each other, just a bit better than acquaintances I suppose. But look at us now, a whole new world has opened up for us."

"You can blame your Father I suppose. If Ross hadn't had that dream you wouldn't have rushed here into my arms..."

"You are right dear. I did rush to you didn't I. I sincerely hope you didn't mind but not being able to see you was the only thought in my head."

Jessica sounded almost sad. Tom attempted a bit of levity.

"Don't worry dear Jessica; I suppose I'll just have to cope with it."

This brought Jessica to life. Punching Tom's arm she replied,

"Just have to cope with it? You'll cope with it alright or I'll want to know the reason why!"

"Pax, Pax!" Tom screamed in a high pitched voice.

"Anyway before you kill me, would you like to know what I have in mind?"

Jessica nodded her head.

"McGregor and I have to go Albury soon. So why don't you come and travel with us?"

"What so that you can see me off at the railway station?"

Jessica commented in a bitter voice.

"Let me finish the rest of my plan dear, golly you

don't half jump in, do you?"

Jessica kept silent but smiled demurely.

"As I said, McGregor and I were going to Albury anyway, Kathleen also has to go home to Melbourne, so what I was going to suggest was if we stay at Mrs. Mainwaring's place overnight while we organise rail tickets required, it should give us enough time to persuade her to travel with us to Melbourne where once Kathleen is settled in we continue to travel on to South Australia."

"Why do we need Elizabeth's Mother to travel with us to Melbourne?"

"Not to Melbourne silly, she's coming all the way to Adelaide and McGregor is staying at her place until we arrive back." Jessica's face cleared.

"You mean you are coming with me all the way home? Oh you are a dear."

Jessica began to kiss Tom all over again. Then she stopped to look at him. A mischievous glint entered her eyes.

"Do we really need to have a chaperone?"

"Yes, we do!" Tom firmly stated.

"It will never be said that I ruined your reputation."

"Of course dear, you are right as usual,"

Jessica replied meekly, although if Tom would've had a good look at her he might've observed that at that moment Jessica's reputation wasn't uppermost in her mind

"Anyway love what I think we should do now..."

"Oh, I'll agree to any idea you come up with you great organiser you."

Tom studied Jessica to see if she was having him on.

"I'm trying to be serious here you know!"

"Of course you are dear, I just love the way your forehead wrinkles when you are concentrating."

Jessica was only barely holding back a giggle.

Tom decided it was best to ignore her and pressed on.

"You should go and see if our plans suit Ross and Elizabeth while I go and talk to McGregor and Kathleen. I suppose I'd better tell the kids and Albert what's happening as I wouldn't want them to be upset because they'll have to do most of the work while I'm away. Well my share anyway."

***

"Goodness gracious me, when you come calling you don't hesitate in bringing everyone do you?"

"It is very nice to see you again Mrs Mainwaring, I sincerely hope we haven't inconvenienced you?"

Tom knew he had overdone it this time but was hoping he could charm Elizabeth's mother into accepting them all.

"I realise there are a few of us but we haven't seen much of you lately and my sister Kathleen wanted desperately to see you again so I thought we'd call in. Of course Elizabeth wanted you to meet her sister-in-law Jessica."

Tom was prodding Kathleen to give him a hand here.

"Yes, Mrs. Mainwaring, I so did want to see you again, because with my career taking off soon, heaven only knows when I would have the opportunity to come down here again. I'm having a meeting with the great Melba next week you see and anything could come from that meeting."

As Kathleen was speaking she placed her arm around the elderly lady and slowly walked her down the passage into the kitchen with the rest of the troupe following.

"We did some shopping before we came so there is no need for you to be concerned about food Mrs. Mainwaring."

Jessica thought that comment might relieve the lady's feelings a bit. Kathleen manoeuvred the lady onto a chair. Tom took over again.

"Mrs. Mainwaring another reason we are here is that I have a proposal for you." This statement made her look up.

"A proposal, surely you aren't offering to marry me, young man?"

Tom and the others laughed.

"You never give up do you Mrs. Mainwaring. I suppose hope springs everlasting. No, no all we want to do is take you away from here for a while."

"Take me away? What do you have in mind for me; it's not the First of April is it?"

The woman showed signs of panic again. Tom realised he'd have done better if he'd come down on his own.

"No, there's nothing to worry yourself about, let me explain it all to you."

In a soothing voice Tom started to tell Mrs. Mainwaring what the visit was about.

The others looked at each other as they saw the lady's face begin to lighten as a smile appeared. Soon she was beaming.

"You want me to travel with you to Melbourne and then go on to Adelaide and dear Mr. McGregor will remain here to look after my home? Why didn't you say so in the first place instead of frightening the wits out of an old lady? I've always wanted to travel and at the same time I can get better acquainted with Jessica." Looking over at Jessica she said,

"Somehow I feel there won't be much time to speak to you here dear." Jessica returned her smile.

Rising from her chair Mrs. Mainwaring began to organise each one of them, chattering all the while, which showed how excited she was. It didn't take long before each one knew which bed he or she was sleeping in.

Tom and Jessica looked at each other while Tom wiped his hand over his forehead as if wiping sweat away then suggested, "A man's work is never done. As the Lands Department is still open for business why don't McGregor and I leave now to attend to our business and on our way home we'll detour by the railway station and see if we can organise the train tickets we require?"

Now when the three women were on their own - it didn't take long before they had a portmanteau open on Mrs. Mainwaring's bed and began busily sorting out what would be required for the time she would be away.

"How is your Father dear? He was ever such a caring man while he was here; I'm quite looking forward to seeing him again."

While Jessica explained the reason why they were visiting her Father, she was thinking that this was the first time she'd ever heard her Father being called a caring man.

***

The rhythmic cadence of the train wheels on the tracks had acted as a sedative on Mrs. Mainwaring. Leaning comfortably against a corner of the apartment which fortunately had no other travellers in it the mature lady sat in silent repose with her eyes closed, her hands resting on her lap breathing regularly the breath of those who are at peace with the world. Tom nudged Jessica, "If our chaperone is not asleep she'd have to be in a cataleptic trance instead, that's for certain. If I was a real cad this would be the time that I could have my wily way with you!"

"Oh no sir, I'm a good girl and remember my Father wouldn't like it!" Jessica whispered in mock horror.

"My little girl it is not your Father I had in mind."

Both of them laughed, snuggling closer together on their seat enjoying the opportunity of being on their own. Mrs. Mainwaring was good company but like all young lovers they loved the time when there was only the two of them. Holding each other close Tom watched the landscape rotate past like a giant wheel. 'Isn't life funny?' Tom thought, 'only a few months ago I was desperately in love with a woman who never was sure she wanted me but I was certain that eventually I could persuade her to change her mind.'

'Well I was wrong, although at the time I thought I was right. Dear Father in heaven how often have you had to listen to that epitaph? Now here I'm in love again but this time I know it is right as Jessica tells me she needs me just as much as I need her.'

Tom wanted to tell Jessica once again how much he loved her but her gentle breathing told him she had fallen asleep. Ah well, he'd just have to wait and tell her later. Tom was looking forward to many more (laters), even if that was not the right way to say it. It sure felt right!

***

"Hello Father!"

Jessica stood on the front door step hanging on to Tom's arm. They'd pulled the front door bell not knowing who'd answer the door and were rather surprised to see the owner open it.

"Jessica! Tom?" The colour drained from the elderly man's face.

"It's a pleasure to make your acquaintance again Sir."

Tom reached out to shake Jessica's Fathers hand.

"Sorry Sir, if we gave you a shock but there was very little time in which to let you know we were coming. Kathleen my sister came down to stay with me and brought Jessica with her, when Ross came over they recognised each other and then Ross had a dream about you - in it you asked him to come here, so we thought you'd be pleased if Jessica came instead. So here we are."

Tom knew he was rambling on but little else came to his mind that would help the situation as Mr. Smith remained standing where he was.

"Jessica, you have returned."

Jessica turned to see an overjoyed Clarence stumble in haste towards her.

"Oh Clarence, you don't know how good it is to see you again!"

They held each other in a bear hug neither one wanting to let go first.

Finally Mr. Smith came to his senses. Apologising for being so rude he invited Tom, Jessica and "Mrs. Mainwaring isn't it nice to see you again" inside, giving his daughter a long welcoming hug as she stepped through the entrance.

"You look so much more confident and mature than the way I recall you dear."

"I suppose having to stand on my own two feet helped me grow up," Jessica replied smilingly giving her Father a squeeze to show she didn't hold anything against him. When she looked at his face she noticed there were tears in his eyes. Clarence slowly ambled back to the job he had been doing ever so pleased that his master had made his daughter welcome. Could be there was change in the air? The old man had changed a lot since his trip away but so far the workers in the district weren't convinced that it was worthwhile applying for work. It took a long time for local people to change their minds. Now that Jessica had returned even if only for a visit the neighbours should be able to work out something had changed for the better. Clarence hoped so anyway, as he was becoming very tired of having to do everything on his own.

"Hello I'm Tom, is there anything I can help you

with? Clarence isn't it? Jessica is busy chatting with her Dad and Mrs. Mainwaring is trying to make herself at home in the kitchen so I thought after having sat in a train for most of the week I'd come and give you a hand."

Clarence looked flabbergasted, never in his born days had any visitors that stayed at the main house ever offered to work. The man didn't hesitate to take the shovel Clarence offered him and without any questions began to work.

"Looks like you know which end of a shovel to use?" Clarence commented.

"Seen plenty of shovels in my day Clarence, Ross made sure of that."

"Ross? You don't mean Ross Smith the boss' son?"

"Yes, Ross and I met up years ago. He caught me trying to pick his pocket. I must admit I was very hungry that day. Anyway he fed me and we became good mates. We are neighbours now which makes it easier to farm as we can use each other's equipment and labour. It saves heaps on costs and works great as long as we remain friends."

Clarence was hungry for news on Ross and kept Tom busy by having to answer all his questions, however it made time move faster and it wasn't long before they were tackling the next job.

Clarence found Tom just as good to work with as when he worked with Ross, no wonder they were good mates. At the end of the day Clarence knew to the head how many animals were on the properties owned by Tom and Ross.

Without Clarence realising it Tom had gleaned a lot of information about Jessica's Father and the state the farm was in.

That night after they had partaken of the meal that both ladies had dished up Mrs Mainwaring excused herself, blaming the long day spent travelling and after apologising retired to her bedroom. Facing each other sitting in comfortable chairs Mr. Smith asked if Tom could explain how Jessica and Tom had come to meet.

"I vaguely remember you, Tom, telling me something while we stood at the front door but I must apologise as I was too shocked to see Jessica appear out of nowhere that I am afraid very little of your story sunk in."

Once again Tom, interrupted by Jessica at times, related the story. When he had finished Mr. Smith sat quietly back in his chair peering at each of them.

"I found it so hard to believe that I had been standing close to Ross before we actually met a few days later, but if you think about it Jessica, a similar thing occurred with you and Ross. The funny part is that your sister, Kathleen I believe is her name," Tom nodded, "and you Tom knew both of my children but never realised there was a connection."

Silence reigned in the room, each one occupied

with their own thoughts. Suddenly the elderly man was overcome with a bout of coughing. When he recovered, now even paler than before, Tom wasn't sure if he had noticed the red spots he thought he'd observed - in Mr. Smith's handkerchief there were spots of blood or was it part of the handkerchief's design?

Jessica, worried at seeing her Father so pale made a yawn, stating that perhaps it wouldn't hurt for all of them to retire.

"There will be plenty of time tomorrow for us to continue our discussions!"

Tom agreed and seeing that it was two against one Mr. Smith began to struggle out of his chair ready to go to his room.

"That's the trouble with a chair that is comfortable," he grumbled, "It refuses to let you go when you want to leave it!"

Chuckling delightedly Tom and Jessica watched her Father leave the room. She still could not believe the change of attitude in her Father.

The two of them remained in the room, standing close together while hugging each other then after a long kiss they broke apart to go to their own bedrooms.

Normally her Father would have been up and around. Jessica had never known him to rise late. She'd been concerned for a while now, at first she thought to give him an extra half hour of sleep as he'd had quite a shock yesterday but now she stood hesitantly at his bedroom door listening to see if she could hear any movement. No, all was still.

Knocking gently on the door brought no results so Jessica began to open it slowly. She did not want to waken her Father unnecessarily.

The door collided with something, pushing a bit harder she found it moved but something was definitely preventing it from opening. It was now open far enough to put her head through so she could see. Oh, dear God no, it was her Father's body which was blocking the door. Letting go of the door she ran down the passage to call Tom who fortunately was still in the kitchen.

Tom, seeing her face knew instantly there was something awry. Rising from his chair so fast that it fell backwards on the tiled floor, Tom ignored the chair and followed Jessica instead who as soon as she knew Tom was coming had turned around to run back to the room.

Mrs. Mainwaring wandered over to the chair and placed it where it belonged, wondering what had happened for Tom to move so fast. It didn't take her long to find out. Pushing his weight against the door Tom found that he could open it far enough for him to enter the room. Placing his finger on Jessica's Father's neck he discovered a weak pulse.

"He's still alive!" Tom whispered to Jessica.

"Thanks be to God! Jessica exclaimed.

He didn't know why he whispered but for some reason found he was doing so. Tom also found that he could hear his own heart pounding in his ears.

"We'll have to get him to a doctor, we'll make him comfortable and then I'll go and get a cart ready with Clarence's assistance, he'll know who your Dad's doctor is and where he lives."

Clarence dropped whatever he was doing and speaking to Tom over his shoulder asked if the patient was sitting or in a prone condition.

"We found Mr. Smith stretched out on the floor, I'm not sure if he would be able to sit or not," Tom answered.

"We'll assume he can't then. We can throw a mattress on this buggy to make the travelling a bit easier for him; at least it is well sprung so the Master will receive a fairly smooth ride." His mind made up he swung his way towards the stables coming back with a horse whose condition showed it would eat the miles at a reasonable fast clip.

"While I organise this why don't you see if you can find a single bed mattress and be ready for me at the front door." Tom left to follow the hand's orders.

"Nothing is changed here thank heavens, since I've placed a pillow under his head he seems to be able to breathe easier. Just take the mattress from the bed in the room which belonged to Ross; I'm sure he won't mind us using it."

Jessica pointed to a door. Clarence entered the

room and the three of them carried Mr. Smith out on a wide plank which in the past had been used to stand on to paint the ceilings.

"Please Mrs. Mainwaring could you stay behind to look after the place just in case someone comes up the drive," was the last instruction Tom gave as Clarence laid the whip over the horse's back, something he had never done before. The horse took off with great speed dislodging loose gravel from the driveway as the vehicle gained speed.

Standing outside the doctor's surgery, Clarence was busily tamping tobacco in his meerschaum pipe. Tom idly kicked the gravel with his shoes wishing he smoked also so that he could keep his fingers busy. He enviously looked at Clarence inhaling his first mouthful of fresh lighted tobacco looking a picture of serenity. Commenting that he was experimenting with cultivating a crop of tobacco Clarence replied,

"Wish, I was working on your farm! The price of tobacco is keeping me poor. At least at your place I could smoke the gleanings after the crop was harvested."

Tom nodded his head thinking that there would most likely be enough tobacco left behind to keep half a dozen smokers happy.

"Did Mr. Smith ever attempt to cultivate a different crop?"

Tom asked amicably.

"No, not him, he was a cattle man. He only

reared horses because they were useful in mustering the cattle and handy for riding or pulling wagons. Ross suggested trying to cultivate grapes at one time but was criticised so heavily he never mentioned it ever again."

"Grapes, now there was a good idea," Tom thought - the climate in the valley should be right for growing grapes. He must read up on it. Nearly as many people who smoked liked to drink. Yes, grapes could be a real money maker!

Jessica accompanied by the doctor came through the front door, her eyes searching for Tom; she smiled as her eyes found his.

"Dad has improved slightly with Doctor Clarke's administrations but he did suggest Dad would be better looked after in a hospital.

"Where is the nearest hospital?" Tom asked.

"That is a problem, the only one which has all the facilities that Dad requires is in Adelaide."

Tom stroked his chin staring into space, and then turned to face the doctor.

"Surely you don't expect us to take him in that jalopy?"

Tom pointed his finger towards the buggy.

"I realise the contraption got us here, all the same I don't think it would take Mr. Smith to Adelaide, at least I don't think he would arrive there in the same condition as he left."

"You are right Tom! It is a lot to expect of that

worn out buggy, but what I had in mind was, that I contact the Ambulance here in Hahndorf and they can take Mr. Smith to Adelaide, that way Mr. Smith receives the care he needs as he requires it."

The doctor had a serious look on his face as he continued speaking directly to Jessica.

"You will have to keep in mind though that there will be a lot of aftercare required. An injury like your Dad has gone through doesn't repair itself overnight!"

Jessica's face changed colour, she knew there was no one else but her that could look after her Father. It wasn't fair! Tom and she had hardly had anytime to be together and now she would have to remain at home to look after her invalid Father. Hundreds of miles apart they would be! Would Tom want to wait? How cruel that sounded, wait for what? Until her Father regained his health, or wait until he passed away? Even more important would Tom still have the same feeling for her after being separated for heavens knows how long?

Tom observed the different emotions pass over Jessica's features. Walking over to her he placed his arm around her to let her know that he was on her side. A difficult decision had to be made and even he could see there was only one way for it to be resolved.

"Organise the ambulance Doctor!" Tom instructed. The doctor went inside.

"Come what may we'll sort this matter out love.

At the moment we have to do what is best for your Father, he comes first. Remember if we don't make the correct decisions now we have to live with our mistakes the rest of our lives. We are still young we can wait a while. Remind me to tell you about the plan that McGregor and I are hatching. When I do tell you, you'll find that a year delay might just put the icing on the cake."

Jessica looking mystified sagged against Tom, wearily happy that some of the decision making had been taken away from her. The doctor came from the building again to inform them that the ambulance should be arriving within the next half hour or so, in the same breath he told them that Mr. Smith was faring better than he expected which would help enormously for the journey ahead. It was decided Jessica would travel with her father and Tom would return with Clarence back home where they would bring Mrs. Mainwaring up to date.

CHAPTER TWENTY-ONE

"**N**o dear, you'll have to take more than this. Here let me do that. You should've asked me in the first place. Never have I met a man yet who knows what to pack for a woman when she is away from home."

Emptying the suitcase Mrs. Mainwaring began to sort out and deftly packed the items which she knew would be required by Jessica. She had worried about the girl whom she liked more each day she spent with her. What were these two youngsters going to do?

Tom had explained the situation at teatime the day he had returned with Clarence from the doctor. She could see from his crestfallen face that he wasn't too happy with what was happening.

"Did you say McGregor is going to live in Albury once his farm is sold?"

Tom looked up enquiringly as the question seemed to come from nowhere.

"Don't look so surprised Tom. It may amaze you that a woman my age might come up with an idea; all the same I think my idea is a good one. Would you like to hear it?"

Studying the woman in the kitchen with him, wondering what she was going to say Tom decided that a bit of flattery wouldn't go astray at this moment.

"Your daughter Elizabeth has come up with some great ideas since I've known her. I'll wager she has inherited a lot of your intelligence. I'm all ears Mrs. Mainwaring."

"Don't overdo it Tom, but you are right my daughter is a very sensible girl."

Tom had the grace to look chastened, so Mrs. Mainwaring carried on.

"I've been thinking that while McGregor is staying in town he could rent my house for the time it takes him to look for a new business venture."

"Where would you be staying then Mrs. Mainwaring?"

"Well you know the quandary you and Jessica are in has been on my mind you see, and suddenly the answer came to me."

Wiping her hands on a towel the lady looked at Tom who just sat at the table staring back at her.

"If I remained here to help Jessica look after her Father, I mean, there isn't a lot for me to do at home since Elizabeth left to start her own family, so I thought we could share the load and Jessica would be able to have some free time to visit you for instance and her brother too of course."

Tom jumped up from his chair to place his arms around the formidable lady giving her two big kisses on each cheek. Blushing faintly she said,

"Hang on Tom; just be a mite careful, you know I'm only a frail old lady who can't take too much excitement. I'm glad you are happy with my idea though."

Tom gave her another big hug.

"You are a genius Mrs. Mainwaring, I'm more than happy with you I'll tell you that for true. You are a godsend, that's what you are."

Looking pleased with herself she said,

"Well if you let me go, and you think everyone will be happy with my idea why don't we continue packing Jessica's things so that you can go and tell her about the new developments." Tom stepped back releasing her.

"Why are we still standing in the kitchen then? Let's go and pack!"

***

Tom looked pleased at being able to see the location which in his mind he called 'Where two rivers meet'. He never realised how much he missed the area until he came back to it again. God had been good in giving him the opportunity to settle here in what Tom knew would be as close as Paradise could be on earth.

Two months it had taken for the time to be right in South Australia before he felt comfortable enough to leave the two women behind. Mr. Smith was recovering steadily and looked like he'd be able to oversee some of the work in a month or so. Clarence had been given an assistant which gave him time to see to the more important work - selling some of the stock had created some capital which according to the accounting books had been sadly neglected.

Best of all, Jessica had promised that in another three months she would have the farm so organised that she'd be able to come down and visit him. Tom gave a heavy sigh; he missed Jessica so much already.

"Are you going to sit there forever?"

At the sound of McGregor's voice Tom came back to earth.

"Sorry mate, I was miles away. Won't the valley look different when your church is built?"

McGregor smiled. "I can see it there already. It is a pity that I won't be able to see it every day."

"You can always come and visit us; you know that you'll always be welcome."

"I know Tom, and it is appreciated I assure you. However let's get down there so that we can begin marking out where all the buildings will be placed. These architectural drawings are burning a hole in my satchel." McGregor patted the bag fondly. Both riders moved their steeds forward to start the downhill stretch home.

Tom had been amazed at the amount of work McGregor had accomplished in the time he had been away. Once again it proved to him that if someone had a dream they were interested in, time became irrelevant to the amount of work that could be achieved. If McGregor had shown the same enthusiasm for his farm he would've become a rich landowner.

Two small figures came running towards them, although Tom thought as his siblings came nearer they weren't that small anymore. Soon he and his brother and sister would have to make a decision on where they wanted to go in this large world. Jumping down from his horse he stood with his arms wide open to welcome the two. Walking back to the homestead he was regaled with all the latest news and happenings. As they stepped onto the veranda Albert stood at the door smiling broadly.

"Welcome home Tom, it is nice to have you back with us again!"

"You are right Albert; it is nice to be back!"

***

"How come you never let me know about these plans before?" Ross was piqued at only now finding out what McGregor and Tom had in mind. Seeing the plans spread out on the table in front of him he had to accede that there wasn't much else he would've done differently from what his two mates had done. Elizabeth was silently staring at the drawings of the proposed school, still too much in awe at what she was seeing. Finding out that her Mother had remained behind with Jessica had come as a real surprise and now seeing what was in front of her hadn't helped much to calm her nerves down either.

"A proper school, complete with classrooms, we'll need another teacher!" She breathed in awe. Turning towards McGregor she said, "You are a saint!"

"No nowhere near a saint, Elizabeth, but I'm very glad you like what we are proposing to do for the valley." His face darkened. "It's sad though that it cost the lives of my two dear children to bring this into existence," he said as he waved his arm towards the drawings scattered on the kitchen table.

What McGregor had said had brought them all to reality. It was true that the death of his two children, mature as they had been, had brought forward the dreams that at this stage only had been in their minds. Tom placed his hand on McGregor's shoulder.

"No worries my friend, the opportunity that you have created will never be forgotten!" A moment of deep silence descended over the people in the room.

***

It was two years later nearly to the date when Tom stood at the foot of the altar. Ross was standing next to him. Both of them looked at the congregation in front of them. Some of them were visitors who had been there for the official opening of the church and had remained for the first celebration to be held in the newly blessed church.

Kathleen sitting next to Jason, who was sitting next to Terry, had broken a contract to sing in London so that she could attend the special function today. It seemed that Jason had sacrificed his career just to be near Kathleen. He now acted as her manager and minder. Tom wondered when his sister would recognise and really appreciate the devotion that Jason held for her.

Mrs. Mainwaring was sitting in the first row with an empty seat next to her. She and Mr. Smith had travelled slowly from South Australia to be able to attend the special day.

Albert dressed in his finery was hovering behind Tom and his best man. Albert had spent so much time around the church when it was being built that he had recognised his feelings for the church had not withered as much as he assumed they had. After much discussion and debates with his superiors they reinstalled him into the priesthood making him the minister of the new church.

So much had happened to the people Tom had met and known during the time he had known Ross.

He knew it hadn't been only Ross who had helped him; much of it was due to the higher authority he had discovered that time in the valley with Ross. Tom knew that he had never looked back since he attuned himself with the great God who ruled everything. God must've been listening as Tom was sure he heard the soft words, Be still; I'll be with you always in his head. Tom felt blessed hearing the words he had heard so often when he was troubled. Now however, he knew that God was close to him on this special day.

Jessica and he had suffered much at being apart from each other and here he was standing waiting for her to come to him once more. What was taking her so long? Tom desperately hoped Jessica hadn't changed her mind.

The small organ began to play the well known tune.

Tom could not keep his eyes off Jessica who beautifully dressed in white, was escorted to the altar by her Father who looked pale but walked straight backed with a faint smile on his face glancing proudly at his daughter. Mavis followed by Gloria who had made sure that she was able to attend this special day, blushed as people who knew her indicated how pretty she looked.

Finally standing at the altar Albert moved forward to say,

"Who giveth away this woman?"

"I do!" Jessica's Father declared in a firm voice, and then stepped backward to sit next to Mrs. Mainwaring.

Elizabeth discreetly wiped her eyes as the great love she had for the two young people overcame her. It hadn't been that long ago that she had stood in front of a crowd to openly declare the love she had for Ross. Grabbing Ross' hand she fervently hoped Tom and Jessica would be just as happy as she was.

About the Author

Peter Damen in 1954 with the rest of his family immigrated to Australia at only 12 years of age from the Netherlands. Working as a qualified Toolmaker he decided to attend a Sales and Marketing diploma course at night school and became a Product Manager of a large company. Eventually after changing direction again he took ownership of two Health Food shops which he ran with the help of his wife Maureen. He has travelled extensively overseas and throughout Australia and now in retirement helps out with the Welfare Department at the local Salvation Army Corps. Having a love for reading Peter decided that there was an opportunity to share his feelings for Australian history and how it can affect people's daily lives.

Connect with Peter here: peterdamen609@gmail.com